THE DENUDATION

THE DENUDATION

TILOTTAMA MAJUMDER

Translated from the Bengali original *PRAHAAN*
by **Soma Das**

NIYOGI
BOOKS

Published by
NIYOGI BOOKS
D-78, Okhla Industrial Area, Phase-I
New Delhi-110 020, INDIA
Tel: 91-11-26816301, 49327000
Fax: 91-11-26810483, 26813830
email: niyogibooks@gmail.com
website: www.niyogibooksindia.com

Editor: Mohua Mitra
Cover Design: Misha Oberoi
Layout: Sarojini Gosain

ISBN: 978-93-83098-67-5
Year of Publication: 2015

Printed at: Niyogi Offset Pvt. Ltd., New Delhi, India

I

"DON'T kill me! Please don't kill me! I am your friend... am I not? How can you kill me, Sujoy? Are you really going to kill me? Ahh..."

The wall behind rushed up to meet his back. Slogans on democracy and socialism were scrawled along the length of the wall and meandering tracks left by dripping paint disappeared into the two-foot gutter at the bottom. Even the gutter advanced on him menacingly and the ground beneath his feet retreated with extreme hostility, denying hope. All he could do was cry out, "Ahh...ahh..."

"We have known each other since our school days. Tell me...isn't that true? Am I not your childhood chum? How can you kill me? Sujoy...please, listen to me. I will move away, I will leave the party. I swear...I swear on my mother! Oh dear!! Sujoy, please...spare a thought...what will my mother do without me? Agh...ahh...uck..."

And that was where words deserted him. After that, all that his mortal body released were some meaningless garbled utterings, mechanical sounds emitted in the moments prior to annihilation. The gurgling sounds were accompanied by blood which spurted forth and flowed into the gutter below to mingle with its infested water. His lifeless body slid down the wall, his back grazing against its roughness; his feet lifted off the ground which had long ago betrayed his trust; and, he slowly slipped into the gutter, his body an inert slumped mass. The dirty water flowed over and around his slit throat. The same throat which had been his instrument of expression for so long. His eyes were still wide open. The same eyes which had for so long identified friends and enemies. Sujoy Banerjee still remembered how, just before the murky water drowned those eyes, he clearly saw tears trickling down from them. Yes, Pulak was crying.

Was he really crying? It remained a mystery yet. Why? Why would Pulak cry? For his mother perhaps. Huh! No one cried for his mother in the instant before death. Not even for his wife or children. At that moment, a man cried only for himself!

But wait...maybe it was not so. Not at all. Perhaps, one forgot about himself. 'Me' and its existence ceased to exist. All that rushed through the mind was 'them'. One only thought of those near and dear ones with whom his life was entangled, who made up his memories, who made his life worth living. Perhaps one realised the depth of this feeling only when at the threshold of death. Hence, the tears. The pain of eternal estrangement could be felt only by a person who is faced with it; and it was a pain beyond description. The anxious anticipation of death was manifested through the welling up of the eyes. Death—an end to everything, ceasing to exist in every sense. How piercingly painful was the feeling of being wiped out? Tears were possibly the only way of its expression. But all in vain. One could only hope to express...and perhaps fail. Because, another person, who was not in a rendezvous with death at that moment, could only watch and try to feel a meagre sliver of that pain. In all probability, he would not even be able to understand it or believe in it. He would be unable to trust the tear-streaked expression of agony. He could very well think that those tears, which were flowing in tandem with the ebbing life, were not really a conscious expression of any inner feeling; they were nothing but a physiological reaction of the dying body. Could these tears then be associated with crying? Were they not similar to the tears which flowed when dust pricked the eyes?

So today, like the many times before, Sujoy Banerjee could not ascertain whether Pulak had truly been crying. Perhaps, the only person who could clear this doubt was the dead Pulak. Or, could he? Did the brain function in all its capacities till the final moments of death so that a clear description of feelings was possible by the dying? From amidst these thoughts, Sujoy asked, "Pulak, where are you now?"

The car screeched to a sudden halt. Propelled by inertia, Sujoy jerked forward in his seat. Manjil gnashed his teeth and cursed, "Buggers! These bastards are born to die!"

Sujoy looked up to find a little boy just about a couple of inches away from one of the wheels. He looked about four years old, was dirty and near to naked. His eyes almost popped out and he gulped a few times while breathing heavily. Sujoy's gaze was drawn to the boy's throat. Used bus tickets were strewn all around and the boy quickly busied himself collecting those. As Sujoy rolled down his window, he heard a female voice.

"He could have died. Can't you be more careful while you are driving?"

Sujoy traced the voice to a girl on the road while Manjil retorted, "How is it my fault? He flung himself in front of the car."

"Come here." The girl started to pull the boy away by his arm but he twisted free and took to his heels. He spared a quick glance backwards and then kept on running. As if the car could again try to run him over. As though, he was another Pulak

Biswas – or, for that matter, some other being – who needed to escape the moment he saw Sujoy Banerjee in the car for fear of losing his life again.

Manjil drove on and Sujoy sat back comfortably in the rear seat losing himself in his thoughts. While being driven around by Manjil, Sujoy preferred to surrender his well-being into Manjil's hands and weave various thoughts—some logical, some scattered, some self-motivating and others self-destructive, some perhaps without reason.

Sujoy pondered…another Pulak. Another Pulak Biswas. He had already come across many of them. Countless Pulaks in the place of one. It pleased him to note that the Pulaks were back in this world. And, like every other day, he shrugged off the feeling of melancholy and gazed at the crowd of lives. He liked human beings, innumerable human beings. As he rolled up the window, he recalled how Pulak's left hand had been raised. No, not to attack but in an attempt at self-defence. Pulak did not try to retaliate. But why? Well, there could be various reasons. Not far from them, had stood the alert Jayshankar who would unfailingly deliver Sujoy from any untoward or unexpected situation. Or, perhaps, the dagger in Sujoy's hands had filled him with such dread that he did not dare think about retaliation. Also, retaliation usually came with prior mental preparation. And, for Pulak, the concept of Sujoy raising a dagger to him was so implausible that he was not prepared to counter-attack. Pulak was confident that Sujoy Banerjee was capable of raising only a pen or a paint brush. But, even the lowliest creatures have an inborn inclination towards self-defence. Had Pulak been devoid of even that?

No! Sujoy shook his head and concluded, the hand was surely raised out of an inborn tendency to attempt self-protection. But yes, a feeble attempt, no doubt. A while ago, he had witnessed the same and it once again reminded him of Pulak. And, as was the case with him, such incidents always drew him closer to the past. If an incident occurred in the present then it remained just that but when an incident recurred from the past, it snowballed into a prominent event, demanding more attention and analysis. It was in human nature to scrutinise the causes, workings and associations of such events to arrive at conclusions and decisions. Past experiences always contributed towards this in a considerable manner. Knowledge born out of experience shaped a man's present and future. In fact, a man's past often brought him to a mirror which gave him the opportunity to converse with himself.

In Sujoy Banerjee's life, his past was as active as his present. His past was also extremely responsive because it sprang to life at the slightest provocation from the present. For instance, just a while back, when the car was stuck in traffic near Aurobindo Setu, he looked out of the window and noticed an irate mother spanking her daughter on the roadside. The girl was about four but it was hard to home in on the mother's age. Prolonged struggle with penury had given her body a battered look, and beneath it was buried an enraged mother's real age. Could this little girl be Pulak reborn? Perhaps...perhaps not. Let us say, that little boy he saw earlier and this little girl being beaten before him now were both born of Pulak. Let us say, for argument's sake, that there were many such tortured, poverty-stricken and despairing humans around. Then, was it true...could it be true that one person's soul could divide to create numerous human beings? Could one death be the reason behind many births, like in the fairy tales where a thousand devils were born from a single drop of blood lost by one?

The little girl stood there with a head of rough, unkempt hair. Her filthy frock, a few sizes too big on her, repeatedly slid down her shoulders. But for her mother, she had a negligible and weak existence amidst this swell of human beings.

Her mother was taking the rod to her well and hard. Perhaps the girl had been nagging about something, craving some food...perhaps her love for a handful of some roadside treat had landed her in this predicament. Or she could have been naughty, quite expected of a child her age. But her mother, bogged down by poverty, was in no mood to indulge her nagging or make little of her mischief.

Mother and daughter stood before a soil-filled flower tub on the pavement from which a couple of flowering stalks reared their heads. The mother first slapped her daughter and then gave her a rough shove which landed her hard against the flower tub. Then the mother kicked the little girl in her belly, flinging her farther—as if she wanted to squash the tender belly with her foot. She grasped a handful of the child's hair and banged her head against the ground. The girl was crying with her mouth wide open...or, at least, she was trying to cry. Her breath was probably stuck in her throat due to the pain. For quite a while she could not close her mouth or utter a sound. It appeared, she couldn't breathe in enough air to make a sound. She was caught in a strange stranglehold, neither able to inhale nor exhale. And then she was racked by the heartless hiccups which always followed such a bout of choked crying!

The mother continued to rain frenzied blows on her daughter. The girl curled up on the ground in pain, her laboured breath mingled with hiccups. She supported her sprawled body on her right elbow and held up her left hand in a weak show of self-defence against a ferocious assault. Her eyes brimmed with tears as her mother again lifted a foot.... Sujoy closed his eyes, perhaps the only way to detach himself from the cruel scene. He rolled up his window, eyes still tightly shut. Many sounds bounced off the glass windows of his air-conditioned car and everything conspired to remind Sujoy of his daughter, Sree, and wife, Ragini. Ragini and Sree—mother and daughter. Surprisingly, such cruel assaults had no place in their relationship. But why? Perhaps due to the absence of paucity. Was poverty the only thing that could taint the invaluable relationships in this world with assault? No, not really…jealousy could. So could rivalry, and hero-worship… and an extremely insensitive form of selfishness.

In a flash, the familiar posture of self-defence bounded back into his mind. And with it, followed thoughts of Pulak Biswas.

Pulak, you are my childhood chum. We have played together, run through the fields side by side and dressed our kite strings together. We have sat patiently by the pond in each other's company, waiting for fish to bite our baits. Once you split my lip with a blow…another time, I punched you so hard you needed stitches in your cheek. We have been at our worst and at our best with each other. During our exams we helped each other on the sly. We were friends. Yes, we were friends till the day our political leanings differed…till the day each developed his own principle and charted out his own path. Oh Pulak, can different political beliefs truly turn friends into foes?

Rubbish! All this hue and cry about principle and opinion was meaningless. The only thing of any relevance was gaining control and setting a goal. One had to set himself a goal to serve his own interests and then reach it by hook or by crook. He had to overcome all obstacles and take every situation by the scruff of its neck. All competitors had to be bettered and left behind. The way you, Pulak, wanted to deal with me. The way I have dealt with you. We were neither enemies nor friends. We were rivals. And rivalry is filthier and more ferocious than enmity.

"Dada, where to now?"
Sujoy jerked out of his reverie. Had he nodded off? Manjil had stopped the car beside Tala Park. He was not familiar with Rani Harshamukhi Road. Sujoy gave him directions and settled back. This was the first time he was visiting Dibyangana at her home. His art dealer friend, Anjan Kar, had told him about Dibyangana. For that matter, Anjan too had never been to Dibyangana's house. He had only kept himself informed about her. Every year, Prajit Mukherjee, an artist, hosted an exhibition of his students' paintings and till a couple of years back, Dibyangana's paintings had captivated Anjan.

It was not necessary for an art dealer to also be a connoisseur of art but yes, it did help the business manifold if he could be one. The business did not only involve trading of the work of established artists. Fresh talent had to be identified and promoted. If one could be the prologue to a new artist's success story then he could rule over and benefit from that artist's work for years. Also, the manner of trading differed for the works of established and new artists. The works of renowned artists brought in profit but also required more investment. Compared to that, trading the works of upcoming artists was faster moving. There were many buyers in the market, with easy cash at their disposal, who were not too bothered about the artist's claim to fame. Besides, the works of new artists were in much demand for interior decoration purposes, especially in offices.

Hence, it paid to have a trained eye in business. Anjan Kar was blessed with it and made every effort to continuously develop it. His trained eyes had seen the promise of a bright future in the paintings of Dibyangana. Of course, it was a different story that for the past two years Dibyangana had not attended Prajit Mukherjee's classes. Her in-laws were of the opinion that no one got rich painting pictures and this hobby was nothing but an expensive indulgence.

Those who were of such mind-set always had a retort ready to demean the success of anyone who has made a name. Along with pointing out that those celebrities 'were different' these people did not forget to add an insulting line about some shortcoming or the other in their persona or appearance.

Dibyangana's in-laws' place was home to many such discerning experts and they had not noticed any promise in Dibyangana. Hence, she had parted ways with art.

Sujoy learnt these details from Anjan. Anjan heard everything from Prajit. And Prajit was briefed by none other than Dibyangana herself. Over the telephone. She called infrequently, when an opportunity presented itself, because at her in-laws' place she did not enjoy the liberty of dialling a number at her will.

Sujoy had asked Anjan whether Dibyangana had given up painting for good. Anjan replied, "Possibly…not sure. But even if she doesn't pick up a brush for two years, it would hardly make a difference. I have seen her and I have seen her work. That kind of talent does not burn out so easily. You go ahead and ask her to paint for you."

So now, Sujoy was on his way to Dibyangana's house. As a successful businessman, Sujoy nurtured some basic tactics. For example, before facing an unfamiliar situation or an unknown person, he liked to arm himself with as much information as he could gather. He did the same for Dibyangana, and in this too, Anjan proved the worth of their friendship by helping him out. For this Sujoy was grateful to Anjan. Also, it assured him that Anjan's and his lines of business were absolutely different. What Sujoy Banerjee dealt in was ancient, in demand and eternally tarnished. Hosting art exhibitions had been a hobby with him. Just a hobby, though a fair amount of selfish motive was tied with it. And it had developed into a genuine interest gradually.

Dibyangana was around twenty-three or -four. She had lived with her elder brother and his wife after her parents passed away, till she was married off. Her brother was a clerk of lower order in the Food Corporation of India and his wife a dedicated housewife. Her father too had been a government employee, working in the life insurance sector. He had managed to build them a house in Amtala, Howrah and put aside enough for Dibyangana's wedding. It was courtesy the same money that she was now enjoying domesticity as the legally wedded wife of an architect. Her in-laws were quite supercilious and at the same time conservative. Somewhat unrefined too. All they cared for was food, wealth and security. They preferred to regard Dibyangana as a docile and amicable girl without much in the quarters of personality. And, they firmly believed that a peaceful household was only possible when the women in it were timid, cordial and not prone to rebellious behaviour. Besides motherhood, women should not harbour other dreams. Besides the welfare of their husbands, they should not aspire for anything else. Furthermore, they should not complain even in the direst of situations.

Dibyangana's talents began and ended with painting. But her in-laws were oblivious to this fact. So there must have been something else in her which had impressed them. Some attribute which landed an architect husband in her basket. Well, appearance may be taken into account here since, even today, girls are valued against their looks in the marriage market. But, what else? Of course...the seventy-five thousand worth dowry which came from the money left by her father. No, let's not call it dowry. Assistance, perhaps? By calling it dowry we would be affronting the laws of the land. So, assistance it shall be.

Artist Dibyangana was not too keen on marriage in return for lending assistance. But she did not have another option. Her sister-in-law was already over the edge trying to keep this art-crazy girl in control. So, Dibyangana chose this very easy way of freeing her brother and his wife from their responsibilities.

So...? Sujoy Banerjee initiated a conversation with himself.

"So...I can very well plan the killing of Dibyangana. If my art exhibition is successful then the dead artist within me will surely be pacified, besides other things.... But how to get Dibyangana? Her in-laws were sure to object; hence, the plan needs to include a way to dissolve those objections. But what way? Well...the same way I take care of all the obstacles which bar my way in business. By identifying the Achilles' heel of the opponent."

2

UPON Sujoy Banerjee's orders, Manjil got out of the car and pressed the calling bell by the door. Sujoy rolled down his window and watched. It was a two storied, box-like house, stripped of all appeal, whatsoever. The veranda had a grille at the front from floor to ceiling. What could one possibly call this house?

Yes, it was a house. Not a home. Why not? What crime had this house committed to be ineligible for the title 'home'?

A house was simply a shelter. Four thick walls with a roof on top. There was no need to care for or decorate it. Nails could be hammered into walls haphazardly and household paraphernalia hung from them without a care. Everything from clothes, pictures of gods, photographs of deceased family members to mementos collected on the odd holiday found place on these walls. Perhaps a photograph taken in Darjeeling or a fire-spewing monstrous, yet sacred, dragon from Bhutan. The beds were raised on bricks, the number of bricks varying according to need for space under. The peeling paint on the walls was ignored till wedding bells rang in the family. No one spared a thought for the fading curtains or the moss gathering in profusion on the terrace. The damp and musty bathroom sported myriad patches. The soap lay melting in its wet and limp wrapper in the absence of a proper soap-case. At the door corners, there were small mounds of soil dug up by the ants. And termites created their own network of poisonous abode on the walls, gnawing the foundation hollow.

This was a house. An everyday necessity. Like answering the call of nature. A home, on the other hand, involved mental peace and heart's content. A home was set up keeping aesthetics in mind. Various items, carefully collected, occupied positions of honour in a visually pleasing manner. The curtains hung in perfect folds. The paint on the walls, the design on the floor, the furniture and the upholstery complemented each other. Even the shoes had their own place of rest. In a home, the sight revelled in serenity.

So, Sujoy concluded, Dibyangana's in-laws' place was a house. He tried to take in the house with a scrutinising glance. But the time was dusk; moments before, darkness descended in a hurry. Soon the sky would darken, accompanied by the blowing of conch shells—the sound floating in the air. By the houses and along the roadside, the dark blue of the sky would mingle with these sounds. At this point, time stood still for a moment. To ponder whether it should allow the sun to set. And then, inevitably, it let the sun set. The decisions of time never changed. And with every passing day, time swallowed up a sliver of the present.

Sujoy Banerjee looked at his hands. The smooth, taut skin was witness to his thirty-seven rewarding years on earth. When he looked in the mirror, a confident face lined with intelligence, experience and honesty looked back at him. His face appeared as pure as the pink-tinged, fragrant calamine lotion. And, truly, Sujoy Banerjee was yet to touch sin. He was a pure and honest man living a life of solitude. Suddenly, his gaze fell on a little boy of four. Or, was he five? Could be six. Unclothed, except for a loose and tattered pair of pants, the boy walked along twirling the rickety stick he held.

Pulak! You? Again?

There were numerous Pulaks roaming around him. On some days, Sujoy happened to meet quite a few of them. The real Pulak had perhaps been delivered from his sins. Hence, now he was visible in all children around the age of four or so. Presently, all these Pulaks were living the Oedipus complex, having crossed the phases of lust and narcissism. They were gradually retrieving their selves.

Passing through a naïve auto-erotic stage, narcissistic stage and currently through Oedipus complex. Living in the sinless after-state of naïve lust.

What a wonderful elucidation! Whether it was palatable, was a different issue. Sujoy did not have the time to ponder on that. He was truly blessed with superior perceptions! Hence, he was almost unique as a pure and sensitive social personality. His sub-conscious mind revelled in this confidence and his conscious mind had never touched any form of sin. But yes, he was surrounded by sinners. Weren't there any pure and virtuous people around? But then, what was the difference between pure and virtuous?

Pure…or, untouched by sins. And virtuous…or, one who had amassed purity. Kind of like the arrangement of negative and positive numbers with zero in the middle. Purity was a state of zero. Those who sinned along life's path, gradually travelled down the line of negative numbers. While the virtuous people's lives were brightened as they moved up the line of positive numbers.

In that case, who were the pure and who the virtuous around Sujoy Banerjee? Anjan Kar – though a businessman – was a lover of art and a considerate connoisseur too. Hence, he was virtuous! Jayshankar was surely pure—he was untouched by sin. Incidentally, sin never touched man. Man touched sin and in the process became tainted. Sin dwelled in its own realm, it did not pursue anyone. Man was the one who succumbed to the attraction of sin and chased it. In fact, when man touched sin he actually tainted it. So, both man and sin were reciprocally contaminating agents of destruction!

"Who are you looking for?"

A grating voice jerked Sujoy Banerjee back to reality. He heard Manjil ask promptly, "Is this Dibyangana-di's residence?"

A lady's face stuck out through the open window along the staircase. Patches of light and darkness settled over the uneven planes of her crumpled face. Her enquiring glance was full of irrevocable darkness.

"Yes, this is Dibyangana's in-laws' place. Why? What's the matter?"

Manjil now looked at Sujoy who was already getting out of the car.

"*Namaskar*. I am Sujoy Banerjee. I'd like to meet madam to discuss about some pictures."

"Picture? Whose picture? Bouma's?[1] But why?"

The lady appeared glued to the window. Sujoy realised it would take a while to get around her and asked Manjil to park as much to the side as possible. The name of the road belied its actual width and condition. By then, the lady had finally exercised some control over suspicion and opened the door to come and stand in the grilled veranda. The grill door, of course, had a big lock hanging on it. Her dyed hair hung loose, she wore a black sleeveless blouse and a pair of heavy gold earrings, besides other jewellery. Her eyes were thickly outlined with kohl and after inspecting Sujoy, Manjil, the car and, of course, Sujoy's confident demeanour, she unlocked the door and invited him inside. The living room was devoid

1 Generic informal term of address for 'daughter-in-law' in Bengal.

of artistic touch, just as Sujoy had imagined some moments back. Without paying much attention to any invitation to take a seat that the lady might have offered, Sujoy unhurriedly sat down on the sofa. After all, he was there for a discussion which would take time. He heard the same grating voice hollering, "Are you there? Come here...Bouma, can you hear me? Come and see who is here...!"

Her voice carried traces of displeasure and disregard. Perhaps the irritation was due to the fact that a gentleman had arrived, in a car, to meet her daughter-in-law, and talk about some pictures. In a way, this unwarranted attention could very well be a blow to their honour. Sujoy's thoughts travelled along those lines and he became engrossed in them.

A little while later, Dibyangana entered the room and greeted him. She was thin, shrivelled up, yet pretty. Sujoy stood up and returned the greeting. Then he asked the girl to take a seat and sat down in the adjacent sofa, maintaining respectable distance. Sujoy noticed that the simply dressed, unadorned girl's beauty was marked by a faint streak of sindoor. As though, she had applied it quite flippantly, at the command of others. Her cheeks were touched with pallor, her lips devoid of colour and her fingers long and thin like paint brushes. But, the deep, dark pools of her eyes stood out as most prominent amongst her features. Slightly turbid. Like a mirror on which unwanted dust had collected. Sujoy Banerjee started by introducing himself, as a preamble to all that he had to say, "I am Sujoy Banerjee. I am here to talk about your paintings."

"Yes, but I..."

"Art exhibitions and trading of paintings are my hobby. Not a business...not at all. I have been doing this every year for the past seven to eight years."

"But I have never heard..."

"It was a very small affair with paintings of people I know. This year I plan to expand and the event will be organised with young artists. I'd like to concentrate on different age groups every year. For instance, next year we are going to invite teenagers."

Dibyangana's mother-in-law now entered the room and sat down. She switched on the TV and soon sounds and visuals from a serial show filled the room. During commercial breaks, they were subjected to advertisements where the boy grew up fast on Horlicks, where a couple in love cuddled up to each other after brushing their teeth with Colgate. The lady sat with a ball of wool in her lap and started to knit.

Dibyangana glanced at the TV and said, "Yes, but I...I mean, for a long time..."

"I am going to take five paintings from each artist. The dimensions will be specified but the artist is free to choose the medium. There will be complete freedom regarding subject and style but collages will not be accepted."

An aged gentleman, dressed in a lungi and kurta, entered the room with a copy of *The Statesman* in hand. He settled himself on the large bed close to the TV and spread out the paper in front of him. Then he released an order for Dibyangana, "Bouma, get my glasses from upstairs."

Dibyangana excused herself and rushed to follow the order. Sujoy Banerjee thought—if you are an artist then you will need to have patience. You will have to overcome all unwanted and unreasonable hurdles with endurance. Calmly. And Dibyangana, being a girl, was likely to possess these attributes. Sujoy waited. Their conversation had been disrupted, like a commercial break in the midst of a programme. None of the others in the room expressed any desire, whatsoever, to speak to him.

Dibyangana delivered the glasses and returned to her seat. Sujoy skipped mentioning Anjan Kar's name and said, "I heard of you from Prajit-da."

"Mastermoshai[2]! Oh!"

In a flash, the girl's face lit up with festive brilliance. But only for an instant. Then it clouded over with hopelessness, devoid of all pleasure. She said, "But for a long time, I haven't ..."

"I am giving you two months' time. Total five paintings. Minimum three. This will not be simply an exhibition. There will be arrangements to conduct sales and a good painting will not return home."

Sujoy then cleared his throat and added in a louder voice, "If your painting sells then the entire amount is yours. I will deduct a bare minimum as my expenses. Since this is a hobby, and not my business, I do not take in profits. Suppose one of your paintings sells for five thousand, I will deduct ten per cent and hand over the rest to you. And, even if you don't sell any then you have nothing to lose except the hard work you put in. Collection and return of the paintings will be my responsibility."

A young man entered the room and directed an enquiring glance towards Sujoy. Sujoy assumed he was Dibyangana's husband.

The lady said, "Bouma, get Khoka[3] a glass of water. Would you like to have tea?"

Sujoy Banerjee had not been offered tea. For that matter, not even water. Dibyangana again excused herself and returned with two glasses of water, one for Sujoy Banerjee.

---

2 Generic name in show of respect for male teachers or masters.

3 Informal term of address in Bengal, for the son of the house. Used by parents and elders; normally used to refer to little boys and often carried over to adulthood.

Now, her father-in-law interjected, "I am her father-in-law. This house is mine."

"Of course."

Father-in-law: We always encourage Bouma. We always tell her to continue with her painting at home. After all, Bouma is like the daughter of the house.

Mother-in-law: I have also told her to paint in her free time. There isn't much to do at home. Just the usual cooking and cleaning…that is a part of every girl's life.

Father-in-law: But painting involves expense. Pursuing it simply as a pastime…. Do paintings really sell?

Sujoy: They do.

Father-in-law: Yes, I have come across reviews in the papers but never read them. My interest lies in politics!

Sujoy: That's great!

Father-in-law: How much do they fetch?

Sujoy: What?

Father-in-law: I mean, the paintings.

Sujoy: It varies. Anything from five hundred to fifty crores.

Son: But that must be for famous artists. Nandalal Bose, Hemen Majumdar…

Father-in-law: This is my son…Brato. Dibyangana's husband. Bouma, please do the introductions. And she is my wife, Dibyangana's mother-in-law.

Sujoy: Namaskar. Yes, I guessed as much.

Brato: Ganesh Pyne, Prakash Karmakar, Bikash Bhattacharya. Or, if we were to name some from the west then Van Gogh, Picasso…

Sujoy: Great! You seem well-informed!

Brato: Yes…I mean, their paintings can fetch good prices. Who would buy Dibyangana's work?

Sujoy: There are many who are keen to buy the work of new artists.

Brato: Are the prices good?

Mother-in-law: Huh! Bouma never told us that paintings actually sell.

Sujoy: We have our own pricing policy for the works of new artists. No painting is priced at less than a thousand. So, even if Dibyangana's painting sells for the minimum, it will fetch a thousand. Moreover, according to her teacher, if she puts her heart and mind to it then each painting should be worth five thousand.

Father-in-law: Hmm...good. Bouma, give your consent. After all, it is something you love doing!

Having said that, he returned his attention to the newspaper. As if, no work was worthy of love if it did not carry monetary value. If this exhibition had not offered the opportunity for income then this same father-in-law would not have encouraged his daughter-in-law to agree to the proposal. The lure of money even made the mother-in-law release her daughter-in-law from the everyday chores, though temporarily.

Mother-in-law: I'll have Bakul come in to cook.

Then she concentrated on her knitting.

Brato: There you go! You are being offered your dues. Get started!

Brato then turned up the volume of the TV. Dibyangana sat still, biting down hard on her bottom lip. Her face pale. Sujoy Banerjee got up. His work was done. He then said to Dibyangana, "I'll visit again after a month and half with the contract. Do start painting."

Dibyangana looked up. Her expression stirred pity and she appeared in a dilemma. Quite worried. "But I..."

The rest of her words were lost in the cacophony blaring out of the TV. But did she really say anything? Sujoy assured her, "You have not painted in a long time. So what? You will start again."

With that, he walked out of the house. If Dibyangana really did return to painting, and painted well, then this unpleasant evening would bear some fruit. This breed of people, the obloquy, this chagrin, would no longer bother him. Not at all. He already had an arrangement with Anjan—they would buy all of Dibyangana's paintings. So that a promising artist did not suffer an untimely death.

3

"ON his way back, Sujoy felt tired. He knew that this world, the home of humans, was not always favourable. In fact, most of the time, it was unsympathetic. And, most of the humans were, more often than not, disagreeable with one another. Trying to turn around the unfavourable situations through discussions was indeed a tiring process. Irrespective of origin and time, every man possessed some exclusive quality, a different twist. For instance, an individual's thoughts about the sky. If one was to ask each person what she or he thought of the sky then it was quite possible that a few answers would be perturbing, seem even illogical.

Sujoy remembered an old lady from his childhood, who used to come to his family home in Haur to sell dung-cakes. Her sagging skin was crisscrossed with wrinkles; yet, her frame was upright, strong and determined. The children of the house called her 'Mishi-thakuma'[4]. Whenever she arrived, her face was wreathed with an ear to ear grin displaying her dark brown teeth. Apparently, she used *mishi* on her teeth. Till this day, Sujoy had not found out what mishi was. But he guessed it was perhaps some form of tobacco, cheap with intoxicating qualities.

Mishi-thakuma often said, "Do you know what is beyond this village of Haur and the paddy fields? Lord, bless us!"

---

4 Thakuma is the term for paternal grandmother; a term of endearment and respect for a lady old enough to be the caller's grandmother

The children asked, "Is that where God lives?"

Mishi-thakuma put on that almost impossible smile and replied, "Of course! Look, beyond the paddy field you can see nothing but the sky. That is where the earth ends. And what is at the end of our world? Heaven! And who lives in heaven? The Lord!"

"Since heaven is so close, just across the field, why don't you go there?"

She would clamp down her teeth on her dark brown tongue in a gesture of apology and say, "Oh dear! We are not supposed to make haste about such things. He will call us when the time is right. Lord, bless us!"

Once, someone quipped, "It could very well be hell beyond the field. What proof is there that it is heaven?"

Mishi-thakuma's smile vanished. Her face took on a sad look. She said, "Don't say that, dear. The Lord has not created hell. Hell is a creation of man. Only man is capable of such things. After all, it is easy to infuse fear with threats of hell. Take the Lord's name and all fears will ebb."

Around that time, Sujoy had learnt to find places on the globe. He had learnt that the sky was actually a limitless expanse of space and the earth a negligible rotating mass in it, quite like a dung-cake. A bee buzzed in Sujoy's bonnet—how about explaining these facts to Mishi-thakuma?

Mishi-thakuma arrived. Sujoy brought out the painted tin globe, mounted on a wooden stand. Then he launched into a lecture, "Look here, your concept is completely wrong. This is the Earth and this is Haur, where we live…a miniscule speck. The Earth has no edge, no boundary. At every instant, every inch of the Earth shares a boundary with the universe." Mishi-thakuma listened with rapt attention, her features firmly set. Sujoy felt quite encouraged by her silence and continued, "Would you like to see beyond the paddy field? I'll take you."

At that, Mishi-thakuma whimpered, “No dear! I have never set foot outside this village.”

Sujoy said, “Why don’t you take a look? There is no heaven at the end of it. You will find the same kind of ground and fields. Perhaps, even a village and people like us. Many more of them. From there, if you gaze ahead, you will again find the sky at the end of it.”

Mishi-thakuma burst into tears. She sobbed, “Oh dear, I’ll never again talk to you about heaven. Please let me be. This is all I know. How am I to know more? And now, how am I to leave the known behind and set off towards the unknown…?”

Sujoy had laughed a lot that day. With time, Mishi-thakuma faded from his memories. But of late, he remembered her often. Because Mishi-thakuma was an intrinsic part of many of his life’s experiences.

Years later, when Sujoy was in the twelfth standard, he remembered Mishi-thakuma. An Australian boy, a friend of Sujoy’s roommate, Dibakar, came to live with them for a while. At the time, Dibakar-da was in his third year of graduation. One night, the Australian boy, Sam, took out some hashish from his satchel. That was Sujoy’s introduction to the stuff. Hashish—an extremely strong and exceedingly addictive substance. The name seemed quite apt for the nature of the substance, conveying a kind of hushed up and repulsive affair.

The stuff was in the form of a dark brown lump. Dibakar-da waited with a chillum while Sam scraped out powdered hashish from the lump. Dibakar-da lit the chillum while Sam added the powder and took a long drag from it. He appeared unaffected. But when Dibakar-da tried, his insides revolted. His eyes bulged and he started to wheeze, as if choking. Sam added some more powder and took another drag. His eyes glazed over. Then the chillum made its way to Sujoy. He took a drag. Immediately, a ball of sticky smoke swirled in his airway and almost blocked it. He felt as if his chest would burst any minute. The pain was almost unbearable, as if his life was being dragged out of him. Gasping to take in air in an effort to keep his life within himself, Sujoy lay down. And just before darkness enveloped him, he saw Mishi-thakuma's face!

Today, sitting in his slow-moving car, Sujoy inhaled deeply. There was a lot of traffic around him. The road was lined with dusty and formidable buildings, the mark of a big city. At every turn, every corner, hung the odour of man's deep dark resolves. Yet, all the households in a particular society did not share similar resolves and beliefs. In fact, in the bustle of city life, each household was a separate society in itself. And why only a household...each room in a household could claim the status of a distinct social order. Who or what could justify the righteousness of the various rules and concepts? Sujoy's mind circled around these thoughts as the car inched on.

How did Mishi-thakuma arrive at her belief? Where did she adopt it from? Did she conjure it up by herself? We, who believe ourselves to be free thinkers, are actually ignorant of the extent our thoughts are ruled by pre-determined notions. Most of the time, we adopt those pre-established dogmas in our oblivion and carry on manoeuvring ourselves within those set boundaries, assuming that we are self-ruled. For Mishi-thakuma, her belief was the ultimate truth for her. And that 'truth' provided her with mental peace and security. Whenever the indomitability of such truths is threatened, man is led into fallacy. Just as Mishi-thakuma had experienced—in the attempt to clear one misconception, the very foundation of her belief was shaken.

I believe, Pulak too, was a victim of such fallacy. He was my friend and classmate, no doubt, but being a follower of a different doctrine – what we liked to call a different political canon – he started to regard me as an enemy, instead of the friend I was. He vowed to destroy me. Today, I find, the entire world has fallen prey to such misconceptions. Discrimination on the basis of religion, caste and skin colour leads to factional enmities.

Pulak's final days surfaced in Sujoy's mind. Those days, Pulak and Sujoy were busy toiling away for their respective student groups, riding high on excitement. Every year, there were always a handful of students who would busy themselves with this kind of work. These student bodies were formed with student welfare in mind. It was necessary for each body to have different goals and philosophies, so that welfare work in the colleges could be carried out in an unbiased and justified manner. In the light of that, it was not necessary for any of these bodies to be an appendage to any political party. But, in reality, these student bodies came to be the properties of various established political parties. The students fell prey to the virus of political rifts, class-consciousness and the poisonous lure of power.

It is true that if students are properly trained in politics, they can turn out as responsible citizens in the future. But in these times, alongside that, they also learn to misuse power and exploit public resources to suit self-interests. This unfortunate aspect cannot be overlooked.

But then, who knows, maybe the inclination to serve the self with public wealth starts much earlier in life! In relative oblivion! Say, the childhood celebrations of Saraswati Puja by collecting contributions from various households in the neighbourhood. At that time, pilfering is considered a laudable feat. Pinching fruits, vegetables and flowers from various homes is part of the deal. Even the chicken, for the feast on the following day, does not come by honest means.

... But that sort of 'stealing' is not a crime! Such childhood pranks and follies are hardly looked upon as 'offences'.

Most young boys have a few such misconducts listed against their names. At that age, one overflows with energy. More energy than is required for studies, play or even fights. How do they deal with this excess energy? Well...they think of 'appropriate' names for the elderly in the neighbourhood, indulge in mimicry highlighting the little oddities of people in their immediate vicinity, draw caricatures of their teachers in their books and, of course, celebrate Saraswati Puja.

A small idol of goddess Saraswati. A rickety makeshift pandal made of bamboo, twine and loin cloths borrowed from fathers and grandfathers. And, of course, the first smoke! Ten bundles of beedis for the ten young organisers, and one extra bundle. Late in the night, they sat behind the pandal and divided the precious cargo. A bundle each and then a beedi each from the eleventh bundle. Great! True followers of socialism. But what about the extra beedi left over from the eleventh bundle? What would its fate be? Why? It would surely be lit and everyone would get a drag. After all, the Sarawsati Puja fund was no one's family fortune. Everything had to be divided fairly and equally. So, one of the boys lit the beedi, took a drag and passed it on. But what if someone took an extra drag? Or took a longer drag? What if the beedi burnt out before reaching the last member? Oh! What anxiety! The moment one of them took a moment longer than deemed necessary, the others hurried him on, "Hey, come on. Pass it on, quick. We need a turn too." And if, by some twist of fate, one of them was cheated of a turn then a good round of arguments, fights, scuffles, name calling and choicest expletives followed.

Pulak and Sujoy too, were once a part of it all. Partners in crime during their first smoke. But then a rift crept in when they pledged loyalty to different political parties. But wasn't it more due to the hunger for power? Yes, it was. Though, at the root was the political party. Man always tries to bring others around to believe in his chosen path. Because he wants more people on his side—an age-old inclination to form groups. The bigger the group, more the power. But changing times always had an effect on such practices, however old. The effect was usually slow yet all-encompassing. In current times, a group is a gathering of many people and many minds. And the mind does not always follow the same philosophy or doctrine. The group is certainly above the single mind but once in a while a strong mind comes along which has the power to steer the entire group. Such minds are leaders. And the leadership may be effective in the arena of either religion or politics. To be precise, leadership has to choose a path along which the mass will follow indubitably. Religion and politics are the most rewarding choices. Though apparently quite removed from each other, religion and politics share a few major aspects—like leadership, principle and the preaching and spread of the principle.

So, to construct the opinion of the mass, what was more effective…the leadership or the group? Since his college days, Sujoy believed it was the leadership. The general mass did not want to struggle with an ideal plucked out of the sky. They needed a leader who was a living example of the ideal. A leader had the power to alter the course of the followers' beliefs and lead them along his chosen path. Such was the power a strong leader wielded. Pulak was such a leader. And Sujoy too. How could one, of two equally powerful entities, accede defeat at the other's hands?

So? Tell me, Pulak. How could I let you live? If I hadn't killed you then you would have killed me. Or, I would have had to give up politics. Even then you and your party wouldn't have trusted me. Because my strong leadership qualities scared you and your lot. And why would I step down? In fear of you? In fear of your party? Why wouldn't I once try to win the war before succumbing to fear? And Pulak, you were my childhood friend...you knew that I had always been a man of art. People may think such men to be timid and calm, but in reality, they are fighters. An artist called Millet said, "Art is not a pleasure trip. It's a battle." Essentially, each artist is a warrior. War is their doctrine of life. And, one who shies away from that doctrine in fear, is no less than a sinner. Pulak, I am a pure soul; why should I follow the path of sin?

When we were in the first year, you and your group assaulted me. A cruel and terrible assault. You were my childhood friend, couldn't you have warned me of it? What would you have lost by saving me? In fact, what would you have gained by killing me? How much more power? You didn't save me. That day, I was saved by Shyamal, who happened to be from your party. And Jayshankar, of course.

The scene is still vividly clear in my memory. Someone from your group raised a chopper. Shyamal said, "Don't kill him!"

"Bastard!" Spat someone else and kicked me. I was conscious but devoid of strength to save myself. Bleeding from various wounds, I slowly slipped into unconsciousness. That evening, Jayshankar and I had planned to spend time together, drinking our fill. When Jayshankar arrived at my place with the bottles, I wasn't home. Finding it unusual, he started looking for me. We had a strange emotional connection, based on trust. A connection which is still very much alive. Though I don't have much idea about his family, community, problems, pains or, for that matter, anything. But this much we knew, whenever the need arose we would be there for each other. Whereas you, Pulak, despite being my childhood friend, planned to kill me instead of saving me!

That evening, Jayshankar guessed that something untoward had happened. He didn't know why he thought that way, but he did. During his search, he found out from the lady at the tea shop by our college that I had gone towards the BEd department around dusk. She also added that since then she hadn't seen me return the same way. Jayshankar found me in the alley beside the BEd department. By then, I had been unconscious for almost two hours. I spent one and a half months in hospital.

You wanted to give me a good scare. Why? Just because I joined your opposition party? Don't think so. You contributed to the plan of killing me because you yourself were scared. You knew that both of us were equally powerful. So, one would have to go, sooner or later. Or perhaps you wanted to render me physically disabled…with a leg or an arm chopped off. After I recovered, you again planned to kill me. That day too, Shyamal saved me. He scribbled in my book—"You may be attacked. Keep your window open." I did; and managed to jump out of the first floor window and save myself. Pulak, that year luck was with you. I was on the run, trying to save my life at every turn. But the following year….

Sujoy Banerjee heard the sound clearly. The last sounds from Pulak Biswas. Glob…fizz…wooshh…!

Again, Sujoy was in a dilemma. He couldn't be sure if those sounds had actually come out through Pulak's slit throat. Just as, he wasn't sure whether, at that moment, Pulak had really cried. And even if he did, for whom did he cry? Himself or his mother?

That day, Sujoy had flung the bloodied dagger into the muddy gutter. He trembled and sweated profusely. Every instant, he felt as if an iron hand was about to grasp him from behind. Nausea welled up from within. His body and soul felt sin-smeared. Or, perhaps, at that moment, none of his senses were active, no sensation alive. The only thought that surfaced clear was that he had to flee. Flee as fast as possible. He tried his best to keep on walking, stumbling and tripping on the way. Jayshankar followed him, maintaining a safe distance to quell any suspicion of them being together. All these safety measures had been Jayshankar's doing. In fact, he had wanted to take care of the entire matter himself. But Sujoy didn't agree. Jayshankar even expressed doubt about Sujoy's ability to pull through. Hence, he planned the aftermath with care. As decided, they parted ways at a particular juncture.

Much later, when Sujoy lay in the field and gazed up at the sky, contrition crept into his senses. The younger of the two of his elder brothers, Chhotda, left a torch with him; of course, without any clue about his situation, perhaps just on intuition. During those moments, a few pictures formed and immediately faded away in his mind, all of them somehow tinged with the hues of death and murder.

Now, after so long, time had clogged the memory and everything had mingled into a few formless lumps which traversed the path of memory at their own will.

That evening, after parting ways with Jayshankar, the need to escape had urged him to hail a cab. But his sense of practicality stopped him. Keeping to the shadows, he walked along the alley and finally reached the brightly lit main road. There he jumped onto a moving bus. A little later, he got off and took another bus to Howrah, and from there to Haur. By the time he reached his village, evening was giving way to night. The only person he came face to face with was Chhotda.

"What has happened to you?" Chhotda asked.

Being the youngest of three brothers, Sujoy had to endure extra doses of both affection and discipline throughout his childhood. These had shaped him into a rebellious, stubborn and introvert person whose actions bordered on flippancy. As he grew older, these traits became increasingly prominent in him. After a length of time, his family started to keep their distance. Though, this behaviour, on the part of the family, could well be called a kind of affectionate indulgence, to dilute the effects of past discipline which in the present seemed redundant. As for Sujoy, at that age everyone felt a natural inclination to stay away from family members. Though, it was also true that home was a necessity at that age, a haven to return to after the day's struggle with the newly discovered world outside. Caught amidst these conflicting emotions, one grew quite attached to a particular room or corner or even a window in the house.

For Sujoy, the corner room on the ground floor was that retreat. He made good use of the affection, discipline and indulgence meted out to him and clung on to that room the way a child clings to his mother's lap. Though, as with the mother's lap, he had to share the room with one of his brothers. But all his personal belongings, his art materials and books crowded that room, occupying their rightful places.

Their middle-class family home had only two rooms on the first floor. One was their parents' and the other was occupied by Sujoy's eldest brother, Sudeb, or Borda as they called him. On the ground floor, apart from the living room and the kitchen, was this corner room which Sujoy shared with Sumit, his Chhotda. Sujoy didn't mind sharing room space with Sumit, because, though siblings, they also shared a friendship of sorts due to the small difference in ages. It wasn't a very carefree kind of friendship but they understood and had faith in each other. To be honest, the relationship was not free of envy. Close siblings were usually competitive and this gave rise to a considerable amount of envy. Whenever Sujoy bragged about his popularity in college, Sumit countered with jealousy-laced sarcasm.

But, that evening, Sujoy perhaps appeared different. Sumit – a poet at heart – surely noticed the change in his brother's usual demeanour. Sujoy, upon reaching home, had yanked his shirt off feeling extremely warm and rushed to the washroom to throw up. Noticing this unusual behaviour, Sumit had probed. He had asked, "What has happened to you?"

Sujoy's parents and Borda were away. Baba had accompanied Borda to Asansol where he was to join a new job. Immediate employment had become a necessity for Borda because Chhotda had shown no signs of graduating into an earning member of the family. Ma had taken the opportunity of Baba's absence to visit her brother in Pashkura. Chhotda looked after him. Sujoy remembered, as he retched and vomited, Chhotda gently stroked his back, worked the hand pump for water and applied cool compress to the back of his neck.

Sujoy threw up some bitter bile; because, due to the furtive excitement within, he had not eaten through the day. When the bout of throwing up subsided, Sujoy returned to his room with Chhotda's help and lay down. Chhotda switched on the fan and drew the curtains aside. This room, in one corner of their middle class home, had always lacked in light, be it daytime or night. Perhaps, that was why calmness hung heavy in the air of the room. And, at that moment, Sujoy sought shelter from that tranquillity. He lay there as many probing questions washed over him....

Did you eat something disagreeable?

You threw up nothing but bile. Didn't you eat anything during the day?

Why? Didn't you have money?

What have you been up to?

Working for the party?

At this rate, the party will surely benefit but what about you?

Sujoy answered all questions with a wave of his hand. Besides the fact that he probably did not have enough strength to speak, he also did not wish to talk. The acrid smell of blood and the final sounds made by a human body still seemed to chase him. Through the window, he saw the huge expanse of the field in front of their house. A swelling urge to go out to that field filled him. He rose, changed into fresh, clean clothes and walked out. In the field, he stretched out on his back on the grass.

Chhotda followed him. He sat beside Sujoy and rested his hand lightly on Sujoy's forehead. Then he asked, "What is wrong, Joy?"

Sujoy didn't reply. He remained inert and silent. In fact, he was quite listless; unaware of his body and mentally exhausted. As though, whatever had happened was as meaningless as that vast, abandoned stretch of field. Sumit continued, "I won't force you to tell me anything. I just want to know if you are in trouble. And, what kind of trouble. Something related to the party? Or a girl? Anyway, don't lie here for long. Come in soon."

Sumit rose and was about to walk away when Sujoy called him, "Listen…"

Sumit turned around, "Yes?"

"When did Ma leave for Pashkura?"

"Last evening. Why?"

"Nothing…I mean…"

"Tell me…"

"If anyone, including Ma, asks about my whereabouts, say that I returned home in the morning."

"Who else will ask besides Ma?"

"Whoever."

"What is the matter with you, Joy?"

"Chhotda, I want to be left alone for a while."

Sumit left slowly. Perhaps, his poet's heart had felt the apprehensive stirrings of some misfortune. Because, when Sujoy didn't return for long, he again went out to the field with a torch.

Sujoy's gaze was fixed on the stars. And, after a while, the stars and the grass seemed to melt into each other. As if, the soft folds of the sky, like a starry blanket, had gently descended and covered the form lying on the bed of grass below. Sujoy, in the agonising grip of the chastising aftermath of a sinful act, had taken cover under the twinkling blanket and pondered on life's mysteries. What if, eventually, he was identified as Pulak Biswas's murderer? In that case, a life of darkness waited for him. But now, instead of worrying about that possibility, Sujoy Banerjee craved to analyse the various perceptions of human life. He felt, it was not the body but the mind which man could control. But, wasn't it the mind which controlled every moment? Then how could the mind be handled? Perhaps, there was something above the mind... what we called conscience. The ability to discern and judge. Consciously. Knowledge, perception and conscience – residing in more exalted spheres – could control desires and guide the mind in the right direction. So, man was a slave to the mind. The mind was a slave to the conscience. Hence, man had to bear the burden of the mind as well as the conscience.

You are human. You can control your thoughts. I too, am human. My mind and conscience help form my assessments by which I determine every step I take. I am Sujoy because I know and believe that I am Sujoy. My existence is determined and established by my belief.

I believe, I had no other option but to kill Pulak Biswas, and it was not a sin. I believe, I am not a sinner. Much before I developed my own power to think and discern, I was indoctrinated by others into the faith of the Almighty, in my oblivion. It had been instilled in me that all creation and the cycle of past-present-future in this world is the Almighty's will. Hence, I may logically conclude that Pulak Biswas's death was the Almighty's will.

It is difficult to say whether the three primal qualities of man – goodness, spiritedness and ignorance – are directly or indirectly determined by God or man himself. It is almost impossible to come to a conclusion about that. Hence, I will not think of myself as a sinner. I have taken a human life the way I would have killed a snake, a tiger or an elephant, for self-defence. If it stands that human life is of greater value than any other form of life then I will justify my act by saying that I have ended a valuable life to save a more valuable one. For a third person, these two lives – Pulak's and mine – are of the same value. Here, it is important to know who is making the assessment. For every man, there is nothing more valuable to him than his own life.

Dwelling amidst a medley of such thoughts, Sujoy Banerjee saw two extraordinary men—resplendent in heavenly brilliance, yet, dressed ordinarily enough to be able to sit comfortably on the grass. Outlined in their heavenly haloes, Sujoy saw them deeply engrossed in a private conversation. Sujoy had never seen these men before, yet, they did not appear too unfamiliar either. He gazed mesmerised, at the men and their aura. The sight wiped his mind clean of all thoughts about sin and virtue. He caught snatches of simple sentences about trees, flowers and birds. As he lay on the bed of grass, with the moon for a pillow and the star-spangled sky for a blanket, he listened to the conversation. And, as he listened, he noticed that the men addressed each other as Upo and Abhi—both denoting propinquity.

Upo: Heron, heron. When it flies, its wings appear milk white underneath. It rests in the quiet by the waterside. And what an amazing mating ritual! During the mating season, the male develops brown patches on its back. The Pond-heron chooses the same tree for six consecutive years to lay its eggs. It hunts on its own, without a witness; yet, sits atop the trees as a close-knit community. The Pond-heron…an amazing bird!

Abhi: The Pakhiraj too, speaks of extraordinary beauty. Its dense foliage with clusters of red and yellow flowers. The pink-tinged new leaves slowly turn into a coppery purple. And the leaves which are in the throes of youth, are a brilliant green, gradually developing into compound leaves with pointed tips like those of an Ashoka tree, arranged in perfect symmetry along the branches. The blossoms are…somewhat, I should say Upo…like countless bright lamps descended from their heavenly abode. I have seen it several times in the height of spring and also in the depth of summer. I wonder who brought it from Burma and named it Pakhiraj. Has it forgotten the name it had before?

Upo: No, no. The birds, the trees and the flowers … they do not forget anything. They always remember their origins, their land. Think of the migratory birds. What scientific knowledge do they possess by which they perfectly retrace their flight path of thousands of miles? They remember. All the birds which fly in from the Palearctic eco zone during winter do not stay back through the year. They remember and fly back.

Abhi: I once asked the Neelmoni creeper. The *Petrea volubilis*. Which arrived from a faraway land in South America to make a home in Rabindranath Tagore's home.

Tagore had named it 'Neelmoni'...from *Petrea volubilis* to Neelmoni. I asked it, "O beautiful *Petrea*, do you like your new life as Neelmoni?" She said, "Yes. There is love here. And if there is love then even a foreign land can be made home." I asked, "Tell me, do you really not feel homesick?" She replied, "Of course I do! After all, that is my motherland. But here too I am greatly loved and cared for. Trees too have feelings. They know how to love. They love humans."

Upo: But, not all humans love trees. They cruelly chop them down. They kill birds and rejoice in the display of their valour. Yet, those very birds give so much to the world. The Black-headed mountain sibia, the sunbirds and flowerpeckers, the mynahs and the bulbuls pollinate numerous flowers and scatter the seeds of fruit-bearing trees across the country. My mother had a pet Chandana – a Rose-ringed parakeet. It was not bound by chains, yet, it never left her. Once in a while it took off to the skies, pranced on branches...but always returned to my mother. It had tasted love.

Abhi: Trees too know love. Plant two saplings of the same tree in different places. Make water, sunlight, air and nutrients available to both. But talk to only one of them. Tell it affectionately, "Grow up, be healthy. Spread your branches wide." You will find that sapling growing faster than the other.

Upo: Spread your love, trees, birds and flowers...spread your love.

Abhi: Spread your love, plants, birds and blossoms... spread your love.

Upo: Victory to you, trees, birds and flowers...may victory be yours.

Abhi: Victory to you, plants, birds and blossoms...may victory be yours.

Sujoy distinctly heard someone calling out to him.

He opened his eyes, and immediately, the haloed men disappeared from his vision. The star-spangled blanket fell away; the moon ceased to be a comforting pillow and returned to being nothing but the Earth's satellite. In a flash, everything was relegated to the corner of his mind reserved for forgotten dreams. Sumit enveloped him in a hug and the brothers spent the night in silent slumber. Sujoy woke in the wee hours. And painted pictures in the dark....

Soon, Sujoy found himself in a disturbing situation when news of Pulak Biswas's death reached Haur and Sumit put two and two together. Sujoy was still at home, three days after the incident, nursing a fever. Hence, Sumit was able to pull up Sujoy and ask agitatedly, "You knew?"

"Yes, I did."

Sumit clutched a pillow tightly to himself and sobbed profusely. Then he sprang up and said, "When will you leave the party? Joy, please leave the party!"

"I will. Once I leave college. For sure."

They did not talk about it anymore. Though police enquiries found their way to Haur, Sumit's alibi saved Sujoy from becoming a suspect. Furthermore, since the police was burdened with numerous murder cases, they heaved sighs of relief if they could close a few by stamping them as political. In such instances, they hardly showed interest in solving the cases.

4

SREE opened the door and asked, "Did you find her, Bapi?"

"Yes."

"Did she accept? Will she paint for us?"

"Sort of. Will need to find out in about six weeks."

The subject of this conversation was Dibyangana. Sujoy liked to share his ideas and projects with his daughter, Sree, who in turn cooperated and contributed like a matured adult. Sree was more matured than others of her age group. Sujoy tried to give this maturity its due importance rather than brush it aside as inappropriate. As a result, Sree too was quite frank with her ideas, demands and opinions. Sree was Sujoy Banerjee's daughter as well as friend, his faith and joy, his present and also his future. Sree was the reason he wanted to live, the satisfaction he derived from his work and the only thread of conversation between him and Ragini!

Sujoy ruffled Sree's hair and asked, "Why are you looking so dishevelled?"

"Bapi, next year I have to take the board exams. When you are not at home, I use the time to study. You know, once you return, I don't get any studying done!"

"You mean, I disturb you?"

"You don't. But I get disturbed anyway."

Sujoy tweaked his daughter's nose. Sree hung on to Sujoy's arm and walked with him into the living room. They discussed about Dibyangana. But Sujoy kept all talk related to the purchase of Dibyangana's paintings out of the conversation. As a successful businessman, he was well aware of how much to reveal in which quarter. Life's experiences had taught him a few things. Just as the amount of trust one could reserve for someone differed from person to person, so also, how far one could trust someone depended on the matter at hand. According to Sujoy, trust was blind and without doubt. But it was divided and layered, according to situation and person, resembling the mass of water on the Earth's surface.

All of Sujoy Banerjee's opinions and principles were well-thought-out and they played an active role in the decisions he took in life.

Sujoy Banerjee's family hardly fit the bill for an ideal family. All three – Ragini, Sree and Sujoy – knew that they could not live without one another. But, at the same time, disregarding the social and marital norms, they had separate bedrooms. Since Sree's birth, Ragini and Sujoy had not resumed normal sexual relations. Ragini did not want another child. But, to draw the curtain on their sexual life because of that, seemed quite contrary to modern mind-set. The variety of available contraceptives could have easily been a part of their life. But Ragini harboured a weird belief that Sujoy would have somehow got an upper hand over all contraceptives and impregnated her.

Sujoy too, had never exercised his husbandly rights to demand marital sex. He believed that a lover had every right to nurse an ego. And so, he did not discard arrogance and beg sexual favour. Ragini, according to her will and need, invited Sujoy to her bed during the 'safe' days of her menstruation. Sujoy did honour the invitation a few times but had returned with the bitter taste of displeasure. Being intimate with menstrual blood had repulsed him. Hence, their respective refusals kept them apart indefinitely.

Since Ragini could have taken birth-control pills and resolved the issue at her end, it seemed irrelevant that she was not comfortable with the idea of Sujoy using the normal male contraceptive. But Ragini was averse to pills. Pills were believed to be instrumental in adding extra pounds and Ragini went into a frenzy at the slightest threat to physical beauty. In the eighth month of her pregnancy, while on a routine pre-natal check-up at the doctor's, she suddenly felt that she looked quite ugly. She feared that she would never regain her pre-pregnancy figure and beauty. And, for some reason, she blamed the doctor for it and attacked him, scratching his neck and face. She threw the paper weight and broke the glass top of the table. And even attempted to jump out of the window; but the nurse saved her just in time. From that day, till she delivered the baby, Ragini was kept under strict vigil, in the care of a psychiatrist. After Sree was born, Ragini refused to feed the baby at her breast. On being told that the baby might die from lack of nourishment, she finally agreed to nurse Sree. Then, gradually, while taking care of the new-born Sree, she returned to being her normal self and also set her mind on regaining her lost beauty.

Sujoy believed that when someone behaved like a mad person, he or she actually succumbed to lunacy. In fact, Sujoy's belief was actually based on scientific facts. The term 'like a mad person' apparently had no relevance. A person was either mad or he wasn't. Madness was related to a particular stratum of a person's mental state. He could dwell in that stratum permanently or temporarily. There were some social rules and doctrines which decided the acceptability of a mental state as normal or abnormal. But who could guarantee the authenticity of those doctrines? Who could say that the life which we took to be normal was not, in all essence, a madness of sorts?

In Ragini's proximity, Sujoy had developed a certain opinion about human nature and relationship in wedlock. Of course, it would be better suited to say that the opinion related more to his own behaviour than human nature. Sujoy often tried to arrive at unique conclusions about human nature by studying other people in the light of analyses drawn from his own behaviour. Thus, the conclusions acquired greater depth and alluded to human nature in general rather than a particular person's behaviour.

Often, he felt that some of his actions had no connection with his conscience or his soul. To be honest, being alive seemed nothing more than just that—something as mundane and meaningless as scratching an itchy patch or exchanging a polite smile with a neighbour in the lift.

At other times, life seemed worth every moment. His existence seemed indispensable. He felt, had he not existed, many of the world's changes would not have been possible. These feelings usually surfaced when Sree was with him or when he felt a sudden rush of emotions for Ragini.

Rush of emotions for Ragini—that too, was a wonder. In their sexually deprived marriage of sixteen years, Sujoy often felt that he loved Ragini deeply. But then again, he felt that love was after all a personal engagement and choice. The fact that one human being would love another, connoted nothing beyond a personal decision. Initiated by that decision, a sense of longing and other related emotions took shape. The emotions were solely attached to that pre-determined one person. Often, the emotions died soon enough and were transferred to another human being, for a new lease of life.

The love which blossoms between a man and a woman, follows the laws of nature and is geared towards a sexual fruition. The love shared with parents, offspring and friends is not relevant in this context. The love between man and woman, for Sujoy Banerjee, was but a temporary state of life. Its tenure was short, like the first burst of youth. For Sujoy though, the short period had extended to sixteen long years. The memories of the sexual attraction which had bound Sujoy and Ragini in the early years of their marriage were still sweet. In the light of that, Sujoy believed that, though love was temporary, sex was not indispensable to the existence of love. To express the fact that he was capable of love, man needed another entity. For Sujoy, Ragini was that entity. He had given his love to Ragini and was yet to take it back.

Sree rubbed her cheek against Sujoy's and said, "I'm off to study a bit."

"Ok. Where's your mother?"

"Ma is painting. She said she is going to paint through the night. No one is to disturb her. The exhibition is round the corner and she is feeling inspired."

"That's good. But, won't she eat?"

"She asked Mashi to make her four chicken sandwiches and a flask of coffee."

'Has she made it?'

"Huh! Is it possible that Mashi will ignore any of Ma's requests? Ma has woven many dreams around her art, hasn't she Bapi?"

"Yes. Many...people will know her all over the country..."

"She will attend exhibitions abroad...be awarded.... What do you think is the standard of her paintings, Bapi? Do they have it in them to be famous?"

Sujoy was taken aback. Sree was expressing doubts about her mother!

Was Sree trying to test him? Did she have a motive behind asking such a question? Usually, Sree and Ragini were blind to each other's shortcomings. Of course, only in the area of talent. Because, often, when Sujoy and Ragini fought, Sree took her father's side. Although, it was rarely that they fought openly as such incidents sent Sree into bouts of depression. It was for Sree's benefit that Sujoy and Ragini tried not to cross each other's paths too often. And as Sree grew older, maintaining this distance became easier.

As far as talent was concerned, both Ragini and Sree believed themselves to be extremely gifted artists. But Sree was matured enough to judge Ragini as a person without bias and so, she happened to take Sujoy's side every now and then. In fact, father and daughter had struck up a sort of endearing friendship. Yet, Sujoy often felt that Sree was a mirror image of her mother. Or, perhaps, Sree complemented and completed Ragini's existence. Sujoy's relationship with Sree was quite different from the one he shared with Ragini. Between Sree and Sujoy, there was happiness, trust and dependence. But between Ragini and Sujoy, there existed mistrust, disagreement and suspicion. Yet, there was dependence too. And love. Love always existed. Sujoy and Ragini's marital life, which revolved around Sree, appeared quite an ideal one to the outside world. And, of course, it was valuable to them as well. Else, each would not have felt the other's need in life. But, just as a sphere was made up of innumerable smaller spheres, so also, Sujoy knew that his family was made up of numerous smaller families. Made up of mother and daughter. Where, often, he did not find a place. Especially, when mother and daughter needed to come to a decision involving either or both of them. At those times, Sujoy's opinion was usually not sought or completely ignored or rejected outright.

The first year of marriage was spent in the grip of sexual fever. After that, when the spell was broken, started the accumulation of neglect. Since then, he had been carrying the burden of disregard and insult. For the past sixteen years.

That was the reason he could understand how closely bound he was to Sree and Ragini. Because, if they were not close to his heart, they wouldn't have been able to hurt him. Sujoy Banerjee was a successful man of thirty-seven. Who else but his own people had the right to hurt him?

So why was Sree questioning her mother's talent while in the father-daughter sphere? The question unnerved Sujoy. He became cautious. Was his daughter trying to test him? Had she been put to the task by her mother? Was this in any way related to his visit to Dibyangana regarding the upcoming exhibition? Sujoy allowed praise to flow freely. He said, "There can be no doubt about your mother's talent."

"She has been painting for a long time now. There have been many reviews and previews. But to what effect?"

"You know how things work in this country, don't you? Until one is acknowledged abroad, he or she is not awarded any recognition at home. Moreover, Ragini's work has not been written about in any leading newspaper or magazine. I'm going to try this time."

"Bapi, I think your generation does not understand Ma's paintings. Yet, for me…the younger generation… her paintings are greatly inspirational. They appeal to me immensely. So, Ma is actually well ahead of her times. And that is why she is so lonely…and in pain."

"Do you really understand so much, dear? Not only your mother but you, too, are amazing! I guess, all talented people are slightly loony."

"Oh Bapi! Come on, talk sense! Do I even stand in comparison with Ma in this respect?"

"I am pretty sure that you have inherited your mother's talent, if not more."

"The other day, Ma showed me prints of some paintings by K.K. Hebbar. What fantastic paintings! Bapi, I have to paint stuff like those. Ma says her inspiration comes from Rossetti. Well, I feel no one can paint better than Ma."

"As you see more paintings, you shall have clearer concepts. Don't look at your mother's work as her daughter. Think of your mother as an individual and an artist while judging her work."

Sree rubbed her cheek against her father's again and went to her room. Sujoy too retired to his room. The table was laden with food, ready for dinner. Mashi would readily serve and offer a plate of food to any member, if requested; or, one could easily help himself to it. In this family, the tradition of sitting down to dinner together did not exist. On the odd occasion, as though by accident, Sujoy, Ragini and Sree met at the dining table. On those evenings, disagreements between Sujoy and Ragini punctuated the meal. The topic would sometimes be business related and at other times not.

The conversation often ran along these lines when Ragini initiated, "I heard you were at Lalbazar?"

Sujoy nodded, "Hmm."

"Did you meet Supratim Bhattacharya?"

"Yes."

"Why?"

"A casual meeting."

"There must be some good reason...perhaps you don't want to share with me."

"Why wouldn't I share?"

"You know better."

"No, I don't."

"Of course you do! Didn't you buy a flat without telling me?"

"So what? You better concentrate on the business. By the way, did I buy the flat for someone else?"

"Oh come on! I know what you were up to!"

"You simply know nothing! Why are you so overtly concerned about my whereabouts? Do I question you about yours?"

In such situations, Sree took turns siding with either her mother or her father, in an attempt to mediate.

It was only when they had guests for dinner that the family ate in peace. Ragini sported a charming smile as she spoke and Sujoy replied with equal amiability. They acted the 'exemplary couple' to perfection. When Sree was younger, she prayed for dinner guests every day. Little did she know that had guests been a regular feature at the dinner table, the masks her parents wore, would have dropped off sooner or later.

Sujoy sat down with some important files after taking a shower. His business was doing well. But Sujoy knew that profits could never be increased along the path of complete honesty. In fact, he believed, honesty was surely not the reason behind the more successful businesses in the world. The primary aim of business was profit. To be honest, profits were necessary for a business to be sustainable and to prosper.

Sujoy also believed that business brought with it a kind of social responsibility. The Government of India had been incapable of providing employment to those who had been blessed with jobs created by his business. In the light of that, he was not repentant of the grey areas in his business. He was confident that, in the course of his business, he was not depriving or exploiting anyone. His employees received good salaries. And it was because of the grey areas in business that he was able to offer his employees an annual bonus and afford to host art exhibitions, paying high taxes and clearing all revenues at the same time. During the days when he banked upon honest earnings, his family lacked proper medical care, security, social acknowledgement and respect from society. Familial and social problems abounded. Money had bought out those problems. Yet, difficulties still existed and the demands of those difficulties did not reduce; they never did. Of course, at the same time, his abilities had overtaken many of his inabilities.

To be honest, Sujoy couldn't always identify his own problems. The absence of a sexual relation with his wife was not his only concern and surely he was not the only example of a person deprived of normal conjugal relations. It could hardly be said that, in the presence of normal conjugal relations, his other problems would have vanished. To be honest, problems were adept at procreation, even if solutions for the current ones were close at hand.

Sujoy knew how to get his own way, by means other than solely honest. Yet, he also had certain shortcomings. Alongside his many abilities, resided his various inabilities. He couldn't for example, leave the world of art behind. Though he no longer painted, he had kept himself as closely associated with art as possible. He couldn't ignore Ragini, he couldn't hurt her; neither could he leave her. Why? Ragini's paintings failed to attract him. Yet for some inexplicable reason he had embarked on hosting art exhibitions in order to bring fame at Ragini's doorstep. Else, he would have relegated himself to simply appreciating and purchasing art, and thus maintained proximity to art.

Sujoy could very well gain popularity by proclaiming that the exhibition was only a means to gratify his own desires. The exhibition would lose credibility if word got out that it was also an avenue along which he was trying to lead Ragini to success. Did others get a whiff of the fact that he was trying to establish Ragini as an artist? Perhaps they did. So, to avoid such complexities, Sujoy wanted another artist, besides Ragini, to take part in the exhibition and receive public gaze and acclaim. Let the world know that establishing his wife was not his only aim.

He truly sought new talent. He truly loved art because even after immersing himself in business, many a time he had stood before a blank canvas and felt shivers run through his body. That was one place which provided him respite from the cruelty around, it offered him a haven.

Sujoy Banerjee, like many young men, had initially decided not to tie the knot. He had planned to lead a racy life to keep up appearances and paint alongside to keep calm within. His favourite subject was 'life of a boy'—a young boy's features, thoughts, hopes, desires, pains and loneliness! In between painting young boys he would also attempt some frames from nature. And along with it, he would lead a restless wanderer's life. He had certainly desired the life of a wild horse, without any shackles. He also wanted to immerse himself in an extreme form of dedication. The kind which united his senses with his heart and soul. But alas! He could not become a devotee of that kind; and that fact echoed in the hollow of his heart. One could not push oneself into self-oblivion with conscious efforts; it was a fact. Sujoy Banerjee could not become an artist; that was also a fact. It was the piercing longing to become an artist that eventually led him to become a businessman.

Ragini had crushed, battered and hewn his dreams to pieces till they ceased to exist. She had killed the artist in him like a cruel tornado of destruction.

Was Sujoy more talented than Ragini? He did not know. Ragini's yearning for wealth pushed Sujoy ahead and transformed him into a successful and shrewd tradesman. At the same time, wealth had also made Sujoy stronger in mind. With his wealth, Sujoy had gained control over various luxuries, security and even people, with a hold on their personal lives as well. But he could not get back the artist in him. Was he at peace? Often, when faced with this question, he hardened his jaw and said, "I did not want peace. Because I am not a coward. I am not naïve. There is no peace in this world. And I do not long for that which the world does not have."

Sujoy flipped through the file which was the source of his joy as well as anxieties; though not peace. There was a sound at the door. Sree stood there in a knee-length white nightdress held by spaghetti straps at her shoulders. Sujoy noticed that his daughter's soft slim arms seemed to flow down from her shoulders like cascading milk. The curve of her neck and shoulders was like the curve of a swan's neck. He gazed and thought how fast his daughter was growing up. Just the other day, she was a little girl! His little Sree! Suddenly, a magician seemed to have tapped her with his wand and made her grow up.

The thought that his daughter was no longer a child made him sad. He held out his hand and said, "Come! Did you want something? "

"Bapi, please fasten this."

Sree offered her back to him and he noticed a small zip at the base of her bare back. His daughter bent down while he pulled the zip up, though it would hardly matter if it was left undone. Beneath his hand was a smooth back, like a fresh blank canvas without a mark on it. He stroked the canvas lightly as if pondering what to paint on it. His daughter turned her face to him and smiled. Sujoy's eyes were drawn to the outline of his daughter's small breasts and he felt a pang. He thought to himself, my daughter's breasts are like the swell of the sea shells and the fine lines that the sea etches upon them; my daughter's breasts are a burgeoning truth! Then he tousled her hair and said, "From now on, ask your mother to help you with this dress, okay?"

"Why? Why not you? "

"It is not right."

"Why not?"

"I'm not sure, Sree. Your mother will explain to you."

"To begin with, Bapi, Ma is not free to help me now...she is busy painting and has shut herself in. Secondly, I know why you are saying this. Because I am a grown-up female now. And you are a male. Right?"

"Then you know perfectly well, dear."

"I do...but I don't agree with it."

Sree hugged her father and rubbed her cheek against his. Just as she had been doing since childhood. She did this often and preferred to exercise her rights rather than pay heed to any forbiddance. Then she said, "I know very well but I don't agree. You are my father, my friend. I love you. It would be a sin for me to be shy with you."

Sin! Sujoy felt a stirring of anxiety. The word 'sin' was a weakness with him. He remembered how terrified Sree had been at the sight of blood, during the initial months of the onset of menstruation. She called out for her Bapi from the bathroom. Ragini tried to manage by herself but failed. Hence, Sujoy had to lend a hand and, on many days, ended up being late for work. Sree was only nine when she started her periods, quite early. At the time, out of insecurity, she called out for her father. But, in time, she grew used to the change. Though, even today, she was not at all shy before her father. Often, she asked him to fasten the back buttons of her dress or hook up her bra!

Sin! What was sin! It was nothing but a figment of the mind. Anything, that made one feel guilty, was sin. If shame evoked guilt in Sree then that shame would be sin.

Hence, Sujoy Banerjee kissed his daughter's forehead purely as a parent would. His gaze lingered on as Sree left the room. She looked like young Ragini, of course, sixteen years younger. Almost identical except for a more developed body.

Ragini never possessed such pretty nightdresses. She perhaps wore cheap printed ones bought off the pavement stalls after much haggling over the price. Sujoy lay back, the file on his chest. Old memories flooded his mind. Ragini...! Ragini had married Sujoy by force. But why? In those days, Sujoy was still a student with unemployment looming large in his horizon. Yet, Ragini married him. Their relationship too, was not one of love and romance. Yet.... But why?

Even today, Sujoy drowned in the thoughts which attempted to seek an answer.

5

SUJOY was in his third year and Ragini in her second. Sujoy was doing an honours degree in economics but Ragini did not take up honours in any subject. She wanted to pursue art after graduating. By then, Ragini had trained under various art gurus—Amalesh Chatterjee, Samir Majumdar, Prajit Mukherjee. However, her expectations were not met anywhere. And it couldn't be said for sure that she would have found a path to her liking even if she had studied at the Government Art College. Because the teachers she had already rejected were also professors at Art College. To be honest, Ragini was of restless mind and spirit.

Like everybody else, Sujoy too noticed Ragini in college. There wasn't much of an option. Ragini's beauty was like that of a conch shell, pearly white and perfect. Her complexion, figure and features were perhaps unmatched. She travelled to and from college in a shiny black car. In those days, there weren't many students who had a car at their service. This fact, along with her exceptional beauty, kept Ragini pegged firmly at a different level. And Ragini rarely smiled; her eyes were not youthful and laughing like others' her age. Instead, they spewed unexplained anger. Hence, the boys were afraid of falling in love with her. She didn't have many friends. Just a couple of girls and a few boys, who were grateful to be able to exchange a few words with her. Supriyo, Sreedam, Raju and Amit. The other envious boys took out their frustration on these four by calling them derogatory names.

Besides appreciating her beauty, Sujoy never experienced any pull towards Ragini as a person. He did not have time to waste on girls. After all, he was the successful general secretary of the college students' union. He was on his way to make a name as a good orator and often received urgent summons from political leaders for addressing street corner protest rallies. He was gaining fame as a courageous, friendly and honest student leader. Sujoy Banerjee's uncontested leadership had brought peace to the college campus.

One day, Ragini walked into the students' union room and sought him out.

"I need to talk to you about something important", she said.

Whatever the 'important' matter at hand, Ragini's manner of speech hardly suggested that they were strangers. In fact, her tone hinted at familiarity which had given her the right to approach in this manner. The heated discussion raging in the union room stopped abruptly. All eyes were on Ragini.

"Yes, tell me," said Sujoy.

"It's personal, I need to talk in privacy."

Students from all classes were present in the room. Sujoy glanced at their faces. Everyone, like him, was amazed at the girl's request because it implied an intimate conversation. The request also brought to light the daring streak in the girl's nature and Sujoy always gave courage its due credit. He asked the others to wait and walked out with Ragini. Leading her to a somewhat deserted area near the girls' common room, he said, "You can tell me now."

Ragini bent her head, the flash of courage much dimmed, and said, "The matter is kind of personal. Can you please accompany me?"

"Where?"

"Out of college."

"Why would you want to share something personal with me, Ragini?"

Ragini bit her lip as her eyes welled up. Then she said, "I know I can trust you. It is very urgent. But if you have a problem..."

Teardrops rolled down her cheeks, taking Sujoy by surprise. College was yet to give over and not many people were around. Yet, Sujoy felt self-conscious. He had not expected things to take this turn, especially with Ragini.

He pleaded, "Please don't do this. I'll listen to what you have to say...but not today."

Ragini wiped her eyes with her dupatta. "When?" she asked.

"Any other day. Tomorrow...day after."

"Tomorrow?"

"Fine. What time?"

"I have classes till three. Will you have time after that?"

"Ok. I'll be in the union room. Please come and find me when you are done."

The following day, after three, they got into the car waiting outside college. A well-built middle-aged man was in the driver's seat. Ragini addressed him, "Girin-da, please take us to Victoria."[5]

Then she turned to Sujoy and asked, "Hope you don't mind accompanying me to Victoria, Sujoy-da?"

"No, that's entirely up to you."

"Let's go, Girin-da."

Girin. That was the first time Sujoy saw Girin. At the time, he had no clue that Girin would be a constant presence in his life for the rest of his days. When one meets someone

5 Victoria Memorial is a large marble building in Kolkata built in the memory of Queen Victoria between 1806 and 1821, on the orders of Lord Curzon – the Viceroy of India. It is now a museum and a popular tourist destination set in the large Maidan by the river Hooghly. It has also been a popular lovers' haunt for many years.

for the first time, hardly does he know if his life is going to be associated with that person in any way. Relationships happen out of the blue. In oblivion. Two people...perhaps they had crossed each other's paths, perhaps their gazes had met, their hands had brushed while at the cinema hall or a stadium gallery. They didn't even remember very well. Yet, one day, their lives joined together. As enemies. As friends. Perhaps neither enemy nor friend, just by faith. Or mistrust. Or, no relationship as such, just a regular interaction...like the one with the local fishmonger or the corner shop guy.

Then there were some who recognised the possibility of a relationship at first glance. They felt they had found a dear one. And, truly, someday that person became very close. No one knew how these relations were born. Man and his world were mysteries in their own rights.

But there existed hard reality beyond the realm of these mysteries. People's lives were joined by harsh social obligations and unexplained infatuations. The proactive general secretary, Sujoy Banerjee, never thought he would have to leave this life behind. That he would have to walk away from the intoxicating excitement of party work, the dependence of others on his abilities, the growing crowd of followers...and move on with Girin-da in the driver's seat. That he would have to flow along with Ragini. He never thought he would be a trader; not an artist or a politician or a teacher or an economist. Not even a government employee or a lawyer. From that day, his life came to be controlled by Girin and this car, by Ragini and her bizarre nature.

The car stopped outside Victoria Memorial and Ragini led him inside. Sujoy felt strange, perhaps because this was the first time he was on the grounds of Victoria with a girl to hear out her personal problems. Usually, these grounds were a haven for couples to indulge in some uninterrupted romantic moments. Perhaps, as an artist, Sujoy should have already done the rounds of Victoria but that had not happened. His romanticism had been converted into dynamism which was manifested through political meetings, processions, slogans, lectures and protest marches. In the light of this, Ragini's desire to meet Sujoy in privacy had stirred his friends and followers. They couldn't help but wonder if Ragini's charm and attraction would sweep Sujoy Banerjee away...far away from his life as a leader. They placed their worries before him but Sujoy himself was hardly perturbed. He thought, this too would be a problem in need of resolution, like the various other problems in college. Hence, apart from normal curiosity, wonder and a fair dose of awkwardness, he did not find much in the entire affair to be worried about.

Ragini settled down on the grass by the pond with Sujoy. Her movements well indicated that the place was familiar to her. Though that fact hardly worried Sujoy. For a while, Ragini sat quietly, her head bent low; perhaps expecting Sujoy to initiate a conversation with a question or two. Sujoy did not disappoint her. He leant back on his arms, stretched out his legs and said, "Now tell me."

Ragini said, "Yes, of course."

Sujoy thought, perhaps the girl was still in a dilemma about whether she should really be sharing something personal with an almost stranger. To Sujoy, the dilemma appeared quite natural and his curiosity as a listener remained intact. He said, "I find this quite a surprise."

"What?"

"You hardly know me. Yet, you have brought me all the way here to share your personal issues. Why?"

Ragini looked up and said, "Didn't I tell you that I think I can trust you?"

"How can you be so sure?"

"I know."

Evening descended gradually and the grass looked darker. A grasshopper settled on Ragini's colourful sleeveless top. The last rays of the sun dripped from the flora around and some unknown flower lent its fragrance to the wind. The marble statue of Queen Victoria sat in complete and stark confidence, facing north. The sun played on the thin film of dust which had settled on her face. Many people walked by, some commented, "Victoria reminds one of the Taj Mahal...."

Sujoy and Ragini's conversation picked up after a pause.

Sujoy: How do you know, Ragini?

Ragini: I know. I understand many things. I am an artist. An artist has a third eye.

Sujoy: I too, am an artist. But I don't have a third eye.

Ragini: Then your art will not live for long.

Su: Really? So, what did you see with your third eye? That I can be trusted? I think I'll have to break your trust just to disprove your third eye.

Ra: You won't be able to do that. You will hold back at the last minute.

Su: So much faith?

Ra: Yes.

Su: Very well. But I cannot take any responsibility.

Ra: What do you mean?

Su: Look, I don't know if I am the only one you are sharing your personal issues with. For myself, I can say this much that if I promise then I never spill the beans. But if you have told anyone else and that person breaks your trust then don't blame me.

Ra: Two of my friends know. Karabi and Rikta. They won't tell anyone.

Su: Fine. But I'll still say that I have no responsibility.

Ra: I agree.

Su: Now tell me.

Ra: I'm helpless. Please save me.

Su: How?

Ra: My father has found a match for me. He is an established government employee who has recently joined services after clearing the IAS exam.

Su: Okay!

Ra: I cannot accept him.

Su: Tell your father. Or ask for some more time to think.

Ra: That won't help. I have no option. That's why I have come to you, Sujoy-da.

Su: Why don't you have an option? Is your father adamant?

Ra: Our marriage was registered two months back.

Su: I see!

Ra: It has been decided that after a year, once his younger sister is married, we will have a social wedding.

Su: That's good news! What's his name?

Ra: Bikash Purokayastha. But it's not good news.

Su: Why?

Ra: I have spent quite some time with him…for three months before the registration and after. I realised he is going to torture me. I will not live if I am married to him.

Su: Is he that bad a man? Then why don't you tell your father?

Ra: That's not possible.

Su: Fine, then tell your mother.

Ra: I can't tell anyone. No one will understand.

Su: But why? And what exactly have you seen in him?

Ra: It's a feeling, Sujoy-da. Just a realisation.

Su: What rubbish! How can you bank on a feeling and come to such an extreme conclusion about a person? That's wrong!

Ra: You are right! But Sujoy-da…please try to understand. I'm helpless. Please save me!

Su: How can I save you? What can I do? You don't have any valid evidence against him.

Ra: I do! After our registration, I went out to a movie with him, and that's when I realised...

Su: Did he misbehave?

Ra: No, no. While sitting beside him, I had visions of my past life. I saw him clearly...he was my husband and he was subjecting me to extreme torture. Oh God!

Ragini covered her face with her hands. Sujoy thought the girl was mad. Raving mad. He gritted his teeth.

Su: I don't understand what you are saying, Ragini.

Ra: Believe me, honestly, I can understand and foresee a great deal. My clairvoyance is very strong. I saw death before my grandmother died. I had a sister when I was ten. Every time I saw her, I felt she wouldn't live...I saw her dead face. When I told my mother, she beat me up and said I was jealous of my sister!

Su: Stop, Ragini...stop!

Ra: My sister died. From nephritis. My father couldn't save her in spite of all his wealth. My mother almost went mad.

Su: Just a co-incidence, Ragini. You are reading too much into it.

Ra: Then what about my brothers?

Su: What about them?

Ra: My brothers were in boarding school in Darjeeling. When my sister died, they came home for a while. The day they were to return, I had a vision of their car rolling down into a gorge...

Su: This is unbelievable, Ragini...

Ra: I told my mother and she stopped them from travelling. My father was angry but she refused to let them go. Later we came to know...

Su: What?

Ra: That day, a car actually fell into the gorge.

Sujoy was dumbstruck. Were there really such things in the world which defied reality? He was almost sure that the girl had lost her wits. Or, perhaps, her overactive imagination had crossed all boundaries to create an unnatural world for her. Ragini broke into his silence.

Ra: You don't believe in life after death, so you cannot bring yourself to believe me. You don't have faith on man's transcendental powers. But man is capable of many such things which cannot be explained by logic and common sense. Moreover, life after death is mentioned in our scriptures.

Evening was upon them. How long could they sit there? Yet, he didn't feel like leaving. He didn't feel like doing anything; an evening as this was a rarity in his life. He felt like sitting there, listening to the crazy rants. ".... trust me. I believe in life after death and karma. I believe in the existence of souls. Any conventional 'Sanatan' Hindu[6] would."

Finally, Sujoy found something to say.

Su: Am I an orthodox Sanatan Hindu? I have never given it a thought. Is it really something to ponder over?

Ra: Why should you not ponder? You should. Religion is a part of man's existence. Isn't it? Do you know what the doctrine of rebirth is?

Sujoy stared at Ragini, somewhat absent-mindedly. A trace smile rose in the depths of his mind. Back home, in Haur, there was a man called Sanatan. People called him Crazy Sanatan. Maintaining testimony to his craziness, the moment he met someone, he asked, "Hey, who are you?"

And then, irrespective of a response, he said, "Hmm... you seem somewhat familiar." Every time Sujoy heard the

---

6 Refers to a person following the 'eternal laws' and the original perception of Truth guiding the Hindu way of life.

name 'Sanatan' he associated it with madness; he had never thought that the word actually had a different meaning.

He suppressed the smile and re-joined the conversation.

Su: No, tell me.

Ra: Sure.

Su: Ragini, do you mind if I lie down on the grass?

Ra: Not at all. It's quite common here. Now listen to what the doctrine of rebirth has to say. The souls of all beings ultimately mingle with the Supreme Soul. But along the way to that ultimate union, are various births and rebirths. After death, the soul leaves the lifeless body and enters another body. A person's karma decides how, where, in what form he will be reborn. You do believe in the connection between one's deeds and the results he gains, don't you? You reap what you sow, in plainspeak. Well, following this causality, man has to bear the results of both his honest and dishonest deeds. All deeds, whether good or bad, reap consequences. Some people think, only a sinner suffers rebirth. That is not completely true. If a good deed is driven by lust then it leads to rebirth as well. Concentration and deeper delving into these concepts help make them clearer. But not many understand. And, even if they do, they cannot bring themselves to accept the same. After all, not all humans have the same level of willpower and intelligence. Do they?'

Sujoy sat up, somewhat angry and irritated.

Su: Let's not discuss the scriptures, biding time here in the evening, Ragini. Instead, come straight to the point. What kind of help do you want from me?

Ra: I wanted to help you understand the doctrine of rebirth. Unless you understand that, you will not be able to appreciate my problem. And, if I can't make you appreciate my problem then how will I ask for your help?

Su: There is no need for a lecture on rebirth. I have understood. The point is, for some reason or the other, you do not like Bikash Purokayastha. What can *I* do in this matter? Explain to your father. You have not been wedded socially yet.

Ra: I can't tell my father. Please try to understand!

Su: Tell your mother. She believes in your extraordinary powers and clairvoyance.

Ra: It's of no use. Ma has hardly any authority in our family. Father is the decision maker and listens to no one.

Su: In that case, what can I do?

Ra: You believe me, don't you, Sujoy-da? Tell me you trust me!

Su: Ragini, listen to me…it is more important for me to understand what exactly you want from me.

Ra: Please help me.

Su: You have been saying this for quite some time now. But, what help?

Ra: You can put pressure on Bikash to divorce me.

Su: Impossible.

Ra: Why?

Su: Why should I wash such dirty linen for you?

Ra: To save me. Won't you save me?

Su: It's not as easy as that. You say he is a high-ranking government official. He must be an influential man! Moreover, divorce is not child's play that I can scare him into agreeing to it. One has to go to court.

Ra: Please bring him around so that he approaches my father to call off this wedding.

Su: Why would he listen to me? And why should I get involved at all?

Ra: Save me. Please save me. Only you can save me.

Su: But how? Of course, there is no point asking you that anymore…

Ra: If you don't save me then I'll have to commit suicide.

Su: Okay, okay…now stop. Give me a couple of days to

think it over. You said that I can't tell anyone, but I'll have to discuss with a couple of friends.

Ragini agreed. Sujoy shared the problem with Jayshankar and two other trusted friends. After some deliberation, it was decided that they would help Ragini. All said and done, it was quite evident that the girl was not at all keen on the marriage. Sujoy and his friends did not read too much into the problem and did not burn the midnight candle pondering over it. They were actually quite appreciative of Ragini's revolt against her father's decision to deliver her into an unhappy married life.

Jayshankar was the one most experienced and trustworthy in such matters. He made a plan and, accordingly, followed Bikash Purokayastha for about three days. And then, one evening, as Bikash stepped out of his workplace, he was cleverly ushered into a waiting car. They drove with him to a deserted stretch in Salt Lake, quite conducive to such errands. Jayshankar had arranged for a car with dark windows and he held a knife to Bikash's belly, threatening to stab if he made a sound. Bikash did not utter a word. The car drove a route from Salt Lake to Princep Ghat and eventually to Jayshankar's house. Along the way, Bikash was made to realise why he had been kidnapped. He was a short, stocky man of naïve nature. Breaking into a nervous sweat, he agreed to all conditions placed before him…without any hesitation.

If you tell anyone about the kidnapping then…

If you contact the police then…

If you try to be clever then…

If you approach Ragini's father for help then…

If you do not release Ragini within a month then…

If you somehow manage to send us to prison, even then…

Sweat rained down Bikash's forehead and his fleshy, pampered cheeks. Sujoy Banerjee had scraped the sweat from his forehead with a sharp, glinting blade. He had not noticed a little pimple on Bikash's forehead. In the process, the blade cut into it and a few drops of blood escaped, though they had had no intention of shedding a single drop of blood. Bikash began to tremble.

Much before they reached Khidirpur, Bikash agreed to all the conditions. They then decided to drop him back at Salt Lake.

Bikash Purokayastha – short and plump, dark and pampered, courteous and gentle, timid and scared for his life – curled up and retreated like an insignificant worm or a tiny beetle, and hastily detached himself from Ragini's life.

Twenty days after Bikash left her, Ragini again sought out Sujoy. In the meanwhile, Sujoy expressed no curiosity or interest towards Ragini. He did not ask Ragini how her family took the entire matter and what exactly unfolded. The day after they threatened Bikash, Ragini was informed that if the result was not favourable then she was to let Sujoy know.

Now, Sujoy realised that perhaps his decision to get involved in the matter was a shallow one, egged on by the inexperience of youth. Yet, that very decision had been controlling every moment of his life till date. The entire episode was like a tremendous turmoil which gave no hint of what could be the future impact of such a decision.

When Ragini approached him the second time, he received her with ease. A kind of heroic arrogance played within him and, in Ragini's presence, he felt quite powerful. Indomitable. And the girl, who had been instrumental in fetching him this self-satisfaction, said, "I am extremely grateful to you. I don't think I shall ever be able to repay you in any way. Yet, here I am with my last request. If you turn me away then I shall be at a complete loss..."

She fished out a few strips of sleeping pills and said, "I always keep these with me. I will die sometime soon..."

Sujoy's sixth sense perked up. He felt anxious, as well as irritated. Why did this girl always demand help with her life on the stake! And why did she choose him as one of the players of her game?

Sujoy replied harshly, "The last time you said that if Bikash was not removed from your life your only option would be death.... Well, you got what you wanted. Now you are trying to say something else. I think you are unwell. Why should I cater to your needs time and again? And how?'

Ragini: Sujoy-da, please...

Sujoy: Hope this time you are not here to say that now you want Bikash back in your life!

Ra: Please help me, Sujoy-da. Please!

Su: Ragini, no way! I cannot spare so much time for you.

Ra: I know, you will help me. I can see it...in my vision. You are a man of greatness. There is simply no one like you in my life.

Su: This is meaningless! I have done nothing great. Don't you try to pamper my ego to get your way. It is a cheap ploy.

Ra: I know you are great. I can see it. I believe in it.

Su: How can I be great? I exercise certain political powers within the boundaries of this college. If I am not here, someone else will step into my shoes. The way I took the place of others. I appear to stand tall because my realm is so small. In reality, it is nothing!

Ra: I was talking about your humane side. Your political influence has no connection with it.

Su: Ragini, I have to sit for my Part II exams in six weeks. I have not prepared at all. My father is not rich like yours.

The moment I clear college, I will have to apply for clerical jobs. Now don't sour my mood with your gibberish. I have to get back to the hostel and study.

Ra: A clerk is no less a human being. But you have a lot in you. You are not meant to spend your life as a clerk.

Su: Is this also an observation of your third eye, Ragini? Since, you are so specially gifted, why don't you solve your own problems? Of course, I don't know what your recent problem is.

Ra: Will you believe me?

Su: We'll come to that later, Ragini. I cannot promise anything beforehand.

Ra: Won't you believe what I have to say?

Su: Please Ragini…

Ra: Promise me, you won't turn me away.

Su: I cannot promise till I have heard what you have to say.

Ra: But…but…

Su: I am running out of patience, Ragini. I have to leave…

Ra: Please lend me a shelter, Sujoy-da. Please…please marry me. I can't take it anymore.

At that instant, if the girl had asked for Sujoy's life, he wouldn't have been as stunned. To be honest, there wasn't another proposal in the world more bizarre than this! Hence, Sujoy was dumbstruck for quite a while. Today too, they were at the same place, near the pond in the grounds of Victoria Memorial. The time too was similar. But the difference between the two meetings was that, during the earlier one, Sujoy was more or less an audience and today the focus was on him. This realisation brought his thoughts to an abrupt halt.

The only thing that registered with him was the sun preparing to set in the horizon beyond the race course. The tiny tufts of clouds were spotted with a vibrant red. The greens of Victoria were gradually becoming darker. There were many other faces around them; all cocooned in love. Couples, headily in love, sat wrapped in each other. An angel descended to earth and folded her wings as she sat down before him. Who had brought these angels to earth? Who had then left them behind? The angel wept as she sat there. Sujoy longed to capture the scene with a paint brush. The dusk hues, the clouds, the dark greenery, the pairs of lovers, the love around...his heart jolted! Love! He had never before thought about this word.

Today, why were these unsolicited words and some unwanted things crowding his mind? His colours and brushes always wanted to paint pictures of little boys, of nature. Or of penury and death. But love!

A cruel query tore at him—was Ragini in love with him? Did Ragini adore him? If so, then what was the haste? Why did she say that she couldn't bear it anymore? What about the sleeping pills? Why couldn't she come clean?

Sujoy was at a loss. He wondered what love was about. Was it only an attachment between a man and a woman? Was it that trivial? Was it only a means to make good use of an opportunity? Did it only aim at bringing two people physically close? Sujoy gripped his hair with both hands; then he covered his face with his hands. Restless. Perhaps he was trying to build up a revolution of sorts against the unknown future. He felt extremely insignificant and helpless.

Su: What do you think of yourself? You think you can get whatever you want? Is the world at your beck and call? How dare you put such a proposal before me?

Ra: Marry me, Sujoy-da. Save me.

Su: What do you take me to be? Why are you proposing something so absurd? Are you out of your mind?

Ra: Yes, I have gone mad. Believe me, my circumstances have made me go mad. Save me, Sujoy-da. Only you can.

Su: Ragini, you are a beautiful girl and men find you attractive. Your father will find an excellent match for you. Why are you behaving this way?

Ra: Can I call you by your first name only?

Su: Please do. But stop acting crazy.

Ra: I have gone mad, Sujoy. Make me better.

Su: I don't even know you very well, Ragini. How can you think this way? And marriage...can't even think about it...I have to leave now.

Ra: No, no, please don't leave. If you leave now, I'll spend the night sitting here. Would you like that?

Su: Ragini, why are you after me? I helped you according to your request. So why this?

Ra: Sujoy, you may not know me but I know you well. At some point in life you would have thought of marriage... so why not now?

Su: I am not in love with you. I don't desire you. You are not even a friend. Ragini, for me, you are not even a nightmare as a wife. You are nothing.

Ra: I want you. I want to be your wife. Because, only you have the power to save me.

Su: Impossible! Incredible!

Ra: Why? Tell me, why?

Su: I am still a student. I haven't even cleared my Part II exams. I am not even twenty-one. My future is anybody's guess! I have two older brothers who are yet to be married... Ragini, you are knocking on the wrong door. I can't take this. Why did you do what you did with Bikash? He is an innocent man...why did you make those excuses? Why did you insult him so?

Ra: No, not innocent! He is a torturer, an opportunist. A lascivious man. You know nothing, Sujoy...nothing!

Su: I don't need to know. I'll leave now.

Ra: Marry me, Sujoy. I don't want anything else. I'll...I'll give you time to establish yourself. I am pregnant, Sujoy. I...

Sujoy shoved Ragini away from him. Ragini fell on her side, an almost imperceptible whimper escaping from her. Sujoy's control was slipping away fast. Patience, courtesy, education...everything. "Disgusting!" he blurted out. "You are disgusting! Do you think you can trade all men with your beauty? You go around sinning and I am supposed to take responsibility for them?"

Ragini flared up, "What sin? He was my husband in my previous life. What sin are you talking about?"

"Then go back to that husband of yours from your previous life. Why are you after me?"

"I would...if I could."

"If you can't then make other arrangements...you are rich people. The exams are in six weeks. Don't bother me now."

Ragini stood up and said, "Very well. I will never approach you again. I will never bother you again."

"What melodrama!"

Ragini walked along, her head bent. Neither spoke a word. When they reached the car, Sujoy said, "I'll make my own way back."

Ragini did not respond. But Girin measured him with a chilling look which angered Sujoy. It enraged him immensely.

The following day, Sujoy reached college and got the news. Ragini was in hospital. Girin informed that Ragini had taken sleeping pills. Her behaviour had perhaps alerted her family that something was amiss so her mother had kept an eye on her. When Ragini fell off the bed unconscious, her mother was around. They took her to the hospital in the wee hours of the morning. Under her pillow was a note—*Sujoy, I am leaving. No one is responsible for my death. – Ragini.*

Sujoy visited the hospital with Girin. Ragini was in a delirious state, pale and fatigued. Her ashen appearance veiled by a deathly gloom. She had lost an unexpected amount of blood.

Ragini's mother, Mahamaya, held Sujoy's hands in hers and said, "Accept her, dear. Take my crazy daughter. She has told me all about you."

What did the words mean? Sujoy could not fathom anything. All he felt was a profound and strong pain. Immense pain. Dark and deep clots of the pain dotted his entire existence. Gradually, the essence of love dawned on him. It was only love that could mete out pain of this magnitude.

6

ANJAN Kar purchased all five of Dibyangana's paintings from the exhibition. Each painting was priced at five thousand rupees. Sujoy deducted ten per cent and sent a cheque for eighteen thousand rupees to Dibyangana's house. Dibyangana had painted on a single subject—shackled women. Though, in different settings with varying features. She used colours like dark green, white, black and a touch of yellow to express pain and pathos. Anger and sorrow. Repulsion and motherhood. After studying the work done in various media, Anjan Kar said, "Dibyangana is gradually finding her individuality. Perhaps she is better off without the influence of a guru."

Prior to this, Sujoy had not seen Dibyangana's work. Hence, he could hardly offer an opinion. Nevertheless, he was awed. Dibyangana's strokes were confident and strong with not a shade of uncertainty about them, yet they were not incomprehensible. The paintings radiated the artist's personality and conviction.

Sujoy knew that every artist had his or her own characteristic style, just like the various personality traits of different human beings. But most artists failed to express that unique trait due to an inclination towards imitation and lack of self-confidence. These were sometimes interdependent. The need to copy the work of others was often born of lack of self-confidence or inability of self-expression. Often, an artist was influenced by the work of another without realising the fact. For an artist, every brush stroke was an adventure, which had to be tackled with courage and confidence. After examining Dibyangana's work, Sujoy too felt that she held promise.

So, to welcome this new-found promise, Sujoy had visited Dibyangana to hand over the cheque. But, once there, he learnt that she did not have a bank account to her name. Dibyangana's father-in-law requested cash payment; or, a cheque in her husband's name. Sujoy suppressed a smile and informed that those were not possible options. Dibyangana sat with her head lowered while her father-in-law enquired about the possibility of more such exhibitions and sale of paintings.

Sujoy was not sure whether the eighteen thousand rupees would make a difference in Dibyangana's life. But Anjan Kar was hopeful, he said, "I think her in-laws will now give her ample time to paint."

Sujoy pushed a bundle of notes towards Anjan and said, "Keep this."

"No, no..." Anjan objected. "There is no need. Please... Can't I purchase Ragini's work?"

Sujoy waved his hand dismissively. This discussion was an extremely confidential and important one as far as the purchase of the paintings was concerned. He said, "As we decided, the paintings will remain with you. You think mother and daughter would let me be if Ragini's paintings were not priced higher than Dibyangana's?"

"Very well...only the extra amount in that case. Not the full price."

"No, the entire amount. Anjan, you may be my friend but you are also a businessman. We should stick to the contract."

"No. There will be no business contract between us. I am sure I will be able to sell off Ragini's paintings. There are various kinds of buyers. Don't worry about them."

"Fine. You can return the money once they are sold."

"Okay."

Anjan poured whisky into the glasses. Their third round. They were in a flat in a deserted stretch of Kaikhali; almost away from civilisation. Beyond these premises was marshland and then paddy fields. The view from the flat in daylight was wonderful, punctuated by silence and solitude. Precisely the reasons they had bought the two flats on the second floor of this four storied building. On the ground floor were the parking lot and a small room where Jishu, the caretaker, lived. The first floor flats served as the distributor's office of a cosmetic goods company. The third floor flats were still under construction, work progressing quite slowly.

The only people who knew about these flats were their solicitor and accountant. If, suddenly, Sujoy and Anjan were to die at the same time, their wives – Ragini and Debola respectively – would be the surprised owners of these properties, quite unexpectedly.

Sujoy walked to the window with his glass. Dim orbs of light flickered in the distance, as though fatigued by the gradual repletion of their resources as they tried to light up the city. His gaze rested on their cars parked below on the street. They had not used the building's parking space as they were due to leave soon. But how soon? A couple of hours? Three...four? There were times when they stayed put here from six in the evening till eleven at night.

Manjil and Jishu sat on the low boundary wall chatting with Anjan Kar's driver Jitu. The surroundings were mostly enveloped in darkness. But it would hardly remain this way for very long. The lights of civilisation would gradually eat into the darkness. And then, Sujoy would be out searching for a new patch of darkness and solitude. But this flat was his own. If he were to escape to the solitude within its walls then who could deprive him? And if he really needed darkness and isolation then he could always go to Haur. Their house in Haur was now deserted. The fields still rolled away into darkness from the premises. But he rarely visited Haur. The house, the fields, the sky, the sound of trains chugging past...everything in Haur reminded him too much of Chhotda.

Suddenly, a thought struck Sujoy—couldn't the whisky be shared with Jitu, Jishu and Manjil? It was quite possible that a peg or two would help all of them cross the barriers of qualms and urban artifice, and bring them closer. Moreover, their indefinite wait for their masters could be transformed into an enjoyable evening. Sujoy's heart overflowed with sympathy for the trio. He called Manjil and asked him to make good use of a bottle from the car boot. As Manjil hurried to fulfil his master's command, Sujoy's mind came up with the picture of Girin. Girin was in a manner associated with Sujoy's ownership of this flat, he always would be. In fact, Sujoy, Ragini and Girin were entwined for life.

At that instant, Anjan's cell phone rang in his pocket. Sujoy immersed himself in thoughts of Girin-Manjil-Jitu. His thoughts and Anjan's voice mingled and jostled breathlessly in the solid darkness of Kaikhali.

"Hello, yes, tell me."

...are they able to make ends meet with the salary I give them?

"Yes, it's me. Who else would answer my cell phone?"

...there was a time when I earned almost the same and struggled to make ends meet. Today it seems impossible. Of course, a decade back, the amount was worth more.

"Can't say. It's evening and early enough...how can I say when I will be back?"

...so what? There was no end to hardships. Coming from wealth, Ragini was unable to manage. I had to think twice before buying an extra tin of baby food. They too must be doing the same. But then, it is all about habit!

"Yes, I am busy."

...I shall give everyone a raise next month.

"Of course, for a city like Kolkata, eight is still evening."

...how much would it affect my expenses! Would have to talk to the accountant. What was I to do with so much wealth? Wealth should be put to good use. Yes, Ragini would be angry, but who cared! Not a big deal. She believed, if employees were paid too much then they ceased to be at the employer's beck and call. They should be kept wanting! The surprising fact was, even after I gave them a raise, their wants would not be met.

"Yes, I am with Sujoy."

...once the salary was increased, it could not be decreased again.

"Okay, fine."

...was Ragini right? Ragini's father believed, one could never satisfy an employee because employees always kept an eye on the master's gains. Hence, trying to satisfy an employee was nothing but madness. One should always strive to squeeze out maximum work by parting with minimum wage.

"I told you...if you don't believe me then stay with me through the day from tomorrow."

...Ragini believed, one should always make the employees feel that they were at the master's mercy. But why? Didn't they work for a wage? Where did mercy come in? Ragini was an artist but devoid of compassion. She wasn't sensitive. How could she then be successful?

"Why are you going on about it, Debola? There are people here...I am in the middle of something important. Won't you give me a moment's peace?"

...was I compassionate? Did I love other humans? How genuine was my benevolence? Did I feel for others in order to be able to criticise Ragini more? Or, did I help people in order to feel self-satisfaction?

"Bye."

Sujoy: Is everything alright?

Anjan: Can everything ever be alright for married people?

Sujoy: People or men?

Anjan: Of course, men! What worries do women have? They don't have to deal with any problems, be it at home or outside. They sit around miffed, surrounded by mountains of grievance, grief and gloominess!

Su: Is it right to generalise?

An: They are all the same! As soon as they reach middle age, they become either cynical or paranoid!

Su: Calm down, calm down! Not all women are the same.

An: Perhaps. But, sometimes, the entire world leaves me with a bitter taste. Can you tell me who invented the cell phone?

Su: Dr Martin Cooper. Former General Manager Systems with Motorola. He struck success first in 1973. Do you know who he first called from his invention?

An: I hope, not his wife.

Su: No, he called his competitor researcher.

An: Dr Martin Cooper was either divorced or widowed. Perhaps a dedicated bachelor.

Su: Why?

An: Had he been in the company of a woman, he would not have been able to invent the cell phone.

Su: Well said, Anjan! Ha ha...

An: I was thinking...

Su: Tell me.

An: How about setting up a permanent art gallery?

Su: What about the one you have at home?

An: That cannot be called a proper gallery. It's more of a store. I made arrangements for display so that it was easier to show the stuff to buyers. I was thinking of a permanent gallery where exhibitions would run round the year. Kind of a business diversion, you could say.

Su: Good idea.

An: In Salt Lake. Or maybe...

Su: I think Salt Lake is best. There are a few good galleries in south and central Calcutta already.

An: Are you with me? It's a big leap...am not confident on my own.

Su: Of course, Anjan. But you will have to take the responsibility of taking the project forward and managing it. I will share half the costs.

An: As long as you are with me...should I take the leap?

Su: Sure. Start looking for a place first. Then we will deal with the rest .

An: But Ragini?

Su: Since it's an art gallery, Sree and Ragini won't object. Also, we can make Ragini our partner.

They helped themselves to a fourth round of whisky.

The moon had, meanwhile, climbed the sky to be level with the window. Sujoy remembered the small fourth floor flat in Kasba. In spite of the congested neighbourhood, the flat was calm and quiet. It was the only tall building in the area and the cacophony and dust laden air did not reach the flat. There was a big pond behind the building, and it looked lovely during the rains. He had bought the flat to serve the needs of a secret and vibrant life, with a subtle business motive. Not to avail peace and solitude, like at the Kaikhali flat.

There were many people who he had to keep happy for business needs. He had set up this flat to cater to the needs of those people who wanted to spend a few hours with a dear companion, away from prying eyes and without the fear of exposition. Sujoy had opened the doors of the flat for many famous and celebrated persons. Policemen. Litterateurs. Artists. Officials of the tax department.

Among the artists, Amalesh Chatterjee was the one who visited the Kasba flat most often. He changed partners like clothes. Though quite an unattractive man, he had an arresting personality. At the time, Sujoy was always on the go and maintained contact with people from various spheres. He met Amalesh through Ragini and struck up quite a rapport. But, in time, they drifted apart. Intimacy was something which revolved along an elliptical path around a relationship—sometimes close to the core, at other times far from it. That was how life went on. Then there were those unbreakable relationships which did not travel any set path. Two people were bound in such a manner when their cores coincided and matched. Such relationships were rare, but not impossible. Like Sujoy and Jayshankar. Like Sujoy and Anjan.

Sujoy was sure that, even today, Amalesh changed partners with as much flippancy and could boast the same magnetism. They met from time to time, the ageing Amalesh always with a beautiful lady on his arm.

There was another regular visitor to the flat. Supratim Bhattacharjee—a well-placed and responsible officer in the police force. As different from Amalesh as possible. For Supratim, love was a sacred emotion. He was in love with his dead brother's wife. His brother died in an accident leaving behind a child. Supratim had wanted to marry his sister-in-law but his parents did not agree. Eventually, he married Meena, a girl chosen for him by his parents. But, he remained honest and dedicated in love to his sister-in-law.

One day, after downing a few pegs, he had lost control over his emotions and revealed his thoughts.

"I don't love Meena", he had confessed. "I have only taken social responsibility for her. Do you know what a loveless marriage means? It is nothing but legalisation of sex. And responsibility, to an extent, born of humanity and some selfish motives. Meena is my sexual partner, the mother of my child. She is dear to me. But my love lies with someone else; and just because I have married elsewhere, I cannot ask for that love to be returned. Can I? I have loved Sona...Sonali...I still do. Do you know why I bring her to this flat? My parents and Meena do not want me to visit her. Sonali does not live with us. My family looks after her needs but want to keep me away from her. They fear a scandal! Human minds bear a lot of filth. I have never touched Sonali, she believes in the sanctity of the body. She was not averse to marriage...but without a marriage, how could I ask her to...? I did not want to hurt her beliefs. Moreover, the body is not eternal, is it? I feel very happy when I am with her. I enjoy talking to her the most, nothing can compare to it. We can spend time in peace in this flat of yours. I don't want anything else...nothing actually...."

Different people! Different lives! So many different hearts! The Kasba flat had taken him through an array of experiences. But Sujoy did not drag the same to the Kaikhali flat. He no longer liked chaos and noise around him. Moreover, favour-seekers had started to home in on him. At this point in life, he did not want them buzzing around him. Neither did he need to pacify many people to serve his business interests. Now, he could avail the services of many illustrious and powerful persons without much ado. Experience enriched a person and now, Sujoy was a successful and confident man.

Yet, often when he was at the Kaikhali flat, Sujoy felt a pang for the flat in Kasba. Like the pain of being estranged from a dear friend. Such feelings would not have taken hold had he sold off the flat under normal circumstances. But the flat had brought him much shame.

Sujoy had never sought the company of any woman besides Ragini. Even today, after all that had happened, his regard for Ragini was strong and honest. Till the day he felt this way, how could he knock on anyone else's door? He did not care for loveless physical relationships. Not every one who visited the Kasba flat with partners, was bound by eternal and profound love. But that did not worry Sujoy. He believed, everyone had his or her own yardstick of happiness and peace. No two persons could be said to have the same values. Those people came to the flat for a while and returned with joy and content writ large on their faces. There were many who had struck up a rapport with Sujoy only because of the flat. Sujoy gathered satisfaction from their content, happiness from their gratitude. That was all he got out of the arrangement. But Girin spilt some beans before Ragini and she doubted Sujoy.

Mistrust. Well, that was not the first time. Sujoy and Ragini's relationship had been dotted with mistrust from the word go. For trust to take root, love had to be exchanged. Ragini had never loved Sujoy. Then why did she marry him? Sujoy shook his head and muttered, "I don't know...don't know why she married me. Perhaps obstinacy, or to mask her weaknesses...or perhaps just upon a whim..."

Ragini had always enjoyed limitless pampering from her parents. She was used to making stubborn demands and getting her way with everything. She may well claim that her father was a determined man, but Sujoy had seen how she could bring him around to agree with her. Perhaps the first time she was unable to do so was in the case of Bikash Purokayastha. Because, to start with, both Ragini and her father had agreed on Bikash. But then, to push forth her theory of rebirth she roped in Sujoy and helped herself to his assistance. Where she had to get things done her way, Ragini could be extremely charming and gentle. Suddenly, Sujoy felt anxious—wasn't Sree equally pampered by Ragini and him?

Many a time Ragini justified her whims with the theory of rebirth. Sujoy remembered an elderly beggar whom Ragini once invited home. A stooped, lean, unclean and starving man. He had perhaps not stepped on a clean floor in ages and was cowered by qualms in their sparkling home. When he expressed a desire to leave, Ragini pleaded with him to stay on. She had also frowned at Sree's objection. Later she started earnestly looking after the old man. In return, the man tended to the potted plants in the house. The weekly gardener was surprised and the maid who watered the plants found respite from the boring job. The old man's health improved in Ragini's care. He did not appear as stooped and his wiry frame filled out a bit. Once, Ragini even made him sit in her studio and sketched his portrait. During the course of all these things, she did not care to once ask for Sujoy's opinion. Soon and quite abruptly, though, she banished the old man from her home.

Just when the poor old man had started to relax in the assurance of Ragini's benevolence, she told him to leave without granting him any time to prepare himself mentally. He broke down, "My dear, for which sin of mine are you punishing me this way..."

His body was wracked with sobs; his expression one of submission as though some divine death awaited him. Then he asked, "Then why did you take me in? I did not ask for your kindness. Why did you give me these few days of fleeting peace?"

Ragini said, "What made you think that I would keep you for the rest of your life?"

The old man managed a crumbling smile and said, "The rest of my life? How much of my life do you think is left, dear? What am I to do now?"

Ragini's cruel retort cut through Sujoy as she said indifferently, "Go back to what you did before...begging."

"Once the habit of begging is broken it is hard to go back to it. You gave me some kindness...now you are taking it back. Very well...I will leave..."

For the next seven days he was nowhere to be seen. On the eighth day, his corpse was found near Sujoy's house. As soon as Ragini heard the news, she started to cry, "I have repaid the debt." What debt? Whose debt?

She continued, "Believe me, the moment I saw him I knew who he was. I know him from my previous birth. I was indebted to him so I cleared the debt."

"Very well, you had a debt to clear and you did it. But why did you have to throw him out of the house?"

"What would he do in my home? An old man like him... all day in this house...moreover..."

"We could have done something. Since you brought him in, we could have spent some money and made arrangements for him in an old age home."

"I cleared the debt in those few days, Sujoy. He did not deserve any more. Had I given him more then he would have been indebted to me and in the next life I would be the beggar at his doorstep. Would you like that? Do you really want that? Isn't it better this way? To clear all dues?"

Accounts and calculation. And deceptions of her imaginary world. The accounts of this life were not yet closed, how could Sujoy even think about the credits and debits of the next life? Hence, Sujoy made arrangements for the last rites of the old man. The local peddler gathered enough pall-bearers while Sujoy bore all expenses.

Expense...price. The only thing that could give all tangible and intangible things a touch of reality. By paying a suitable price one could even buy the guarantee of peace in afterlife. The world, perhaps the entire universe, ran by this doctrine. And by it, one could tag a price to the peaceful journey of the soul.

"Artists are a strange lot", Anjan mused.

Sujoy asked, "Only artists, you mean?"

–No. Perhaps all creative people."

–You are right. But if you were a fly on their wall, you would hear the creative people remark that businessmen are a strange lot. According to them, businessmen are coarse, heartless people and know nothing besides their dealings, their profits. They don't think twice about retrieving money even from a garbage dump! Everything is about profit and loss.

–Huh! Heart! What do they know of the heart? I have seen many artists, writers, poets and actors in my life. For them, a matter of the heart is nothing but pretence...a game.

–Right. They like to pretend that their hearts are overflowing with love. They are the vanguards of the world's cache of love. And that love inspires them.

–The way they go on about the heart and love, it seems as if without those two elements they would become paupers.

–Hmm. They go on about love but do not love. Somewhat like politicians. They rave and rant about the country's welfare but do not have a drop of patriotism in them. There was a time when I was a part of that political madness. The inherent truth of a political party is not the welfare of the nation. It is power. What is a nation? No, it is not only a piece of land, it is also the population of that land. The population which is made of people. And those who cannot love the people cannot be capable of love in any way.

–Imposters! All of them! They claim that they gain inspiration from their various loves. Huh! For inspiration one true love is enough.

Inspiration! The word startled Sujoy. What was inspiration? Wasn't it that which motivated one to do something? Anjan's cell phone rang. An angry shrill sound. Sujoy slowly walked to the window. Numerous stars twinkled in the sky. Stars had no inspiration. They shone on their own. What was the inspiration for artists and writers? Ages ago, Aristotle said—the moment of creation is one of divine insanity. Or a circumstance of divine insanity. A state of insanity.

Sujoy believed, there was no better explanation than this. In his mind, man followed the ways of the universe. Whatever experience he gathered, he desired to spread the same. Art was nothing but such an expression. Down the ages, like everything else, the definition of inspiration had also become complex.

The desire of man to express himself has brought about creation from times immemorial. Today though, within the folds of these simple endeavours to express, is hidden a sense of self-deceit. The self becomes larger than the creation. While playing with the lives of others, man himself becomes a pawn.

There was a young poet who often visited Ragini. Like many other admirers, he too sang his praise for her. Ragini had many a time been the muse for his poetry. Sujoy always avoided him; just like he did the other men who buzzed around Ragini. The young man had seen Sree as a child and in time he gladly accepted the role of her tutor. When Sree was about nine, poised at the threshold of maturity, he introduced her to the pleasures of the body under pretence of teaching. Sree gradually became quite captivated and went into a frenzied state if he failed to turn up for a day.

By the time Ragini learnt of it, Sree's budding breasts had already tasted the pleasures which experienced male fingers could provide. Ragini, greatly hurt, wasted no time in severing ties with the poet and threw him out for good. The poet, of course, suffered great loss because Ragini had regularly extended financial help to him...without having any relationship with him in the previous life. The young poet believed that besides writing poetry and reading books, no other work was deserving of his attention. To him, business was a sin. Though, he had no qualms about accepting the help which came his way from business sources. He did not feel the need for self-dignity in order to be a poet. Nor did he hesitate to molest the young daughter of his muse and benefactor. He was one of the worst wonders Sujoy ever came across. But, wasn't Ragini a greater wonder?

After being thrown out, the poet spread filth about Ragini in the creative people's circle. Perhaps that was the easiest way for him to avenge himself. Sujoy considered the possibility of taking him to task but he found that Ragini was still soft towards him. She still pampered him. Though she no longer invited him home, she met him outside frequently. After short outings with him, Ragini returned home and shut herself in the studio to paint. As if, banishing him from her home was punishment enough for the young man's slight slip from decency. Hence, he was forgiven.

The reason? Well, the young poet was a source of inspiration for Ragini. Something more valuable than self-respect.

At the time, Sujoy felt extremely hurt. It pained him greatly to think of his daughter. And surprisingly, for Ragini as well. For some reason beyond his comprehension, he felt a strong desire to protect Ragini. He felt as if Sree and Ragini would be lost without him. The world would see to it that they were left without a way of return.

...they were so soft, so blind, so prone to emotions. Their wits were drowned in their emotions. Inexperienced, they did not know what was good for them! Who, besides me, could protect them selflessly? The selfish world would feed on them like a school of piranhas. How could I let that happen?

So, Sujoy approached Jayshankar to protect his wife. Both Ragini and Sree were unaware that Jayshankar's men still kept a tab on their whereabouts. Jayshankar and Sujoy's friendship went back years and so did Jayshankar's loyalty towards Sujoy. Although Sujoy paid him for his services, it was not the only means of exchange for the love and trust they shared. In his thirty-seven years, Sujoy had found that some relationships were wrapped in trust, love, loyalty and understanding without any apparent logical reason. His relationships with Jayshankar and Anjan were somewhat similar.

Ragini's ties with the budding poet were severed in time, without any further brouhaha. By the standards of creativity, the attraction fizzled out and changed tracks. The poet's luck did not favour him much. He had signed a contract with a celebrated writer to share some of his workload, and now wrote dialogues for a television soap. As a sub-writer. Not that it mattered much to Sujoy. He knew, even the big shoe manufacturers contracted some smaller shoemakers to cater to the demands of the huge population. The only drawback was that sometimes it spread hatred. But Sujoy was in a way grateful to the poet. Ragini and Sree were the poet's inspiration and the poet in turn, was

Ragini's inspiration. In spite of many unfulfilled desires, Sujoy realised that Ragini and Sree were his inspiration to live. Prior to this, he had not felt the need for this realisation.

Anjan ended his phone call. He looked quite tired.

The conversation was a repeat of the last and if they stayed on for another hour, it would be repeated again. Debola called her husband Anjan every hour. As the day rolled into evening, her calls became more frequent. Debola doubted Anjan.

Debola doubted Anjan, Ragini doubted Sujoy. But Ragini and Debola were nothing more than acquaintances; they were in no way close to each other. Yet, they were made from the same mould. Would it really matter to Debola if Anjan got involved with another woman? In case Sujoy did the same, would Ragini care? No. To be honest, it would not affect them. Theirs was nothing but a feeling of insecurity. They wanted hen-pecked husbands who would provide them with all the goodies of life with unquestionable loyalty.

Anjan and Sujoy had so long avoided discussing each other's personal lives in detail. They understood quite a bit without uttering a word. Yet, often enough, they wanted to know more, to break down the strong walls guarding their personal lives.

They poured themselves a fifth round of drinks. Anjan looked up with pitiful eyes and blurted out, "You know, my wife...Debola...does not trust me."

Sujoy shed his urban mask. In this flat, he and Anjan were two people who understood each other deeply. They had never clashed due to business driven reasons; neither had their financial dealings bred mistrust. What harm could the sharing of personal woes and joys do? Though he was thirty-seven, Sujoy could still be candid. Couldn't he? Sujoy placed a hand on Anjan's shoulder and immediately Anjan's face twisted with a rush of emotions. Sujoy kept silent and gave Anjan time to collect himself. He looked outside to where Jishu, Jitu and Manjil were engaged in intimate conversation. They seemed at ease, sharing their woes and joys without hesitation. Like friends. Sujoy realised—love, lust, blood did not build good relationships; the world's most beautiful relationship was that of friendship. Yes, friendship had envy, suspicion and mistrust. It had bloodshed and filthy enmity. But when these were scarce, friendship was an unmatched and unique relationship. Full of mutual affection, respect and trust; selfless and extraordinary. Sujoy felt he shared that kind of friendship with Anjan and Jayshankar. His heart melted. He felt like crying for Anjan and Jayshankar, shedding the kind of tears laced with joys, sorrows, pain and affection which he sometimes cried for Ragini. Not a whimper came from him, neither did his body tremble. Only a drop or two of tears rolled down his smooth cheeks. They fell on his shirt and left damp spots.

Anjan sighed and said, "Sometimes I feel I won't be able to take anymore. I feel like dying."

Sujoy said with brotherly affection, "Don't think about dying. Suicide is a crime. Just wait and watch…life is deeply mysterious!"

"Trust me, I am not worried about sins. I live like a robot. I live for my children…they are still very little. I can't leave their responsibility with Debola."

"Hm…true. They are very small. The younger one is three…how old is the other one?"

"Seven!"

"Anjan, not only your children, you love Debola too. You are wealthy, you are not involved with another woman…

do you wonder why you have never thought of divorcing Debola? Instead, you have thought of death..."

Anjan looked at him for some time, his gaze hard and steady. Then his eyes smouldered for a moment and he said, "Doesn't Ragini doubt you?"

"She does."

"I know somewhat of Ragini's wayward activities. Don't you feel humiliated?"

"Yes."

"Are you not wealthy?"

"I am."

"Do you have another woman?"

"No."

"Why can't you divorce Ragini? Fool. We are fools, Sujoy. We are wasting away in the name of love. Useless sentiments, useless values! This darned feeling of love is useless. I have earned a lot. More than my family can spend. Even if I were to have fun with a different woman every day, Debola would have no say! But I can't...I just can't. My conscience doesn't let me. Still, my wife doesn't trust me. Actually...actually, I have sold myself, Sujoy..."

The two men sat in silence, bound in empathy. Anjan took the opportunity to prepare the sixth round of drinks. The evening aged and darkness deepened. The tiny lights in the distance flickered. Just a couple of minutes from the flat was the city—an arrogant and loud expression of civilisation.

Anjan asked in a low voice, "Do you trust me?"

"Completely."

Then, in a slurred voice, he said, "I too trust you, completely. Yet, people say that businessmen don't know how to trust."

Sujoy: Human existence is divided. In some parts there is love and in some there is the absence of it. There is trust somewhere and distrust elsewhere. With all these things surrounding him, man is a helpless earthly creature who wonders about his very own existence.

Anjan: Sometimes, I feel quite awed.

Sujoy: Why?

Anjan: You and me. We are businessmen, both matured men without any addiction except the occasional peg, both married with children...and, certainly not homosexual...

Sujoy: Ha ha! Certainly not!

Anjan: How did we become friends?

Su: Yet, our wives could not be our friends. We joined our lives with them, united with them to give birth to our children and let our goals and aims become tangled with theirs...yet, distrust and suspicion remained.

An: What is the meaning of a relationship like this? Debola used to write poetry...

Su: Yes, I know. She made quite a name for herself.

An: Yes, she did. She had talent. But talent with beauty is a dangerous combination. Taken up with good looks, one often fails to understand which should be the priority, looks or talent. Most people cannot ignore the attraction of beauty and end up neglecting talent. Debola was so mesmerised by her own beauty that she humiliated her real self, and me too. Now, she does not write poetry anymore and people say, it is because of me. Apparently, I have not provided enough inspiration! Debola has lost her poetry after getting married. But I have never forced her to surrender to the demands of domesticity. I had a job at the post office and painted a bit in my spare time. Debola married me with great expectations. She would be a poet and I would be an artist. We would receive many awards, gain fame and earn a lot! But I did not have that kind of talent, Sujoy. I failed!

Su: Did you paint? What medium? What subject did you like?

An: Watercolour. Anything from hens to buffaloes. But I had a tendency to copy and was not very good at dimensions. Sujoy, I have seen your paintings at your house in Haur. You had talent. More than Ragini did, I believe. But for me, I knew my limits. So I tried to keep Debola happy with money. She is so beautiful, she looked out of place amidst mediocre surroundings. So I started trading in art, you see.

Su: Carry on, Anjan. It's your day.

An: Well, you know how difficult it is to find a firm foothold in any business. Art trading is no exception. At the time, my elder son had just been born and finances were tight. Debola offered to help and said she would introduce me to Aniruddha Kanjilal.

Su: Aniruddha Kanjilal! Big shot! Did Debola know him?

An: Yes. In those days, each of Aniruddha Kanjilal's paintings fetched a minimum of fifty to sixty thousand. Debola visited him regularly for about four to five months. Then she took me to him. Such a celebrated person yet, his behaviour was a pleasant surprise. He signed a contract for fifteen paintings at unbelievably low rates. In fact, I didn't have to put down any cash. He assured me that I could pay him as and when the paintings sold. I felt like I had had a visit from God. After all, God resides in humans in various forms, right?

Su: Wonderful! Anjan, we are like a pair of cursed princes. Our hearts and our lives are so similar.

An: Kanjilal helped me find my foothold and I became a wealthy man! Other artists did not hesitate to give their paintings to someone who traded Kanjilal's work. Customers too, flocked to my door. I gave up my job at the post office. In time, I noticed that Debola did not visit Kanjilal anymore. But Kanjilal's attitude did not change. So I did not pay much attention to Debola because I knew how whimsical she was.

Su: Just like Ragini!

An: One day, Debola brought home a photographer she had met at the Academy of Fine Arts. He wanted Debola to model for him, mainly to model sarees.

Su: A poet and an artist.

An: I could not agree. I told her there was no need for her to model, we were quite well off. But Debola...the married mother of a child...was in the grip of beauty. After Kajal left...

Su: Kajal...the photographer?

An: Yes. After Kajal left, we got into an argument. She accused me of interfering with her independence. I defended myself by saying that I was just offering an opinion, the way she could also offer one. The argument built up and became a full-fledged fight...much agitation and lots of screaming and shouting. Eventually, I learnt...

In spite of smouldering repellent sticks, mosquitoes were galore. Sujoy lit another stick while Anjan prepared the seventh round of drinks. After taking a long swig, Anjan said, "Debola had gifted Kanjilal her nudity. To get me the deal."

Su: Anjan, I wish I could give you a comforting hug and take away your pain! When did our lives become reflections of each other?

An: I was sold. Small. Insignificant. A complete human being—I became an insignificant creature in a moment. But I did not want it this way, did I? Yes, I did want to be rich but I could have persevered...worked hard for it. My father had taken a loan from his Providend Fund to help me out, I would have gradually but certainly managed to pay him back in due time.

Su: I know, I know, Anjan. Humanity does not support one human being selling off another. A man, with the minimum self-respect, would not sell his wife. I know, Anjan, you did not want it this way.

An: After that, I did not stop Debola. I felt like committing suicide. But that was the time when money had started to flow in and it was that money which steered me towards life. I forced myself to forget everything. Around that time, I chanced upon some wonderful paintings in an old aristocratic house in Bardhaman. I busied myself with those. Kajal started visiting our house. Debola gave up poetry and took to modelling. Her photos were printed in magazines and she gazed at herself in awe. Slowly, my home became a hell hole. People called me up with indecent proposals, asking my wife's rate...

Su: Anjan, stop...please stop. You don't have to say this.

An: Let me say, Sujoy. I so want to share these things but there is no one.

Anjan's phone rang. He looked at the number flashing on the screen and handed the phone to Sujoy, saying, "You answer it. I don't feel like taking the call."

Sujoy: Hello!

Debola: Why aren't you home yet? Where are you? I am scared. Hello, why aren't you speaking?

Su: Debola, this is Sujoy. What is wrong? Any problem?

De: Where is he? Why didn't he pick up?

Su: Anjan is in an important discussion. Our meeting is almost over.

De: Where are you? Whose house?

Su: We are in Tollygunj.

De: Who else is with you? I can hear female voices.

Su: You are wrong, madam. There is no female here. We are in a meeting with a gruff promoter.

De: Promoter? Why?

Su: Anjan will explain to you later. Okay? I'll hang up now.

An: Switch off the phone. I am not in the mood. What was that about the promoter?

Su: Why? Don't you need a promoter for your art gallery?

An: Sujoy, will you sponsor something selflessly?

Su: What?

An: An old age home.

Su: Sure, if you say so.

An: Yes, I know you will. You and I...we will do this. We will sponsor an old age home and help out poor artists. I was unable to do anything for my parents.

Su: Why Anjan?

An: My parents refused to take money from me because Debola was into modelling. They thought I had pushed Debola into modelling for money...they refused to believe me. My father never took back the money he loaned for me. I deposited the amount into his bank account but he did not use it.

Su: Awful!

An: I have so much money, yet my father died in the general ward of a government hospital.

Su: Come, Anjan, let's go home. Debola is getting anxious.

An: Let her...let her be anxious. Please sit for a while more, Sujoy. I am not done.

Su: Very well, tell me.

An: I visited many places with Debola, Putush and Kajal. Every time we made a plan as a family, Debola requested for Kajal to be invited along. I agreed. Kajal was a jolly chap, somewhat melancholic too. I felt sorry for him.

Su: Here, we are different. I have never had warm feelings for any of Ragini's friends.

An: Debola asked for a divorce one day. She wanted to marry Kajal. Apparently, by then, they were quite involved.

Su: Here too, our stories are different. Ragini does get involved but never asks for divorce.

An: I felt as if I was falling into a bottomless expanse of space. I collected myself and tried to make Debola understand, to consider Putush at least, if not me. But she was adamant. I explained to her that Kajal was still not established and it was very difficult to carve a career as a freelance photographer. Moreover, would his family accept a once-divorced mother of a child as his wife? She said that she had already met and had a discussion with Kajal's mother. Kajal had been schizophrenic and had undergone treatment in a mental asylum for a couple of years. Having gone through hard times during her son's rehabilitation, Kajal's mother posed no objection to her son's choice of life partner. After hearing everything, I simply wanted to end my miserable life...

Su: I too have wanted to die. Many times. But what good would suicide do? Instead, I thought to myself, let me see how many times I wish to die and how many times I want to live on in this world.

An: I thought of killing myself along with Putush. I would kill him first and then commit suicide.

Su: Oh, Anjan! Please! I have never thought of killing Sree. I will never be able to do that.

An: But then, I calmed down. I hugged Putush to myself nightlong and thought of him. He was our child, we brought him into the world with our dreams and love. Why should he be deprived of life in this world? Similarly, Debola was my wife. Perhaps a bit whimsical and different. But who would save her if I didn't? Gradually, everything became clear to me. Kajal was a schizophrenic, who would marry him? Debola was beautiful and loved him. Why would Kajal's mother object?

Su: Oh God!

An: One day, I visited Kajal in his studio without informing Debola. I asked him how much money he would take to leave Debola alone. But he refused, saying that he only wanted Debola. I reminded him that Debola was my wife and the mother of a child, how could he think of having her as his wife? But according to him, just because she was a wife and mother, she needed not to lose the right to be loved. He asked me to let Debola go. Then, I changed tracks and offered to refurbish his studio, get him a nice digital camera and a computer. In return for Debola. And, he agreed.

Su: He agreed?

An: Yes, he agreed. But the next day, we heard that he had hanged himself in the studio.

Su: How shocking! Anjan, why did you make him that offer? But…I guess, you too were not in your senses then.

An: I wanted to buy my wife, Sujoy. I wanted to set a price for her. But Kajal made me realise that love cannot be bought. Being a businessman, I had wanted to buy Debola.

Su: But Anjan, you did it for her good. You needn't be sad! Kajal was schizophrenic, he could have done this anytime. What would have become of Debola then?

An: I don't know if it did Debola any good. She gave up modelling and poetry. She clung to me in helplessness, without loving me. I accepted it. She did not know what I said to Kajal. We had another child, Kutush. But what a difference there was between the births of our two children.

Su: Let it be, Anjan. This is life. There is no set rhythm to life. Relationships too, go through various phases. We have to accept it. Nothing is constant. Sometimes, our own reflections appear unfamiliar.

An: But I feel suffocated, Sujoy. She complains that I don't love her like before. I stress that I do but she doesn't believe me. Often, she sits in the dark and cries and says that nowadays I don't like spending the evenings with her. But those were different times, long ago...I used to work at the post office then and had lots of time. Where do I have the time now? Moreover, I am past the age of sticking to my wife at all hours. With time, the purpose of marriage changes. But Debola doesn't think so. She hardly socialises. All that interests her is her appearance. She has three people to come and groom her. A beautician, a masseur and a yoga therapist. She is in constant fear that her beauty will fade.

Su: Ragini too is overly concerned about her beauty. And, she too knows how to use her looks cleverly. Will tell you some other day. Are you feeling a bit better now, Anjan? After sharing everything?

An: Yes, much better.

They downed their eighth drink. It was eleven at night.

7

QUITE often, Sujoy perceived Girin while looking at Manjil. The salt-pepper hair, broad shoulders, half-sleeve shirt…but then, the vision vanished in a flash and there would be Manjil before him. Could it be Girin's ghost? His wandering soul? Sujoy's thoughts started to travel along various imaginary paths.

Did ghosts really exist? Hindus believed in ghosts and afterlife. But Sujoy, though a Hindu, did not believe in those. He was indifferent to them. Yet, in India, there were millions of people who lived life by these beliefs. Back in their hostel, there was a cook from Odisha called Keshto-da. Often, they found that Keshto-da had shaved his head—a sign of mourning for the death of a family member. He followed this ritual not only for close family but for distant relations as well.

Once Sujoy asked him, "Who is it for this time?"

Keshto replied, "My father-in-law."

Sujoy was surprised. And seeing the surprise on his face, Keshto said, "I am not very strict about these things. In our village, whenever anyone dies, all males shave their heads… related or not. The other day, the wife of one of my distant grandnephews died. All the males of the village shaved their head but I didn't. I get away with a few things because I live in the city. After all, we are pure Hindus."

Sujoy thought for a while. Pure Hindus! Did that mean, the city people were not pure Hindus? Or was urban Hinduism different from its rural form?

Sujoy was the kind of man who found mass mournings awkward and didn't believe in ghosts or the theory of afterlife and past life memories. He had his own world of beliefs and experiences, far removed from that of the worldly crowd. As a child, Sujoy was frightened every time he heard the word 'ghost'. The house in Haur did not have electricity and the rural darkness was very dense. The word 'ghost' made him visualise a tall figure towering over the palm trees, running towards him with its stick-like limbs. When a house in the village was robbed and the thieves could not be found, Sujoy felt sure that it was the work of ghosts. While growing up, along with fear he also felt anger towards the invisible community of ghosts.

Perhaps, the intangible workings of the ghosts and souls had remained embedded in the recesses of his mind. And they sometimes surfaced to turn Manjil into Girin. Manjil was trustworthy and loyal towards Sujoy. Yet, Ragini treated him with indifference; perhaps, she acted the employer with him. Or, it could be that Ragini couldn't stand anyone in Girin's place. Manjil too did not like driving Ragini around. Manjil was trustworthy and honest, yet he sometimes changed into Girin.

It could very well be believed that had Girin been able to return from the land of the dead, he would have killed Sujoy. Because ghosts were aware of everything and nothing was impossible for them. Hence, killing Sujoy would be child's play for Girin. If he took the driver's seat and orchestrated an accident to kill Sujoy, no one would suspect it to be the act of a ghost. There was no Girin in this world. There was no ghost, no land of the dead. And soul? Well, was there really something called soul? And, what about chants or mantras? Did those really work? No...there was no such thing. Sujoy did not believe in them but Ragini did. And, since Ragini believed, Sujoy too was forced to accept some of it. Ragini had zero trust on humans, especially Sujoy. But for illusory matters, her trust was deep. Soul, afterlife, ghost, witchcraft, black magic...these were essential parts of Ragini's life. Not Sujoy's.

Yet, in spite of all the logic, Girin occupied Sujoy's thoughts just like Pulak did. Girin. Girinda. He was the one who told Ragini about the Kasba flat. After being sure that the flat belonged to Sujoy, he told Ragini, "Your husband frolics with other women."

Ragini had pounced on Sujoy. She rained blows and even sank her teeth into his belly. Egged on by anger and envy. Humiliation and defeat. Sujoy had bled from her bite; the marks were yet to fade.

Sujoy had tried his best to calm her down and make her understand that there was no other woman in his life. But she refused to accept it. She had pulled her eight-year-old daughter out of bed in the middle of the night and pointed at Sujoy, "Look, that's your father! Adept at debauchery! He has finished and devoured me, given birth to you...now he likes to enjoy and devour other women!" She screamed and tore at her hair. Their daughter did not understand much and started to bawl. The following day the child ran a fever and mumbled repeatedly in delirium, "Other women...other women...Kasba flat..."

But Ragini was neither ashamed nor did she calm down. Her frenzied behaviour continued for a week. Eventually, she knocked on her father's door and her fury was somewhat quelled. But the anger found home in her father. To pacify the rage, he shouted down the phone at Sujoy, "I will kill you. You are what you are because of me! How dare you misbehave with my daughter?" Sujoy sank into silence due to the insult raining on him. His father-in-law ordered, "I want to check all accounts...you will reduce my daughter to a pauper..."

That was eight years back; Sujoy's financial standing was not as stable. Wealth had started to trickle in slowly and their lifestyle was gradually taking on a shine. His father-in-law had loaned him money to start business. When Sujoy wanted to repay the debt, he had refused by saying that Sujoy's hard work had made him very happy and he had been paid back in full. At the time Sujoy had felt extremely satisfied. But then the same man had exercised his power and asked to see the accounts. When he divided all assets and made Sujoy sell the Kasba flat, Sujoy felt he had actually been purchased. It hadn't been a loan, it was the price handed out to buy him.

Sujoy had no regret that he had to transfer half his wealth to Ragini's name. He would have done it anyway to escape the complex issues of income tax. What he could not tolerate was the insult and the fetters on his independence. He bore everything with gritted teeth and vowed to himself that he would get back twice what he had lost. Perhaps it was this doggedness which fetched fame for many people. Doggedness and dedication. Dedication and intelligence. Intelligence and talent. Sujoy promised himself name and fame with his doggedness and dedication, his passion for growth, his intelligence and talent.

The dark and crooked alleyways of art trading had earned him more insight and wile. Sujoy's accountant maintained various different kinds of accounts. For the government, for Ragini, for his father-in-law and one for Sujoy. But Sujoy did not place complete trust with this accountant. He always liked to remember that any day, for any reason, this accountant might cross over to Ragini's side. And he had informed Jayshankar accordingly. A part of Sujoy's personal profits was kept aside for Jayshankar. But Sujoy knew that it was a small price to pay for Jayshankar's friendship, loyalty and trust. In fact, hundred times the amount would still be too little! Not every service in this world could have a price tag. One could easily determine the price for the service of the nurse who didn't spare a moment's thought on the patient's likes and dislikes but simply did her duty by bringing food and water on time and sticking the needle in according to orders. But, what about the nurse who went out of duty's way to stroke your forehead and ask if you were feeling alright? Could one put a price tag on those moments of caring?

After the division of wealth, one day, Sujoy returned home to find Ragini preparing for a religious ritual. Their household did not observe such rituals regularly. Such things too, were slave to Ragini's whims and moods. Her mother-in-law had given her a brass figurine of goddess Lakshmi and asked her to worship the same every Thursday...but Ragini never did. Yet, once in a while, she made a big song and dance about observing Lakshmi Puja at home in a grand way. Many an artist had been invited to it and many a delicate finger had gingerly lifted morsels of grain from the delicious vegetable pulao distributed as divine offerings from the goddess—her prasaad. That day, Sujoy wondered which god had been lucky enough to be remembered by Ragini. But soon, his misunderstanding came to light.

The nightlong puja was being performed by a sadhu from Tarapith. Various strange drawings of trees, birds, animals and humans had been drawn on the bedroom floor with a paste of rice flour. On it were arranged numerous and varied articles to be used for the ritual. Sree, still pale and weak from the fever, lay on one side of the arrangements. She still suffered bouts of fever every now and then and remained quite morose and irritable. The doctor said that her condition was due to mental trauma and she would recover soon if kept in a soothing environment. Children were by nature sensitive and they had their own understandings and rulings about the surroundings. Untoward changes in the surroundings could leave lasting marks on a child's future life. Members of a family should never fight or resort to cruelty in the presence of a child.

Fighting! Spats! The words registered with Ragini and Sujoy. Sree too heard them being said. The doctor said, "Even animals can sense such things. And the young of humans were far more intelligent...there was no doubt!"

He recounted the case of an Alsatian dog. The dog was very depressed and so the couple, who owned it, took it to a vet. The vet stated that surely the couple fought a lot at home. The couple had nothing to say, they were guilty of the same. The lack of amicability between the two humans robbed the animal of its desire to live. Then there was the young boy who repeatedly hit himself with a stick. Initially, his parents thought that he was being beaten in school but soon they learnt otherwise. The boy's father was a wealthy farmer and spent a lot of money taking his son to various psychologists. Eventually, it was learnt that in their home, when the cows did not produce the desired quantity of milk, their hind legs were tied to a post and then they were beaten mercilessly with thick bunches of coarse rope. The helpless creatures had no way of escaping the torture; their eyes overflowed with tears and their bodies trembled from the assault. This scene had so shocked and pained the young boy's tender mind that he took to hitting himself to feel the pain of those mute animals. Perhaps, it was his way of repentance on behalf of entire mankind.

These stories troubled Sujoy and reminded him of scenes involving his mother. His mother ready to butcher a hen, holding its neck at her cutting blade. The hen listless in anticipation of death. She sat in the courtyard with Sujoy's Chhotda squatting by her, watching. Sujoy clung to his mother's saree and sobbed, "Don't kill it, ma. Don't kill it, please!" His mother snapped, "Go inside! Who else is going to kill it if I don't?'

Another time, he watched his mother cooking over a flaming clay oven. Cockroaches crowded and crawled around her. Whenever one came too near, she held it up by its feelers and chucked it into the roaring fire. Sujoy watched and gulped.

Killing snakes too was no big deal for his mother. She had an iron pipe with which she used to blow into the fire to feed the flames. It was also what she used once to crush a snake's head while its body writhed and shuddered.

His affectionate and compassionate mother was quite the cruel exterminator when it came to pests and insects in the natural world. She did not bat an eyelid when she drowned the mice trapped in a mouse-trap. But all these settled in layers on Sujoy's mind. Gradually, he grew averse to his mother and the distance between them increased. Sujoy was lonely. Though he was surrounded by family, he was a lonely boy growing up through a lonely childhood.

Today, Sujoy felt out of place in his home. He realised, he was unaware of many things which went on in the nooks and corners of his household. He looked enquiringly at Ragini. She was dressed in a red saree and had put a red bindi[7] on her forehead. The tightly-draped saree accentuating the perfect curves of her well-cared-for body made her appear like a fiery flame. Ragini asked him to take a shower and join them for the rituals. But Sujoy refused immediately.

---

7 A red spot of sindoor or a red paste of kumkum on the forehead, usually of married Hindu women, considered to be inherently an auspicious symbol of chastitiy and an embodiment of divine power, enhancing the beauty and grace of a woman.

However, little Sree called out to him, "Bapi, please sit by me. I am scared." Sree was the apple of his eye and he could not ignore her request. He showered and dressed in red, as ordered. Quite awed by this new look of his, he sat beside his daughter. Sree touched his thigh lightly and closed her eyes, as though, all her fears and worries had ebbed and she was at peace with herself. In this way, many a time Sree became her father's darling from being her mother's daughter. Especially during trying times! No one could say for sure which parent a child would crave for in which situation.

The sadhu started chanting mantras to plead and lure and, perhaps, force the evil out of Sree's body. The evil which was gnawing away at her health. So, was there no need of doctors? No need of the medical tests and medicines prescribed for Sree? It appeared, only mantras were enough to free the child of the curse of ill health.

The surroundings angered Sujoy. Ragini, his father-in-law and this environment wreaked havoc within him. Every moment, Ragini was driving home the fact that Sujoy was there only to earn and provide security. Sujoy too, wondered if he was actually anything more. He felt it necessary to prove himself and his existence. Sitting there, in the midst of the rituals, he analysed and planned various things. He concluded that Ragini's belief in the paranormal, her feeling of insecurity, her dominating nature, her lack of regard for Sujoy and her various unexplainable conducts were gradually pushing him towards destruction.

His freedom was in the wall he had erected between his work life and his domestic life. Had that wall not been there, he would have been no better than any used household commodity, almost junk. At that moment, his inner voice and his perception ability reminded and cautioned him against Girin.

The sadhu from Tarapith finished chanting and asked Sree to be taken back to her bed. Manasi, the girl who had been employed to look after Sree, laid the half asleep girl on the bed.

Manasi too, had been brought into their home from Ragini's parents' house. Perhaps with the intention that Manasi's unwavering loyalty towards Ragini would pose a hurdle in Sujoy's wayward ways. Sitting in that environment of rituals and chants, Sujoy remembered the times before Manasi came into the house. At the time, they had a live-in lady cook. Her daughter, Amala did the petty household chores. The girl arrived in the morning by herself and worked through the day. At night, her mother saw her home and then returned to look after Sree through the night. Ragini was not at all fond of Amala because she was a girl of about nineteen or twenty and had a jolly nature.

When Amala's marriage was fixed, her mother requested Ragini for some financial assistance. But Ragini refused saying that she was already paying them well over. Mother and daughter did not lose hope. They waited for Sujoy at the nearby crossroad; not an easy task because Sujoy often came home as late as eleven in the night. The lady decided to wait at the crossroad for half an hour everyday, till they met Sujoy. For this, she could have returned late for her duties and well been sacked by Ragini. But, having found a good match for her daughter, she was determined.

When Sujoy saw the mother-daughter duo standing by the road waving at him, he initially suspected some bad news. Girin stopped the car. Upon hearing of Amala's wedding, Sujoy assured them of financial help. When Amala's mother shared with Sujoy that Ragini had refused help, he asked them not to divulge anything to her. But Ragini came to know of it anyway, from Girin. Within a month, she fired both mother and daughter, and brought in Manasi.

Keeping to his word, Sujoy sent money to Amala's house. Girin wasted no time in conveying this bit of news to Ragini who, in turn, easily associated Amala and her mother with Sujoy's suspected indecent ways.

Sujoy remembered many such incidents orchestrated by Girin as the sadhu chanted more mantras aimed towards overpowering him. A clay representation of Sujoy had been made and the chants were aimed at it. Essentially, the mantras were to make him lustful of Ragini once again and crave physical relation with her. They were to rekindle the passion in him so that his carnal desires were stirred and they could resume their conjugal sexual life.

Sujoy could not understand the relevance of the ritual when Ragini herself was averse to sharing his bed. Was Ragini then keen to re-establish their sexual relations? Or was it just for the sake of the ritual. Sujoy tried to understand whether the chants were having any effect on him; whether he was getting aroused!

The ritual was complex and awe-inspiring, involving the sprinkling of Sujoy's clay replica with sand and flowers, burning sandalwood and even piercing Ragini's left forefinger for drops of her blood. Once the elaborate ritual came to an end, the sadhu asked Ragini to place the clay model under her bed. Ragini complied and then followed the sadhu's orders and chanted various other mantras to bring Sujoy within the realm of her control.

While this was going on, Sujoy remained quiet and inert. He sank into self-meditation and his thoughts dwelt on various philosophies about the body and the soul. He also concentrated on the real meaning of one's religion.

...that which ushers freedom and joy into human life, that which releases the mind, is religion. Evolution had made man superior to all creatures and one of man's distinctive characteristics was self-realisation. Humans were independent, intelligent and conscious of their own rights. Without freedom man did not feel happy. Hence, I would get rid of all that posed a threat to my rights, independence and intellect. Here, Girin was a hindrance to my rights, my happiness and my freedom. Hence…

Hence, next day, Sujoy arrived at Jayshankar's doorstep. Jayshankar advised Sujoy to leave Kolkata for a few days. So, Sujoy visited Haur for three days with his family. Ragini agreed because she quite liked the idea of spending some time in the tranquil rural environment. Moreover, she was keen to project themselves as a close-knit happy family. Girin drove them to Haur and then, after covering the car with a tarpaulin sheet, he returned home. He was to come after three days and drive them back to the city. But Girin never came. Because, while travelling to Haur by train, his foot slipped and he fell out of the running train.

Ragini was deeply hurt. She had known Girin since her childhood and his death not only pained her but also inspired her to paint. She painted quite a few pictures; all of them projecting death in some way. Sujoy consoled her with the affection and concern of an ideal husband. He knew that, as far as his affection and concern were concerned, there was no insincerity involved. Accompanied by Ragini, he visited Girin's family in Shibpur and extended financial assistance. Girin was fifty when he died. Estimating that he would have worked for another twenty years, Sujoy calculated the amount his family deserved. Two thousand rupees a month; twenty four thousand rupees a year; for twenty years…

But Sujoy handed a cheque for fifty thousand rupees to Girin's wife. This though, pleased Ragini and for quite some time she remained calm and grateful to him. During that time, Sujoy's content knew no bounds and his joy was evident in his expressions. Ragini thought it to be the effect of the sadhu's mantras. Till date, Ragini visited Tarapith every year and met the sadhu. Apparently, the sadhu's horoscope proclaimed that he would live to be hundred. Hence, Ragini rested assured. She took Sree along with her and performed the same ritual every year, introducing and educating Sree to the various rituals and their effects. But through everything, she herself remained completely independent and beyond anyone's control.

After Girin, about four or five drivers put in short appearances. Due to various likes and dislikes, none before Manjil could hold on to the job. At the time, they had only one car. Later, when Sujoy bought another car for Ragini's use, her father sent over a driver called Sudhakar.

So far Manjil had been trustworthy. But sometimes, Manjil's head, shoulders and back would be influenced by Girin. Sujoy also noticed traces of Girin in every beggar boy he came across. Girin's rebirth as a beggar pleased him but his taking over Manjil did not. Sujoy knew that it was nothing but an illusion; yet, he could not escape the worry associated with it. Ghosts, souls, sins, rebirth and divinity chased him around. His logical reasoning remained intact and he did not believe in unscientific explanations and issues. Yet, the illusion did not leave him alone. He thought...

...the fact that I have had Girin killed, was it a sin? Was it an act of selfish injustice? Did God really exist? Did he judge humans by their sins and punish them? Was Girin then, not a sinner? Was he not dishonest? No one could see God; how were humans to understand His will? God was in the human soul. Hence, God's will and man's will were not different. Or, perhaps, if the wills clashed then one could doubt the existence of God in the soul. Or, it could well be thought that in certain situations, God kept his existence in the soul impassive. But how? Wasn't God ever active? Not a leaf could shed without His will. Millions of things happened in the world at the same instant. That meant, God professed millions of wills every instant; and, some of them were sure to be contradictory. In this manner, just as Girin playing the spy was God's will, so was my punishing him. Then how could I be a sinner? How could I be unjust? The concept of injustice was relative. It changed with place, time and situation. And, was accepted or rejected by all accordingly. What was rejected by all could well be acceptable to me. I have acted by my own intellect and understanding. I have resorted to murder in self-defence. Essentially, I was the medium of an ageless course of events because birth and death were inevitable events of life. In this ever-changing world of ours, death was an inescapable end. Hence by hastening an inevitable event, I might be a killer but surely not a sinner. I cannot be a sinner. I am what I think myself to be. I am of the ultimate pure soul, beyond reform and attainment of any purer form. My conscience is active and laudable. My mind and wit are dedicated. My intelligence is sharp. My soul is pure because I am non-violent. It is only for self-defence that I resort to violence. Amicability, an essential part of non-violence, resides in me. Mercy, the most important part of non-violence, is abundant in me.

I am not a sinner because I am true to my word. I am true to my word because I do not deceive myself in any way.

I am not a sinner because I have not taken to theft. Only for the sake of establishing the business have I resorted to a negligible amount of deceit. I would not be able to trade if I did not please government employees with bribes. And I can afford bribes only when I hide some accounting facts from the government. Hence, I deceive the government only to serve them. The greed of government employees makes me indulge in cheating. Where I do not need to bribe, I walk the path of honesty.

I am not a sinner because my mind is not under anyone's influence. I am virtuous and clean. Good paintings cleanse my mind. The children of this world please me. My daughter's proximity sanctifies my soul.

I am not a sinner because I am mentally calm. My senses are completely in my control. They are not influenced by outside forces to become uncontrollable.

I am not a sinner because I do not harbour any discontent. I am happy with my wife and daughter. There was no end to the desires and grievances of human beings; sorrow was born when humans failed to achieve their endless wants. I do not indulge wants and complaints.

I am not a sinner because my cardinal passions were suppressed. Lust, anger, greed, desire, addiction and envy lead people along dishonest paths. I have controlled lust. Conquered anger. Greed has not got the better of me. Desire has not taken me over. Addiction has not dulled my senses. I am not envious of anyone. For ages, a fit and able man like me has not enjoyed sex. And yet I have not desired any other woman. I am not driven over the edge by lust. I have never wanted to take my wife against her wishes.

Dear God, where will you get another man whose virtues surpass those of the average individual? Who else but me? Hence, O God, how can I be a sinner?

8

SREE bagged the tenth place in the Madhyamik[8] board exams. There had never been any doubt about Sree's intelligence but Sujoy never imagined that she would find place among the first ten. His paternal pride made the world appear more beautiful. His joy knew no bounds, though he was completely uninformed about Sree's everyday studies. He shared the news with Anjan and Jayshankar. He pulled Sree close and said, "I have never been so happy! How did you do it?"

"Not a big deal, Bapi," said Sree. "I should have come second, to say the least. It would have meant something."

"Did you know you would come this far?"

"Hmm, I did."

"But first or second…? Can anyone be so assured?"

"Well, the preliminary test results of a good school hold promise. Moreover, I am only forty marks behind the first boy, Nabhoneel. I did not join the race to win. Had I prepared myself in that manner, nothing would have been impossible. Mental preparation is a big challenge."

"True. But a difference of forty marks with Nabhoneel is quite a difference, I must say. After a stage, every mark counts."

"How does it matter, Bapi? I was not in the race. In our school, unless one scores above eighty per cent, admission in

---

8 School-leaving board examination – awarding pass certificate – held at the end of the 10th standard of school. This is followed by two years of senior high school leading on to college.

class eleven is difficult. My target was eighty so that I did not have to change school. I got ninety three. What can I do?"

"You are crazy! How can you be so flippant about it? Coming tenth among so many is not child's play. Now you will have to work harder."

"Do you think now I will join the race?"

"Of course."

"No. You are wrong. I don't need to do that. Look, most of the top scorers are boys from middle class families. They need to be in the race. They need good results to get good jobs. Unless they have a good job they won't have a car, a flat in a posh neighbourhood and a pretty wife. Their lives will be spent in middle class trivia. Hence, they will race. But why should I? I will study according to my wish. And I will paint."

"Do you have a car? A flat?"

"My parents do. Anyway, girls have fewer problems. If they have some brains with beauty then they are set for life. And if the girl's father is rich then an NRI husband is a sure shot. Most such girls will tie the knot and fly away. And those who stay back in this country will dress in expensive clothes and drive to their children's schools in expensive cars, making other moms go green with envy. They will go to the gym to shed fat and to the beauty parlour for pedicures."

"You mean you will do the same?"

"Marriage doesn't attract me too much. Moreover, if I am not here then you and Ma will fight each other to death. So, to save you, I need a husband who will stay with us."

"A live-in son-in-law?"

"Yes. Kind of a dim-witted simpleton will do. There's another thing...I can't stay away from you."

"You crazy girl! Every girl thinks that way when she is young. Later, when she finds her perfect partner in that dim-witted simpleton of a man, she easily forgets her old parents. Okay, tell me...what kind of a simpleton do you want? Someone like me? Someone who will obey your every command like I do your mother's? Anyway, now tell me... what are you going to study? What subjects are you thinking of taking up? We can think about a husband later."

"Yes, there is plenty of time. Moreover, in that matter the final choice will be mine. And about my choice of subjects...I am going to take up easy ones. Philosophy, history, education and pol science. I just want to somehow finish my graduation and then drop the curtain on studies."

"What are you saying? You think history and philosophy are easy?"

"Oh Bapi! If you want you can make everything easy. And if you don't then nothing will ever be easy. The level of difficulty depends on how detailed and in-depth the study is."

"How can one of the toppers speak this way?"

"Why not? Just because I have stood tenth doesn't mean that I will have to shoulder an extreme burden of knowledge. Can't I have the freedom to choose how much I would like to study?"

"Of course. Let your mother return..."

"Ma knows."

"Has she agreed?"

"Yes. Ma doesn't interfere in the independence of others."

"Very well. So what are you going to do after graduation?"

"Why, I will look after the art gallery you and Uncle Anjan are going to set up. And paint, of course."

"Then study art."

"Huh! Art is something you do. It cannot be an interesting subject to study."

"Gosh! Your thoughts are quite novel! When is your mother going to return?"

"Anytime now. There is another piece of good news."

"What?"

"Aniruddha Kanjilal has asked Ma to meet him."

Sujoy was amazed, and somewhat apprehensive too. Aniruddha Kanjilal was a name; an institution; a persona. Those associated with the world of art knew of Aniruddha Kanjilal and the kind of prices his work fetched. Sujoy knew of the man and his work through Anjan—Aniruddha Kanjilal was powerful and controlled the market of art. The works of upcoming artists depended on his valuation. Kanjilal had magical powers and wielded an attraction by which, besides being an artist, he was kind of a godfather in the national art scene, determining the destinies of many.

Sujoy recalled a famous painting by Aniruddha Kanjilal. A colourful bird sitting atop a stooping bamboo plant, its beak sharp and a worm its prey. But the main attraction was in the bird's eye. The eye took up about one-third of the picture and portrayed alertness, triumph and delight at lording over the insect world. Like the eyes of Hitler or Nero. If one stared at the eye for a while, it appeared quite real; almost as if it had just blinked. Alongside the triumph and the feeling of being the master and the pleasure of preying, something else came forth—terror. Behind the arrogant façade of victory lay terror. Sujoy knew, if one side of the coin was triumph then the other side was panic and terror. Because everyone who wielded power knew how terrible the lack of it could be. The powerful were the masters of those without power, the weak. But power and weakness were temporary. At any point of time, they could interchange positions. And terror was born of this possibility.

It was true that Kanjilal had established his superiority by painting the eye. And contemporary times had rewarded him suitably. But he was not the best of the nation's artists. Sujoy could name five other artists whose works had the same value, finesse and heart-touching quality. Among them,

Prajit Mukherjee could well top the list, but he chose to give more importance to himself as a teacher than as an artist. There was one thing that could not be refuted though. Most artists could stick a price tag to their own work only. But Aniruddha Kanjilal could stick a tag to his own work as well as that of others.

Some people had this deep and inherent tendency to play king. Aniruddha Kanjilal was one such man. His desire to be the master was indomitable. To feed this desire he needed power. He also needed a tribe of followers to play the role of bearers of that power. And he needed to display his authority to collect that tribe. His control over the valuation of an artist's work was nothing but a display of his authority. For about two decades he had extended a helping hand towards young artists and bought their allegiance. Of course, in that respect, women had an edge over men. Because, besides allegiance, women had something else to offer Kanjilal. In return, they also benefitted suitably from a handsome, famous, talented and powerful man.

Ragini's amazing arrogance had always kept her from approaching Aniruddha Kanjilal. Sujoy knew that Ragini's haughtiness did not allow her to succumb to any form of weakness. This time though, Ragini had been invited and the look of sheer content that he imagined on her face alarmed Sujoy. So far Ragini had been in control of all her relationships. But now, she was to make the acquaintance of a person who sat in the master's chair. This would be the first time Ragini faced a different situation. How would she react to it? Sujoy panicked because he remembered Debola. But what could he do? Ragini was not in his control! It was true that due to Ragini's dominating nature, Sujoy faced humiliation and pain. Yet, that was the role he preferred Ragini in; it kept him assured. Ragini was going to Kanjilal with her covert wishes of gaining fame and popularity on foreign shores. The same could well be the tools with which Kanjilal would be able to keep Ragini in his control.

"Why have you gone all serious?"

Sree's query startled Sujoy and he turned his attention to her. Sree continued, "What's wrong, Bapi? Are you jealous of Ma?"

"Why should I be jealous? And of your Ma?"

"Ma is famous. So you are jealous. You used to paint at one time but couldn't continue. While Ma is making a name for herself. I think Ma can see jealousy in your eyes."

"You mean to say I have not contributed in any way towards your mother's fame?"

"No no...I am not saying anything. I was just quoting Ma. Of course you have contributed with all the exhibitions. But only exhibitions cannot fetch fame. Of late, Ma has been praised highly in all the reviews published so far."

Sujoy smiled. He realised that a change of topic was necessary. Because, he could not share with Sree how he and Anjan had pulled a few strings to publish appreciative reviews of Ragini's works. These things were always possible if one knew the right avenue of approach. Sujoy's line of trade helped; those who could not be offered direct cash bribes could be made happy in kind with his business products. Few people had qualms about accepting a bribe in kind as those could be explained simply as innocent gifts. Sujoy found the foreign-made goods he offered as bribes to be highly effective. Their effect was instantaneous and dependable. But this was not something he wished to discuss with Sree; so he steered the conversation away. They talked about art and literature, about matters which motivated frenzied creations.

Sree spoke very fast. When she spoke, her curly and unkempt hair bounced around her face. A crooked smile hung at her lips. She looked an exact copy of Ragini in her college days. Sujoy watched her while his heart lovingly and beautifully painted her portrait with colourful brushstrokes.

"Creation inspires self-expression," said Sree. "As man is capable of myriad coherent thoughts, he is filled with immense wonder about his own existence. Through his creations he recreates himself and tries to determine who he actually is. And why he is the way he is! Art, literature, music...everything is the creator's self-expression."

Sujoy asked, "In that case, how do those, who neither paint nor write, get so much pleasure out of seeing and reading? What role do the spectators and the readers have to play?"

Sree: They gain pleasure because they too desire to express themselves. But they are incapable of expressing. So, they try desperately to find themselves in the creations of others.

Sujoy: Why is it that one man can create while another can't?

Sree: Actually, everyone is capable of creation. They are sometimes unable to hit upon the correct medium. Or, they are unable to understand their own selves. The human soul has three levels of understanding—*satyam* or 'I am', *gnyanam* or 'I know' and *anantam* or 'I express'. Perhaps by nature's discretion, some individuals are blessed with extra power over all three.

Sujoy: Is that extra power what you call talent?

Sree: Yes. That is talent, a gift of nature. And, not only artists and writers, scientists too fall in that category.

Sujoy: But what about genes? No one can be infused with talent from outside. Talent has to be acquired genetically.

Sree: Of course, gene is a factor. You and Ma paint, so I paint. But, today, if I were to become a Picasso then that extraordinary talent would be a gift of nature.

Sujoy: But...how did you know about *satyam, gnyanam, anantam*? Just the other day you were only a little girl!

Sree: Bapi, these are concepts from the Upanishads. I have read Tagore's critique on the topic. And what I just said about talent is my very own opinion.

Sujoy: You are like your mother. She used to know so many things!

Sree: She still does.

Sujoy: True. But you are still very young...so I find it unbelievable, somewhat. But then, one who is ranked tenth in the board exams can well spark wonder! Okay...tell me, don't you ever feel that talent is an expression of extra power?

Sree: How so?

Sujoy: You may have noticed that some children are hyperactive. They are always on the move all through their waking hours. As if they have unlimited energy! They don't know what to do with so much energy. Talent is the same! When someone has too much energy, sometimes the energy gushes out as talent.

Sree: Nah! I can't agree on that!

Sujoy: Let's say, some people have an inclination... whether they like it or not, they just *have* to do a particular thing. Perhaps, if they don't express their talent then they will die. They write or paint for the sake of their lives.

Sree: Bapi, this doesn't sound right.

Sujoy: Hmm...how about this? Man always wants to bind himself in relationships with others, establish a connection. This is man's natural desire. There is an amazing quote by Tolstoy on this. 'Art is one of the means of intercourse between man and man.'

Sree: This is the problem with people like you. Quoting Tolstoy, Kant, Marshall, Baldwin. Don't you have anything of your own to say?

Sujoy: Then what about all that you quoted from the Upanishads? That too was written by someone else.

Sree smiled a little, perhaps at being caught red-handed. The doorbell pealed. Nayan-mashi, their housekeeper, answered the door and returned to inform, "Some people from the newspapers are here. They want to talk to Sree." Sree laughed while Sujoy gazed at her with affectionate pride. Just at that moment, Ragini returned home. They heard her talking in the living room and soon she called out, "Sree...Sree..."

Sree left and Sujoy too, set off towards his room. Today he had returned home early but with a lot of pending work. They had started work on an art gallery in Salt Lake's HB block. Besides Anjan and himself, Ragini's father also had some financial stake in it. Perhaps upon Ragini's advice.

Near to the upcoming art gallery was an old age home. Anjan and Sujoy had shouldered some responsibilities for the home. Besides these, there were the day-to-day nitty-gritties of his business to take care of. An opportunity had arisen to open a branch in Siliguri. Sujoy sat for a while and then lay back on the bed. His legs, knee downwards, hung off the bed and his toes touched the floor. He stared at the clean ceiling and wondered how his daughter had managed to be among the top ten. Self-satisfaction washed over him. Wouldn't Sree's success touch him in some way too?

When he first started trading goods, he had to bear the brunt of much humiliation and disregard. Many of his friends could not accept the fact that an artist could become a trader just to earn a few pennies. According to them, an artist was better off committing suicide due to penury; that was more socially respectable. Initially, they avoided him. Even his Chhotda, Sumit Banerjee.

Sumit had never taken up a job in order to travel the path of literature. Apparently, this self-sacrifice was far nobler than Sujoy's trading. Sumit started a local monthly magazine with a section on literature. In the initial stages, local small businesses advertised in it. Borda, their elder brother, too lent some financial help. But soon the advertisers lost interest as they did not have much to benefit from the fifty odd people who read the paper. Hence, the publication became irregular. Borda also withdrew the financial assistance due to mounting responsibilities. Having little idea about the concept of the 'little mag', Borda had thought this magazine would, in time, be a source of income for Sumit. When he finally realised that nothing of that sort was going to happen, he declared that he abhorred voluntary joblessness. Their father was still alive and had some savings in which Sumit had a share. But Sumit never demanded it. The magazine had fetched him some local fame and given him recognition as a poet. So, even if the magazine was published once in every six months, he found no reason to pick up a calculator. For him, that would amount to a detestable crime.

At that time, Sujoy decided to help himself. No one except Borda understood his financial need and praised his decision to get into business. Though he did say, "Couldn't you have found a better business?"

But what? That was not clear from Borda's words. Sujoy paid no attention to the support or lack of it that he got from people around him. He realised that it would be impossible to live a life of paucity with Ragini. Momentary lapse of good sense and vaulting emotions made him Ragini's slave. His deep love commanded him to turn his attention towards domesticity and he took up a job. But the insufficient income from that job brought anger, dissatisfaction and humiliation into his home. Disrespect became his companion. At social functions at his in-laws' place, Sujoy's cheap gifts lay in neglect amidst the abundant gold ornaments and other expensive items. When Sree fell ill, his only option was to wait for as long as possible and then avail the cheapest medical facility. Ragini suffered;

the daily trial of trying to adjust to the penniless lifestyle almost made her physically sick. In impatience, she beat Sree. And Sujoy burned in its wake. Once, when he expressed a desire to be physically intimate, Ragini retorted, "Oh! So you *are* a male, after all? You can't provide your wife with the minimum luxury...you have given birth to a child but can't pay for her medical treatment...! What kind of a man are you?"

Sujoy recoiled, lying awake the entire night, his only companion his ashamed shrunken manhood. Often, out of pity, Ragini's father sent across household necessities for his daughter. Ragini's mother invited them for lavish meals frequently, in a show of felicitation for her son-in-law, but mainly to give a loving treat to her daughter. A car would come from his in-laws' place to ferry them to and fro. One day Ragini remarked, "You're enjoying sumptuous meals at my parents' place every other day...those large tiger prawns... do you know how much they cost? Almost what you earn in two days! I must say you quite enjoyed the dish. And, as an icing on the cake, you have a beautiful mother-in-law fussing over you. What a wonderful life!"

Sujoy was filled with self-repulsion. Like Anjan Kar, he felt an urge to commit suicide. But soon that feeling was replaced by a fighting spirit. Why couldn't he do it? Why not...if he tried his best? He realised that it was his love for Sree and Ragini which inspired him to live on. Though Ragini did not reciprocate the love. Sujoy refrained from reminding Ragini that she had once promised to be his partner in sorrow too. In fact, she was the one who had proposed marriage to Sujoy. He had simply shouldered responsibility, in silence, and in the process fallen in the eyes of some people.

To be honest, as far as his father-in-law was concerned, Sujoy was indebted to him by choice. Besides financial help, the man had many a time offered advice regarding the workings of a business. Initially, Sujoy's tongue tied up in a knot when it came to offering bribes to government officials for the release of certain sanctions. He did not know how to frame the proposal; his efforts to express his intentions in his mother tongue always sounded very tactless and lewd. In what language did a bribe proposal sound decent? Sujoy tried English. Well, it did sound somewhat better but the proposal was only the tip of the iceberg. Both parties would need to have the proficiency to carry on an entire conversation in English. Hence, it was an extremely complex and unfathomable matter. Upon hearing Sujoy's problem, his father-in-law said, "Had you not stumbled at this point, I would have been quite concerned. What you are going through is absolutely normal."

Later, Sujoy's father-in-law accompanied him and lent his support on many occasions. Under his tutelage, Sujoy picked up the tricks and tools of bribery. Along with some standard and useful approaches. Like...

–We can go to any length, sir.

–Please see to it quickly, sir, and expedite the job as soon as possible. Your holidays will be worthwhile.

–Sir, if you don't look after me then how will I look after you?

He learnt how to modulate the voice and when. When to sit alert and when to relax in the chair with an air of superiority and contentment. Sujoy's father-in-law carefully taught him all the finer points in great detail. But, after acquainting himself with the works, Sujoy realised that what mattered most was the language of the eyes. Now, Sujoy was adept at reading the other person's gaze as well as conveying a lot with his own. Yet, many of his strings were still in his father-in-law's hands due to various instances of indebtedness. In the process, he had to sacrifice his independence quite a few times. Yes, it angered him but, in the end, he accepted everything as natural human behaviour. He found out secret ways of saving some of the self-dignity and the independence which he had sold to his father-in-law. He built up his own savings and freedom, away from the eyes of his family. Not that he did not have to pay a price or was not ruined sometimes. But soon he rebuilt that separate world.

But he knew no way of escaping the agony of being a slave to Ragini. He did not agree with any of Ragini's decisions; yet, did not have the strength to disagree. It was like a dreadful disease for which the limb had to be sacrificed to save the life. So, he wanted to forgive Ragini and, in the process, forgive himself. To forgive Ragini he convinced himself that Ragini was yet an immature child...or, a little girl in the guise of a matured woman. Someone who did not know right from wrong. And in this way, he developed sympathy for Ragini. But the sympathy was always short-lived because soon Ragini shattered all such illusions and set upon planning various intricate conspiracies with shrewdness. She did that to satisfy her whims as well as protect her reign. She wanted to render Sujoy inferior and incapable; so that, he did not regard her as a female, a wife, an unemployed and weak individual, and try to gain control over her.

Sujoy realised that while growing up as a pampered child, Ragini had mastered the art of establishing herself as superior. This feeling gave birth to repulsion towards Ragini. He felt angry and frightened.

The fear was increasing gradually and had started to take shape. Sujoy could now identify the fear—it was Sree. Ragini reigned over the greater part of Sree's life. She could easily grab and consume the sole existence of their daughter, leaving him out in the cold.

Sujoy found it difficult to breathe. He had not been invited to talk to the reporters from the newspaper. Ragini took full credit for Sree's success. Complete credit. To be honest, Ragini was the one who oversaw Sree's studies and painting. She was the one who guided Sree. Sujoy was but a means of finance. Being the man of the mansion, he was responsible for the upkeep and well-being of his wife and daughter. Hence, the household did not find it necessary to be grateful to him for the vast amounts of money he brought in. It is a universally accepted fact when something was identified as duty, it did not receive any special acknowledgement. While accepting this bitter truth he felt pained. He longed to be in the company of Anjan and Jayshankar. And, he also remembered his Chhotda.

Around the time Sujoy got married, Chhotda had begun to change. His flourishing fame as an editor and a poet had made him detached and self-centred. Or, perhaps, Sujoy's marriage to Ragini had been a cause. Marriage often brought in distance between siblings. Hence, Sujoy had experienced both the intimate and the indifferent sides of Chhotda. Along with his parents and Borda, Chhotda too was quite disgruntled with the newly married and struggling Sujoy. Perhaps that was the time when changes crept in. Later, when Sujoy started trading in goods, the changes took a turn. Sujoy's promising earnings made his Chhotda turn towards him again. His visits became frequent. He also started digging up the past.

–He was always my pet.

–Till the other day, I was his world.

–He has always been extremely fond of me.

–I love him a lot.

–He is not much younger than me, but I love him like a son.

–As a child, whenever he painted, he followed me around till I praised his work.

–Till a short time ago, he took my advice about painting. He has never ignored my suggestions.

–Till very recently, I have cleaned up after him.

Chhotda's behaviour and reminisces increased to the point where they became quite unbearable. And then their father passed away. Their mother followed within six months. Chhotda was left alone in the house in Haur.

The deaths of parents did not affect them terribly. The time was one of rapid changes and Sujoy could not remember the sequence of events during that period. Surprisingly, Chhotda's sweet, apparent benevolence impressed Ragini and won Sree's heart.

Suddenly, Sujoy felt like throwing up and was startled back to the present. He heard Sree's voice from the adjacent room.

"Ma, come here please. I'm sad; I'm going to cry."

Sujoy guessed the reporters had left. He looked at the clock and realised that he had been lying inert for about forty-five minutes.

Why did Sree want to cry? He felt anxious and walked out of the room. Sree was sitting with her head on Ragini's lap, sobbing profusely. Sujoy asked, "What's wrong? Why is she crying?"

"She is missing her Chhotjethu[9], sad for him. Sree, listen to me…come on, get up…"

Sree lifted her head; her cheeks were smeared black with tears and smudged eyeliner. The moment she saw Sujoy a fresh bout of emotions flooded her. She threw herself onto the floor and wailed—

"Chhotjethu…Chhotjethu, where are you? Why did you die?"

---

9 Term of endearment expressing familial affection for uncle, with the diminutive derivative suffix 'jethu' from 'jyatha' (uncle—father's elder brother) referring to Sujoy's 'Chhotda' Sumit—the younger of his two older brothers.

Sujoy gnashed his teeth and clenched his fists...for a few seconds. Then he sank down onto the floor beside Sree and rested a hand on her back. Ragini too came and sat on the floor and lifted Sree's head onto her lap. Tears rolled down her cheeks too. And, enveloped by her parents, Sree cried on for her Chhotjethu. For a long while.

9

IT is believed that the Serpent was the most cunning of all living creatures walking the face of Earth. In the Garden of Eden, God had permitted Adam and Eve to eat fruits from all the trees except the one in the centre of the garden. The Serpent tempted Eve to have a fruit from this forbidden tree, explaining to Eve God's supposed hidden intent behind forbidding the fruit. Eating it would be an eye-opener for Adam and Eve the Serpent said; they would gain Knowledge and share equal stature with God, all of which He wished to prevent. Eve tasted the fruit and in turn tempted Adam to have a fruit from the same forbidden tree. Immediately the duo perceived their nudity and were flooded with shame; they became conscious of 'right' and 'wrong' and covered themselves with fig leaves. And thus began the process of their eternal doom. Adam and Eve were duly punished by God for their disobedience and the Serpent too was relegated to a life of hardship and permanent enmity with womankind. God condemned Adam, or mankind, to a life of hard labour and stress and Eve, or womankind, to give birth through painful labour, live life in subjugation to her husband and yet be attracted to him.

That was the first sin humans committed due to which they continue to suffer. Before that, mankind had no understanding of right and wrong. That was the embryonic cell of sin from which countless such cells were formed in man, giving him the understanding of sin; of right and wrong and led him to self-destruction and a subsequent erosion of his mind and soul. The fall from grace and the denudation was such that it could sully man's purest relationship.

What was sin? And, what was virtue? Both were creations of the human mind. All those stories about God's rulings were nothing but make-believe tales. Was anyone truly inclined to believe them? No! There was no sin, no virtue; and, so, there was no purity.

Nothing. There was nothing. These things had no existence. The path of non-existence and atheism was a straight and simple one. So, it was easier not to believe than to believe. To believe entailed exercising restraint. And what was more difficult than the practice of restraint? But the inclination and the urge to believe, or have faith, was deeply embedded in human conscience. Its roots ran deep and far, deeper than the firm roots of the tall and stately silk cotton tree. Uprooting that faith was almost impossible. Banishing it was also not possible. Moreover, where was the need to banish it? Man, who was made of sins, virtues and purity, was the only one aware of the rights and the wrongs of his life, the cultivated worries and the freedom from them. Anxiety, worry and liberty. Would man ever be free of this cycle?

Man had not mastered the art of achieving freedom, instead he became a slayer of sins. To wipe out one sin, he ushered in more sins. But...could sin eradicate sin? No. That which assisted eradication, could not be sin. It was but a reason, a means.

When a girl is raped, the rapist is punished. He is sent to prison. But imprisonment was not punishment; the real punishment would be death. The rapist should die. But death means the annihilation of life. And, annihilation of life is a sin. Then why is the punishment for one sin death? Why another sin? Because sin destroys sin. Sin provokes sin. Though, a sin which eradicates another sin is surely a lesser one. The actual sin is much more complex and deep-rooted. Then, do sins exist in various layers? How are those layers determined? Also, if there are layers then there are surely limits too. What are those limits? For example, not every murder is a sin. Killing a human being is a sin. But killing a sub-human creature is not. So, if you were to commit an act due to which you were decreed sub-human, then the act of my killing you would not be counted as a sin. But who are 'you'? 'You' are a human being living in this world. Who is this 'I'? 'I' is also a human being living in this world. These two humans are both sinners and lawmakers.

Just like Sujoy and Sumit—both sinners as well as lawmakers. Sumit committed such a sin that his brother, Sujoy, had to sentence him to death. But, for Sujoy that was not a sin.

Sin was like a germ-laden breeze, it happened to catch you. But did it manifest itself through visible eruptions on your body? No. Yet, man believed that there was no escape from the venomous lashes of sin. Even then, Sujoy assured himself that none of the killings he had committed were acts of sin. He was untouched by sin. Through his thirty-eight-year life no sin had touched him.

It happened long ago. Sree was about nine. Sujoy's business had given him unprecedented money and that money changed his life. He had created an uproar with the art exhibitions he hosted. At that time, all those friends who had once abandoned him, flocked back to bask in his success. Chhotda too.

Their relationship was poised to turn for the better. Sumit lived alone in the house in Haur. Borda sometimes visited from Asansol and Sujoy too, dropped by occasionally. Taking advantage of the opportunity which had presented itself, Sumit expressed a desire to revive his magazine. The conversation between the two brothers ran somewhat like this...

Sumit: If you can give me about five thousand a month, I'll manage the rest. If I include some Kolkata-related articles then more advertisements will come in.

Sujoy: How do you manage your own expenses?

Sumit: There is a monthly income of about three thousand from Baba's savings. Borda and I are entitled to one and a half thousand each but Borda has given me his share. If you write off your share to me...I will be able to manage well for myself.

Sujoy: Okay. But if you want a job then you can join me.

Sumit: No...I won't be able to do a job. Moreover...that kind of environment!

Sujoy: Oh!

Sumit: Did you mind? Actually, I want a free life. My life should not be any different from a bird's.

Sujoy: Sorry, I won't be able to give five thousand a month, Chhotda.

Sumit: What! But you are loaded! And, you will get more from your father-in-law! What will you do with so much money? You used to be fond of art. Why don't you do your bit for literature and culture now?

Sujoy: I don't hanker after my father-in-law's fortunes. Chhotda, why don't you bring out your magazine trimonthly? The cost will be less.

Sumit: Will you be able to meet that expense?

Sujoy: I'll try.

Sumit: Very well...since you say so...!

Every time Sumit visited Sujoy's house, it was to ask for money. But somehow, Sumit fell in love with little Sree. In return, Sree too became her Chhotjethu's pet and stuck to him. This pleased and suited Ragini well. Leaving Sree in Sumit's care, she could spend more time in the world that waited for her. Those days, Manasi worked for them. She was the one who first complained about Sumit to Ragini. But Ragini did not pay much attention. Perhaps, except for Sujoy, no other name could invoke suspicion in her. So, Ragini accused Manasi of retarded thinking. Manasi did not have the guts to protest further verbally but she continued to fight with her honesty.

One day, when Sree was twelve, Manasi approached Sujoy. Ragini was out; Oindrila Ray was tutoring Sree in another room. Sumit too was away; since he was a bachelor, no one thought much about his erratic arrivals and sudden departures.

Manasi had been brought into their home by Ragini, so Sujoy felt quite apprehensive when Manasi came to him. Manasi, though not pretty, was a healthy presentable girl. Sujoy asked her to draw apart the curtains at the door before she came in.

Manasi said, "I wanted to tell you a few things. I tried telling Ragini-didi but she wouldn't listen."

Sujoy asked, "In that case, why do you want to tell me? Why would I listen?"

Manasi replied, "If you don't listen to me then Sree might be harmed. I am not going to be around for long. I have looked after Sree for all these years...she is like a younger sister to me."

Manasi was soon to be married. Once she left, her mother would take her place in the household.

Sujoy: Okay, tell me quickly.

Manasi appeared hesitant. She twisted the end of her dupatta around her fingers. For the past few years, Ragini had seen to it that Manasi became literate. Now, Manasi was a girl basking in the light of education. The young man who came to tutor Manasi was the one she was tying the knot with. He had landed a job in a primary school and Manasi was due to leave the household soon. Would this home feel her absence? Sujoy harshly suppressed the rush of emotion that threatened to surface. It was something he did well, since his college days of politics.

Manasi: Please don't take offence if I am taking too much liberty. Please keep Sree safe when Chhotda is here. Chhotda is not a decent man and he lacks integrity of character!

Sujoy was stunned. The unexpected blow dealt by Manasi's words made his voice rough and sharp.

Sujoy: What are you saying? How dare you!

Manasi: Didi too, reacted similarly. But trust me, Sree is suffering.

Manasi's patient manner of speech swayed Sujoy. Moreover, the slightest threat to Sree's wellbeing always agitated him.

Su: What's wrong?

Ma: Chhotda is not like you. You are like an elder brother. But Chhotda is not like an elder brother or an uncle. He touches a lot. He tried it with me too, but couldn't do much. Ma told me that, in our kind of work, we would have to face these things. She taught me how to keep myself safe without breaking down mentally.

Su: What were you saying about Sree?

Ma: Whenever Chhotda used to come and none of you would be home, I used to escape to the neighbour's.

Su: Tell me about Sree.

Ma: How does one say it...I mean...Chhotda. Please don't misunderstand! Chhotda...he touches Sree.

Su: What do you mean!

Sujoy was deeply hurt. He felt restless, agitated and furious. He felt as if he would burst into a million smithereens. The room...the ceiling and the floor...appeared splattered with his blood.

Ma: Please believe me. I have seen it myself. It has been going on for quite a while now. From the time Girin-kaka died....

Su: Impossible! Chhotda...impossible.

Though Sujoy said that it was impossible, in his mind he knew that nothing was impossible. Nothing in this world was impossible. Yet, denial often brought respite from agony. Sometimes believing proved extremely painful...

Ma: Before I came to this house, there was someone who visited often...some poet. The way he used to behave...

Su: Who told you all that?

Ma: Sree told me herself. When all of you visit Haur or when Chhotda comes here, he does it to Sree...Sree has become addicted to it. Now she wants it.

Sujoy crumpled up inside. His soul cried out. He felt he was going mad. He could not understand anything. He touched his forehead and felt the sweat there. Though not a god-fearing man, he sought refuge in His name.

Su: How did you know?

Ma: Sree told me. She shares everything with me. I too try to find out. The first time, she was scared...

The first time, Sree was scared. She was lying beside Chhotjethu in their ancestral Haur house. When she turned over, Chhotjethu rested a hand on her. The hand felt heavy but she couldn't say anything. She didn't know why her throat felt dry. Was it Sree's Chhotjethu's hand or was it Sumit

Banerjee's hand which crept up her chest? The hand felt, pressed and squeezed her breasts the way Sree often tested the ripeness of a fruit. Her breasts hurt. The newly formed tiny mounds sorely hurt even when she herself touched them. Sree remembered Snehasish. Snehasish had taught her to do these things; he had also taught her not to tell anyone. Sree also thought of her mother who had been very angry at Snehasish. She had told Sree, "Yes, one does do these things, but not now. When one is much older. At your age this is a sin."

Why would it not be a sin later? Sree failed to comprehend. Her mother taught her that if someone made such advances on her, she should move away and tell her mother. But Sree did not move away. She did not protest aloud. She did not call her mother. Was she then turning into a sinner? A strange pleasure mingled with the fear in her kept her rooted. She felt limp and it was a nice, lingering feeling. What could she do except lie there, pretending to be asleep? And that is what she did. She lay inert and tried not to let slip her wakefulness. She felt Chhotjethu's damp hand tremble a bit. It felt kind of warm as it slid down over her belly and slipped into her panties. Then the hand became restless. It clutched her soft young growth and the skin beneath. And that was when Sree jerked out of the daze and started to feel bad. Disgusted. Repulsed. She pushed Chhotjethu away. But he pretended to have just woken up. He pulled Sree closer and asked, "What's wrong?"

"Leave me. Let me go. I want to go to Ma."

"Did you have a bad dream? Come...come closer to me."

Sree sat up and wrenched her hand free before leaving the bed in a hurry to go out to the veranda. Her throat felt parched with fear and anxiety. She spent the night in the veranda. But she did not share the experience with her mother. Why?

Manasi said, "That was the beginning. Since then it has happened many times. She is addicted to it. I advised her to tell her mother. But she said that it hardly mattered because she liked it. She laughed and said that she had offered her love to her Chhotjethu. She wanted the stars, the seas and the trees to know of it."

Sujoy saw a vision of himself—blood oozing out of his ears, nose and eyes. It was boiling hot like molten lava.

Su: Why didn't you say anything all these days?

Ma: I told Sree that if she didn't say anything then I would disclose everything. But she threatened me...she said that if I opened my mouth then she would claim I taught her to do these things. And, you know Didi...she would have fired me. My mother is so poor...

Su: You may go now. Don't tell anyone that you have told me everything. If you do, I'll make sure your mouth is sealed forever.

Ma: Perhaps you don't believe me. But please keep an eye on Sree. She is a brilliant student. I wish her well. What do I stand to gain by tainting Chhotda's reputation?

Manasi never spilt the beans, till date. Perhaps she had shared the story with her husband during an intimate night while she lay resting her head on his chest. The story of cruel human malice. Before leaving, Manasi fell at Ragini's feet and said, "You are my god." Ragini had made her what she was today. She made sure Manasi was educated and well-groomed. Because she believed that the person who would be responsible for the well-being of her daughter needed to possess basic sophistication. Ragini gifted Manasi gold ornaments and a Benarasi saree for the wedding. The same Ragini, who had previously refused to help another girl in the same situation, was now Manasi's idol. Ragini was full of contradictions. But then, though unrelated and employed merely as a paid care-giver for Sree, Manasi had always wished Ragini's daughter well.

Sujoy waited for Chhotda to turn up. He thought of the Chhotda from his childhood. Chhotda, who shielded Sujoy during Pulak's case. Chhotda, who distanced himself when Sujoy decided to marry Ragini. Chhotda, who was disgusted with Sujoy's line of business. Was Chhotda the same even at that time? So perverted and crooked! Or had he changed? Did man really change or did his dormant natural tendencies one day spew forth like hidden viruses? All they needed was a favourable breeding ground.

Sumit's financial demands had increased. His trimonthly magazine did not attract many advertisements. At the same time, if it was not published, Sumit's very existence appeared threatened. Sujoy thought back to his childhood years when Chhotda had taught him to solve certain difficult math problems by back calculation. A clever trick. Now, Sujoy did some back calculation. He remembered that whenever he hesitated to give Chhotda money, Sree always pleaded on her Chhotjethu's behalf, "Please, Bapi, give him the money..."

Also, whenever Sumit sensed such hesitation in Sujoy, he promptly reminded his younger brother of the past in the presence of Ragini and Sree.

"Remember your mental condition when you were to get married...?"

"Do you remember Pulak's death...?"

A deep and dark warning, from a brother to a brother. Sujoy felt the vibes. He could see the devil's horns on Sumit's head and sharp fangs hanging over his chin. Three blood red horses surrounded him and schools of predatory fish were at his beck and call. All heartless bloodsucking creatures were in his control. A brain-sucking flower dangled from his left ear and a bird with a coarse call perched on his right hand feeding on a young boy's liver. Dark wings of night, their delicate weave chequered by black veins, sprouted out of Sumit's back.

–He, who carried sin with him, was the devil. Sumit Banerjee was a carrier of sin.

–He, who troubled beauty, was the devil. Sumit Banerjee tortured beauty.

–He, who was the cause of destruction, was the devil. Sumit Banerjee was the destructive force which tainted the purity of the home.

–He, who was against civilisation, was the devil. Sumit had violated the pureness of the father-daughter relationship.

–He, who was against nature, was the devil. Sumit Banerjee was unnatural, perverted and crooked in the mind.

Sujoy pondered. What punishment would be most suitable for Sumit Banerjee?

That night, Sujoy switched off the lights in his room and waited. Ragini's, Sree's and his bedrooms were arranged around the dining room in the centre of their house. The night darkened and deepened. Sujoy waited, still and silent. Finally he spotted Sumit rise from the couch in the living room and approach Sree's bedroom stealthily. Sree...! Sujoy felt like crushing Sumit to death then and there. Like a bedbug. Or an insignificant fly or ant. But he did not want to burden Sree or Ragini with unnatural melodrama. This was a potion of sin which he preferred to swallow himself. His head hurt. His chest burned. And his eyes...

***Sumit*: This time I need more money. There are some prospects** for the magazine. If I can change the look and launch it...! I am due to receive the Kabi Animesh Basu Award. That will fetch fifteen thousand. If you give me another fifteen then the rest…

Sujoy: I have already given you about a lakh, Chhotda. Can't give anymore.

Sumit: You didn't give me the entire amount at one go, did you? To ease the expenses for you, I made the magazine trimonthly. Why are you calculating in this manner? One lakh!

Sujoy: I do. And henceforth I will do it this way. I have to slog for money. Baba's savings are already in your name. What more do you want?

Sumit: No, no…of course, you will have to keep a tab on your money. But, Sree is still young, her mind tender. I am planning to write an article on human relationships. And Sree loves me a lot and reads everything I write.

Sujoy: Exactly what are you trying to say?

Sumit: Nothing much. Your and Ragini's marriage could be an example of human relationship, but for Sree that could…

Sujoy: Don't stoop so low, Chhotda! You are a poet, not a blackmailer!

Sumit: Oh come on, poets will always be sensitive. Do you think I don't understand you? Why are you calling it blackmail? Ragini is overtly emotional and her life is sure to be riddled with mistakes. But you are generous. Knowing everything…

Sujoy: Don't stretch this, Chhotda. You will not gain anything by blackmailing me. It doesn't matter if Sree learns the truth about Ragini. The truth cannot be hidden for long. Moreover, Sree is of modern times. She can take many things easily in her stride. Things that appear important and impossible to you.

Sumit: You are my dear baby brother. I know how righteous you are. Tell me, if I dig up Pulak's case and write about it, will you help me?

Sujoy trembled in rage and agitation. Such venom? But why? Was it envy? Envy towards Sujoy's success? Slowly, he regained his calm and his mind zeroed in on a decision. He felt relieved of all agitation and anxiety. Of love and hatred. No memories from the past remained to soften his resolve. In a very calm and cool voice he said, "Please leave my home, Chhotda."

Sumit: What?

Sujoy: Can't you understand? I am speaking in your own tongue. Leave my home, this very minute.

Sumit: Ragini is surrounded by lovers, she hardly pays you any attention. And your father-in-law has your reins in his hand. What gives you such arrogance? You have married a woman who has been handled by many. Are you sure your daughter is yours?

Sujoy: Don't tempt me to hit you. Get out. Get out now!

Sumit: What you are doing is not right…

Sujoy: Get out!

Sumit: I'll tell Sree everything.

Sujoy: Out!

Sumit: I'll print it in the papers…

Sujoy: Will you leave or not!

Poets are generally soft-hearted, sensitive and emotion-driven. But did that necessarily mean, he couldn't look at females in his family and friend circles in a perverted way? Sujoy was at the verge of amazement but checked himself. Poets were humans too and so they were prone to sinful acts. Every human in this world carried his share of sins. Poets and artists were no exception. And neither were businessmen or, for that matter, petty sweepers.

Hence, how could Sujoy expect his poet brother to possess extra virtue? The protective layers fell away from their fraternal relationship.

Sujoy called up Jayshankar, "Brother, I am in trouble."

Jay: What is wrong, brother? What can I do for you?

Sujoy: Someone is threatening me.

Jay: Just say the name. Should I take care of him?

Su: Yes, Jay. You are like a brother to me.

Jay: Don't say that, brother. I feel ashamed. Do you remind the sun every day that it has to rise in the east?

Su: Thank you, Jay. I will be leaving for Siliguri tomorrow on urgent work for a week. But before the week is over a particular news should force me to return to Kolkata. Better if it is within two days. You will get your dues once I return. Will that do?

Jay: Till date has Jay ever demanded his dues from you?

Su: No, but that is my responsibility.

Jay: Boss, you have made me your brother. Who is the chap you have in mind?

Su: Sumit Banerjee. He lives in Haur. A poet...

Jay: Your second brother!

Not two days. Four days later, a terrified and teary Ragini called him. Sujoy was, of course, waiting for the call. He took the first available flight out of Bagdogra.

The rotting body was sent for post mortem. But nothing could be proved. There weren't any injury marks on the body either. A suicide chit was found beside the body.

It read, 'I am a failed man. I have no right to live. I am a parasite who feeds on others. I do not wish to live at the mercy of others anymore. I have used my father's money without paying my last respects to him. I am a sinful man. And today I relieve myself from such a life. No one is responsible for my death.'

Alcohol was found in his stomach. Jayshankar had threatened and made him drink six pegs within half an hour. Followed by twenty-five pills of Nitrazipam. It didn't take long for Sumit to slip into a deep sleep. But then, anyone could drink alcohol before committing suicide. In the dark, Jayshankar slipped out through the door by the washing area. Before leaving, Jayshankar left the windows open.

The closed door and open windows did not spark any suspicion for the following couple of days. Not hearing from him, the people from his magazine assumed Sumit was in Kolkata. Later, Sumit's cook discovered the open door by the washing area. And then the usual set of incidents followed. Sujoy had wanted a rigorous police investigation but, at that point, Supratim stopped him. He advised, "A police investigation will not be favourable for you. One can never say how far such things will roll. It might even sniff into your business. A bunch of unsolicited problems may crashland! Instead, let me handle this. Which police station serves Haur...?"

Supratim was a blessing. Sujoy felt relieved. Supratim demanded a meagre sum of twenty-five thousand to shelve the case. Apparently that was what it cost to buy the honest protectors of law a round of 'tea'. Had they wanted to have 'sweets' it would have cost slightly more. And if their demand had been of 'mutton curry and rice' then this high profile case would not have been settled below a lakh. Of course, the entire amount was not pocketed by a single person. Everyone, who was connected to the case in some way, received his appropriate dues.

In the end, emerging from the suicide-or-murder dilemma, the people of Haur concluded that it was suicide. After all, suicide by a jobless man, that too a poet, was almost a common social malaise, in no way extraordinary. After cremating Chhotda, Sujoy lay down in the field outside their house in Haur...after many years. Borda came to Haur, but alone. He did not want to involve his wife and children in this tricky and sticky business. He appeared quite dejected as he said, "Was he killed? But who would kill him? Who can be his enemy? He did nothing proper with his life. Do you know if he was in a lot of debt?"

Sujoy asked, "Why do you ask?"

"He called me a few days ago and asked for fifteen thousand rupees. He said it was an urgent need."

"Did you agree to give?"

"No. I told him I couldn't give him anything. I helped him in the past and we also gave him Baba's money. After all, I have a family to look after."

"He asked me too. I refused as well."

"Did he really commit suicide because both of us refused? Poets!"

Sujoy kept silent. Sree sobbed profusely while Ragini tried to calm her down. Sree's crying disturbed Sujoy immensely. When he couldn't take it anymore, he slowly left the room.

As he thought about Sree, his mind came up with a scene from his past. That of his mother thrashing house lizards to death while cleaning the room.

The pathetic creatures ran helter-skelter to save their lives but his mother was ready with a broom poised to strike and kill. Her face had stern concentration and excitement writ large on it. Then his thoughts moved on to his Bengali teacher, Deb-babu. At Deb-babu's wedding reception, guests had been served *khichuri*, or kedgeree—a simple concoction of rice and lentils. One day, while buying a bottle of oil, Deb-babu came across a protest march against the rising price of electricity. He promptly joined the march, his hand still clutching the bottle of oil as he raised it in protest.

Deb-babu used to say, "Rabindranath is a philosopher and Jibanananda[10] a poet." He had no qualms about marking an answer with a zero if it did not meet his expectations. While teaching, he often said, "The times are dire. We need a leader...someone like the Buddha. One who will gain enlightenment and also show us the way. Someone who will guide the wayward in the right direction."

From Deb-babu, Sujoy learnt that love was born only when there was a possibility of hatred. There was no good without the chance of bad. Just as the beginning of creation was also the start of a journey towards destruction. A person's immense success in one field actually brought to light his failures in others.

Chhotda had liked Deb-babu a lot. Chhotda.... Sujoy's eyes welled over.

...Chhotda, you saved my life. Chhotda, you inspired me to become an artist. You saved your lunch money to buy me the biography of Van Gogh. You shielded me in Pulak's case. You were my friend but somehow I couldn't be as close to you. Hence, worthless matters and various sins found their way into the gap between us. Chhotda, when did you start to think of me not as a brother but as someone who could be exploited? When did you start to look upon my child, who could have very well been your own child, with venomous thoughts? When did you become my enemy, Chhotda? From my brother to my friend to my enemy. What could I have done except kill you? Chhotda...Chhotda...have I sinned?

Sujoy's body was wracked by sobs. Suddenly, he found a shining torch making its way towards him. He sat up,

10 Poet Jibanananda Das hailed from Barisal in erstwhile East Bengal of pre-Partition India. One of the most popular Bengali poets, he is often hailed as one of the most prominent precursors of modernist poetry in Bengali literature, after the Romantic era dominated by Rabindranath Tagore.

anxious. It was Ragini. She left the torch with him. In that moment, amidst the tears, the pain, the guilt, Sujoy saw those two divine souls—Abhi and Upo. He tuned in to their conversation as he searched frantically for peace. While listening to them, deep sleep took him over. But, even in sleep, he heard every word clearly.

Abhi: Stars bloom in the sky and flowers on earth. This blossoming makes nature all the more beautiful. Sometimes they look like they are embracing each other, the stars and the flowers. Sometimes they seem to be engaged in a pretend fight. An amicable argument. Have you heard of love been exchanged while in discord?

Upo: Lovers who do not know to fight will never know the true value of togetherness. We had a cock and a hen. They roamed freely but often the cock pounced on the hen and almost strangled it. I felt like killing the cock to save the hen. But my mother said, "Don't hurt it. They are only playing. Don't you roll in the dust with your friends in mock fights? They are doing the same. Don't spoil their game, dear. Everyone in this world has the right to play."

Abhi: I can clearly see the flowers and the stars playing. The star says, "I shine because you bloom." The flower says, "I bloom in the hope that you will shine." That is how the stars in the sky and the flowers on the earth were united. When did this creature called man fall in love with the flower and develop a beautiful heart? When did he decide to make a garden as a symbol of softness? An act through which a new man was born inside him. But his animalistic instinct, from the ancient time when he was an animal, still exists deep down within him. After loving a flower can man still return to his animalistic nature?

Upo: Why are you thinking about man? You will not be able to fathom anything. You will find yourself in such deep darkness that your soul will lose the comfort and peace it gathered from the flower. Your soul will be destroyed.

Abhi: No, no...don't talk about destruction. Talk about flowers and love. They have made life on this earth beautiful.

Upo: You understand the language of the flowers while I understand the language of the birds. Have I ever told you about my very dear Bheemraj[11] bird?

Abhi: Please tell me. Let me see your bird through your eyes.

Upo: Bheemraj. It likes the damp and dense forest. Black in colour with a bluish tinge making its neck and belly shine. It has a white patch on its neck and its eyes are red like a pair of rubies. Its tuft is unkempt...as if it does not like to cross paths with a comb. Its tail is amazing...like the ribbons from a young girl's hair flying free in the wind."

Abhi: Wonderful!

Upo: They move in small flocks. But, in all these days, it has never once come to me from the forest.

Abhi: Really? Then where did you find it?

Upo: I bought it from the bird market. When I took it home, Ma thought it was a crow but then, on a closer look, she said, "This is a Bheemraj!" That was the first time I heard the name. The man who sold it, said it was a Darufingey[12] and would whistle. But Ma brushed aside all such talk.

Abhi: Then? Did it whistle?

Upo: It did call out one day but a very different call. I felt like crying at being cheated by the man. But Ma said, "Feed it

---

11 Racket-tailed drongo (local name—Bheemraj) is an Asian bird with elongated and twisted tail feathers (the rackets, which are more prominent in the case of Greater racket-tailed drongos) with webbing restricted to the tips and an unkempt tuft of curled feathers above the beak. They belong to the family *Dicruridae*, along with other drongos. Found in hilly and forest habitats, especially in the Eastern Himalayan range of North Bengal. It has a loud call and can mimic other birds.

12 Local Bengali name for a common species of the drongo.

lots of cockroaches and other bugs. It will surely whistle." I fed it well and pleaded with it to whistle. And then, one morning, it sang beautifully...almost a heavenly tune. I started to cry. The cat, sitting at my feet, said, "Meeaow." And surprising me no end, the Bheemraj mimicked, "Meeaow! Meeaow!"

Abhi: Oh! I am getting goose bumps!

Upo: It could imitate the calls of cows, dogs, goats, cats and many more animals.

Abhi: Then?

Upo: I let it go.

Abhi: Why?

Upo: I searched high and low to bring it a friend. But I could not find another Bheemraj! The man who sold me this one had also vanished. Finally, one day, I let it go. It did not want to leave and hung around on the custard apple tree for a few days. But by then I had learnt my lesson about freedom.

Abhi: The custard apple tree! A favourite with birds! It has a very sweet and fleshy fruit filled with black seeds; the fruit resembles a cluster of berries. Oh, how wonderful and tasty this fruit is; this particular species of fruit grows out of a multiple fertilisation of a flower—these are cluster fruits.

10

SUJOY did not know all of them by name. Neither did he have the desire to know. He came across them occasionally on the odd Thursday or Sunday. They were Sree's friends from her tutorial class.

Sree had started to follow her usual study routine at home even before the Madhyamik results were out. Except the science tutors, all her previous language tutors of Bengali and English came regularly to give her private coaching at home. But when home tutors were arranged for private coaching in other subjects that she had chosen for high school, Sree declared war. She wanted to join special coaching classes like her friends. Sujoy had thought that during these two very important years of study before college – the eleventh and the twelfth standards – Sree would benefit from one-to-one private tuition at home. But when he expressed as much, Sree, true to her nature, awarded more credit to her own views and compelled others to agree with her. She was well past childhood now and young adulthood was fast moulding her anew. In the tumult of adolescence, Sree was going through a novel yet explosive make-and-break spree. And since she always enjoyed Ragini's support, Sujoy's disapproval hardly mattered. But, as far as tuition classes were concerned, Sujoy stuck to his guns. He went as far as to say, "Which coaching class are you going to join? Mind you, I'll set that class ablaze!"

Sree had retreated to her room quietly. A while later, Nayan-mashi, their previous home help Manasi's mother, screamed in terror, “Oh dear, Ragini-di…Sujoy-da…look what your daughter has done…”

Ragini – in an ethnic black saree, her hair unkempt and make-up incomplete – and Sujoy rushed out of their rooms. Ragini was due to go out soon to honour an appointment with Aniruddha Kanjilal at half past eight and had been dressing. Sujoy had no idea what happened at those meetings; whether they helped one climb the ladder of success faster. As they reached Sree’s room, they found Nayan-mashi trying to hold Sree in an arm lock. Sree struggled to free herself. A blade glittered in her hand and blood ran down her leg. Sree had been slicing the skin of her leg with the blade.

Ragini yelled, “What is this! What’s happening? Sree! Mashi, leave her!”

In the scuffle, Sree’s dress rode up her legs to expose her thighs and then her navel. Ragini cried again, “Sree, what does all this mean?”

Sree appeared quite collected and composed. A wry smile hung at the corner of her lips as she panted an answer, “Bapi is putting restrictions on me, Ma. Of course, he has the right…I am not an adult and I am not self-dependent. But it makes me angry, doesn’t it? And anger should be vented. So, I was simply venting my anger, Ma.”

Ragini fixed Sujoy with a steely gaze. She screamed at the top of her voice and her attractive facial features appeared contorted into ugliness.

“Why don’t you agree? She knows what she wants. She is intelligent enough to take her own decision…’

Sujoy felt as if he had been struck by a thunderbolt. Overpowering pain and extreme self-repulsion made him sink to the floor with a thud. His folded legs were splayed and his forehead was clasped in his hands. He seemed to have lost control over his intelligence, his knowledge, his individuality and his patience. He sobbed with his mouth wide open like a helpless child…or, perhaps, an uncomprehending lunatic. Tears flowed from his eyes, his nose ran phlegm and saliva dripped from his mouth. Nayan-mashi pressed the end of her sari to her eyes and left the room. Sujoy hiccupped as he let the world see him in that state for a couple of minutes. Then he slowly regained control over himself. In a constricted voice, he said, "You are perverted, crazy. You and your daughter. Raving mad. You and your daughter. You are mentally ill. I can't take it anymore. I want to be free Ragini. I want a divorce."

Ragini left the room but returned soon with antiseptic lotion and cotton wool. She locked herself in with Sree in her bedroom as Sujoy went to his room, picked up his wallet and left the house.

After walking around aimlessly for some time in the twilight, Sujoy felt an urge to end his life. He wandered without purpose. And then, he longed to dream. But what dream? A dream, which would put him to sleep, as it had, once before. He had once had a dream but now, he couldn't remember it. He knew it had brought him peace and deep sleep. He tried hard to recollect. What dream was it?

…O dream, please come to me. Please come and deliver me from this agony. What are you? Are you an illusion? An illusion and a self-nurturing indulgence. You are a relief for the distressed soul, a heavenly balm. Dream, you are an earnest plea for clinging on to life.

Slowly, the cool air and the beauty of life on earth caressed his mind and provided Sujoy the much-needed succour to help him shed the momentary yet gripping insanity and fatigue. The flowering trees lining the dimly-lit path returned him to his earthly existence. The starry skies lent him some restraint. He looked at the palatial houses around him. At their feet lay a scattering of run-down dwellings, clinging on like unwanted rotting toe nails. Makeshift houses shrouded in plastic sheets. The waft of a simple evening meal of potato and onion curry being rustled up in these shanty homes – punctuated by the occasional loud abuse and curse word – drifted across. Children played noisily, some even studied in candle light or in the dim light of street lamps. The faces of the boys and girls were somewhat familiar. He knew them from long back. Some eternal souls had returned to life on earth in these new guises. This age-old earth was actually ever-changing, ever-new. The lives and realms of humans, animals, birds and trees made the world beautiful.

Life...home...domesticity! How beautiful!

Sujoy thought fondly of his home and family. Ragini, his wife, was an artist and therefore whimsical; hence, she was complex. He would never tire of watching her. Sree, his daughter, was extraordinary, extremely intelligent and talented...quite a beauty. Adolescence was chasing her around. Perhaps her genius had affected her mental balance, making her revolt. But who would protect Sree if not him? Who else but he would protect Ragini? If he died then who would save these two impractical human beings, who never came to terms with reality?

Hence, Sujoy was again awash with a wave of affection. He felt as if he would be able to paint again. He studied his hands and fingers. His hands were there alright but the artist's fingers were missing. So, other thoughts surfaced in his mind to provide an alternative to painting.

...the entire existence and its expression were intertwined with a variety of matters which were ever-changing. Hence, a limited perspective eventually and gradually spread its wings and crossed barriers. This was a natural reaction of human consciousness. Any attempt to contradict that resulted in despair which time and again gave rise to thoughts of death. And, it was quite meaningless to encourage such thoughts. Why should one slog after the inevitable? Expression has always been a natural desire and a natural product...perhaps, 'satisfaction' was a better word than 'product' here. This expression was a manifestation of the completeness of human existence. It created a unique feeling, starkly different from any other. But this feeling of completeness was momentary. In the very next instant, it was transformed into a new desire or a feeling of despairing incompleteness. No one could escape it. The journey from completeness towards incompleteness commanded human life to follow a set path. Why are we alive? Well, perhaps even trying to formulate an answer to that question was illusory. Being alive was a natural tendency and humans had learnt to accept it that way. There were only three ways in which man could escape from this—love, work and observation. Hence, I have gained this realisation that I love my wife and daughter. Their virtues as well as their vices are acceptable to me. I have dedicated myself to various kinds of work and it is my responsibility to see them through. These actions are close to my heart and will not bear fruit without my assistance. And, when I step out of the realm of love and attachment, work and responsibility, I am a human being who observes the ways of civilisation for self-development.

Sujoy returned home to find Ragini and Sree waiting for him. After informing them that he no longer disagreed with Sree's joining a tuition class, he went to take a shower. A while later, Ragini came to his room and touched his forehead with her left hand. Then she started chanting a *shloka* dedicated to Lord Shiva, trying to calm down his tortured soul and put his passions to rest and at peace.

It surprised Sujoy. Yet, the fact that Ragini had not left to meet Kanjilal did not surprise him. Because Ragini was fickle and beyond comprehension. Sujoy did not expect love through this gentle behaviour of hers. He was enveloped in his own love for her.

Sree had gained many friends through her independent life style. They were primarily from the tuition class. Sujoy's attention had been drawn to one of them; a young man who was poised to become a committed lover. The way he looked at Sree was different. He had beautiful eyes and a profound gaze. His demeanour and manner of speech were bound by a remarkable fusion of intelligence and serenity. Sujoy laughed to himself. He would wait and watch. He was now only an impartial observer.

Today, Sujoy had arranged to meet Jayshankar at his Kaikhali flat. It had been long since he spoke to Jayshankar who had to step out of his own neighbourhood with much caution. In his profession, enemies were many. Jayshankar also did not trust the police officers whom he had already bribed. In his world, trust was absent...and love fleeting. So, out of immense love, he wanted to keep Sujoy Banerjee away from his world. Jayshankar believed in the worldly truth that the enemy's friend was an enemy. And, he wanted to keep Sujoy out of the sight of his enemies. It often alarmed Jayshankar to think that his fellowmen could very well target Sujoy any day, in an act of betrayal. Hence, in matters involving Sujoy, he employed only those who were weak, timid and submissive. Those who could be kept under control easily. In the initial days, they met at Jayshankar's place in Khidirpur. To spend time chatting over a drink or to plan a move or event. But Jayshankar was a clever man and wished Sujoy well. As his enemies increased in number, he curtailed Sujoy's visits to his place in Khidirpur.

For some time they faced difficulties meeting up. But since Sujoy bought the flat in Kasba, those issues were solved. For security reasons, Jayshankar changed his phone number frequently. But his address remained the same. He could be found only in Khidirpur. Those who wanted him, they looked for him and found him there.

It was a strange world, infested with ferocity. A world whose every nook and cranny was not in the know-how of the police force. A world where no one knew who was sealing deals with whom, and against whom, except the persons involved.

Once on the VIP Road, Manjil liked to step on the gas. Sujoy relaxed in the rear seat, taking small and slow sips of whisky. A few days back, their art gallery had opened in Salt Lake. Thanks to Ragini's efforts and Anjan Kar's requests, Aniruddha Kanjilal had graced the occasion and inaugurated the gallery. And his presence roped in the newspapers who published longer-than-necessary reports about the opening. In those reports, Ragini's name found mention because one wall of Room Number Two sported her work. The other three walls had selected works of some budding artists. The gallery, consisting of four exhibition rooms, was planned like the Academy of Fine Arts. In Room Number One, some established artist's work would be displayed for a month at a time. At present, that artist was Prajit Mukherjee. The second room was for new, young artists. But Dibyangana's work was not to be found because she had not responded to the invitation sent to her. The third room could be hired by any artist or artists' guild. At present, a guild called Heptagon had rented it. The fourth room was reserved for sculpture and other forms of art. Currently, it hosted an exhibition of stone, terracotta and wooden art work.

Anjan Kar had been more involved and responsible as far as the rules and regulations of the gallery were concerned. Administration was in his hands. On the day of opening, Anjan Kar looked very happy as he stressed time and again that without Sujoy Banerjee's help it would not have been possible to have the gallery up and running in so short a time. Sujoy was well aware of that fact and the delight on Anjan's face made him happy. There was only one instance when the glow vanished from Anjan's face; when Debola stood close to Aniruddha Kanjilal with his hand on her back. His pink plump hand was splayed on the smooth expanse of her exposed back above the deep semi-circular plunge of the blouse. "Haven't seen you in a long time," he said. "Why don't you come anymore? Do come again, soon..."

Aniruddha Kanjilal was flanked by Ragini on his right and Debola on his left. Two beautiful women dressed to perfection. Hence, he appeared all the more alert, handsome and youthful. But Anjan seemed dull and preoccupied. Sujoy tried to understand himself. How did he feel? Did he have any other role to play besides that of an indifferent observer? He remembered a quote by Goethe. He did not know why it came to mind. The mind was an unfathomable mystery. It was like the impenetrable darkness of an unknown world. One never knew what it would recall and when. Like now, without rhyme or reason, Sujoy thought,

"*Those organs which guide an animal are under man's guidance and control.*"

Ragini was happy; and busy too. The art gallery, the exhibit of her works and Aniruddha Kanjilal's proximity had injected life into her. And Sujoy felt glad seeing her happy. But when he delved deep into his mind, he realised that he was not at peace where Kanjilal was concerned. This was because, not only Ragini, of late Sree too, was drawn to him. Often, she visited Kanjilal with Ragini to show him her work and discuss art. When they returned after a visit to Kanjilal, Sujoy noticed a shine of mesmerised adulation glinting in their eyes. As if, Kanjilal had adorned the eyes of both mother and daughter with the glow of fireflies.

Like Ragini, Sree too, called him Aniruddha-da. Sujoy had exclaimed, "Why are you referring to him as 'dada'? He is quite old…!"

Sree had replied, "I would prefer to call him by his first name. In fact, calling him Aniruddha-da is almost like calling him by first name. I cannot think of him as someone's elderly male relation like an uncle or something…"

Sree was rapidly changing. She was moving fast beyond his comprehension. Was this the 'middle ages of disassociation' during the period of development? Some days ago, Sree presented him with a list of her expenses to justify her pocket money. The amount was equal to Manjil's monthly salary. Sujoy remembered the time when Sree had no idea how to spend her very meagre pocket money. She bought bread with it and fed the stray dogs; that used to be her main expense. Sree could no longer be found on the road, with pieces of bread in her hand.

Meeting her demands, when Sujoy handed her the money, she reminded him, "Only one more year, Bapi. After that, I will keep account of all that you spend on me."

"Why?" asked Sujoy.

Sree: I will be eighteen. By law, then I should be fully responsible for myself. However, that will not be possible in our social system, so I will keep a tab. How much do you spend on me, Bapi?

Sujoy: But didn't you say just a few months back that, since I was loaded, you wouldn't run after money? Have you changed your mind?

Sree: Yes, I have! And why not? Why *should* your money be mine? Ma's money is also not mine. I didn't earn them! Then why should I have any right over them?

Su: But this is our age-old practice. Wealth is transferred down the generations.

Sree: This system is the cause of our lack of independence and our reluctance to work.

Sujoy: Perceptions differ, Sree. In the hereditary transfer of wealth, it is not important what you are taking...why and with what intention you are taking it, is what matters.

Sree: The children in this country do not enjoy mental independence because they are dependent on their parents for money even after coming of age!

Su: In that case, I'll have to donate all my money.

Sree: Of course, if you feel that way. Do you know what Ma has told Dadu[13]?

Su: What?

Sree: To donate Ma's share of his wealth to Bharat Sevashram or some other charity. Ma doesn't want it.

Su: Has Dadu agreed?

---

13 Maternal grandfather

Sree: He hasn't come back yet on that.

Su: Good. Your mother doesn't need a lot of money!

Sree: I need lots and lots of money, Bapi. I want luxury.

Su: Your opinions are changing too fast. I can't keep pace. Am I growing old, Sree?

Sree: No, Bapi. You are not becoming old. You are stuck on a particular value. You see the new world with old eyes. My opinions are changing because I am watching the world straight on and feeling it. I have realised that every individual must have his own means of income. Earning gives a person individuality, independence, self-respect and freedom. I want freedom and I want to experience. I want the best things and the best services from this world. Bapi…I want to savour and enjoy the pinnacles of luxury, contentment and bliss.

Su: What is bliss? What is the pinnacle of luxury?

Sree: The pinnacle of luxury means the heights of bliss. It means being able to do whatever your heart desires. I will live in the poshest neighbourhood in a beautiful flat. The most expensive interior designer will do up my flat. There will be champagne in the cellar. Four or five cars will be lined up. The moment a new model is in the market, it will be mine. I will go to the disco, go gambling. I will have so much money that I will be able to spend without a thought. Bapi, happiness means the power to purchase. Money brings that power. Money is something with which you can buy even a human being.

Su: Then, is the world's richest man also the world's happiest?

Sree: Of course! With money you can buy illness, grief and death.

Su: Death!

Sree: Yes, death. At least, it can be stalled. You can establish a deed of yours with money. Like the Taj Mahal. Shah Jahan had it built for Mumtaz. But what direct role did he play in its construction? Because Shah Jahan had the money his name was etched in history while the actual creator faded into oblivion.

Su: If you have a lot of money, will you do something similar?

Suddenly, Sree put her arms around Sujoy's neck and, rubbing her cheek against his rough stubble, said, "I will run away to Switzerland with my Bapi!"

Sree was changing fast, very fast. Sujoy tried to convince himself that it was the coming of age which was changing her. Maybe, four years later Sree would not say these words. Sometimes, Sujoy felt a deep void within him. He had never been able to touch Ragini's soul; now Sree too, was slipping away. On the other hand, Anjan Kar and Jayshankar, though not related, were closer to him. Much more familiar. They were not shrouded in mystery. They were profound, beautiful and intense with their love.

Ragini was a mysterious woman. Sree too, was gradually developing a veil of mystery. But then, Anjan Kar's mystery was in Debola and Jayshankar's in his family. What was his family like? Sujoy had never thought to find out. He felt quite awed. Friendship was an amazing relationship; it was not a slave to any familial connection. Among all relationships, only friendship was possible without the need of family. And because of that, many friends remained oblivious to each other's families forever. Sujoy decided, today he would find out about Jayshankar's family.

They reached Kaikhali. Sujoy opened his eyes and directed his misty gaze at the star-spangled sky. A torch descended from among the stars. Chhotda lit up the grass with the light from the torch as he approached Sujoy. Beside him was Pulak Biswas. He too, had a torch. Girin walked beside Pulak, his torch flickering on and off.

Chhotda said, "Sujoy, are you asleep?"

"No, tell me."

"I have composed a new poem. Shall I read it out?"

"Yes."

The light from the torch fell on the poem.

"Sujoy, are you asleep?"

"No, tell me."

"You have stopped painting since you moved to Kolkata."

"Yes."

"Why? You should not have got involved in politics. Artists are not made for politics."

"Who said?"

"Politics and art cannot live together. Political shrewdness kills artistic thoughts."

"Nothing in life is beyond politics. Politics is not something untouchable. Every social individual should practise politics. It makes one realise life in a clear way."

"These are all bookish knowledge. I don't believe these. I am sure you will agree that since you took to politics, your art has been suffering."

"I will leave this after this stint of student-politics."

"You will have to value your life more. You have true talent. Don't waste yourself."

"Why didn't you study further? Doesn't one need to study to become a poet?"

"I don't like the conventional way of studying."

"Rabindranath?"

"Sujoy, are you asleep?"

"No, tell me."

"A sky full of stars and a world full of people...which would you prefer?'

Sujoy opened his eyes. Why did they return repeatedly? Why?

Jayshankar was already there. The lights were switched off and he lay on the bed spread-eagled. This was how he liked to have a heart-to-heart.

Sujoy entered the room and sat down in a chair. Then he asked, "Shall I switch on the lights?"

"Give me fifteen minutes, Boss. I am thinking."

"Okay."

Sujoy went about preparing their drinks in silence. His mind wandered to Sree. He recalled Sree saying—"After Higher Secondary I won't study in this country. I'll sit for the SAT exams and go to the US. And if I can't sit for the SAT then I'll finish my graduation and sit for GRE or TOEFL. I will leave this place."

Sujoy muttered to himself, "Sree, if you change yourself so fast then how will I find you? How will I keep up and interact with you? Are you changing under someone's influence?"

Sree was changing very fast in speech, manner and attire. Nowadays, she wore crop tops with a pair of jeans. She was thinking about toning up her body to join modelling. For her, the idea of modelling did not clash with her commendable feat of bagging tenth place in her board examinations. She also had Ragini's support in these matters. Ragini encouraged her having a boyfriend and giving modelling a try. She was teaching her daughter that after eighteen, sex was not taboo. She had even advised her about the use of pills for personal safety. Aniruddha Kanjilal was gradually gathering mother and daughter into his domain. Or, was it the modern times which, like Kanjilal, was swallowing up mother and daughter with its unexplainable realism?

Sujoy felt extremely sad and helpless.

11

SUJOY: I have never asked you anything about your family, Jayshankar.

Jayshankar: Yes, that is the only thing lacking in our friendship. We do not express any interest about each other's family. Though, since you have entrusted me with keeping an eye on the well-being of your wife and daughter, I have gathered some insight into your family life. But you know nothing about mine. It is a fact that true friendship is not dependent on exchange of such information. One can feel the unknown through the emotions involved. That is the power of friendship. But, it is also a fact that there should be no qualms about any matter in friendship. There should be no boundaries.

Both sipped their drinks. Sujoy watched Jayshankar. He wore a kurta over a pair of jeans. He was a bright complexioned man of five feet seven, now sporting a two-day stubble on his rotund face. His hair was cropped short and he wore glasses. By appearance, no one could guess his profession. To be honest, one couldn't arrive at a correct conclusion about him even after talking to him. Contrarily, people would be inclined to think that he was perhaps a teacher, writer or a man of philosophy.

Jayshankar Jha had been living in Kolkata for over twenty-five years. He still spoke Bengali with a different accent and his speech was an odd mixture of Hindi and Bengali vocabulary. Nevertheless, it was laced with affection for Sujoy Banerjee.

And faith too. Jayshankar was devoid of fraud and lies; in his expression, his demeanour and his heart, he was an honest man. His presence, his words and his warmth lent Sujoy a kind of trust. It proved to be a kind of shelter. As if Jayshankar was conveying with his entire being, "I am here. Don't worry. I am here for you." From the depths of his own fearlessness, Sujoy reserved high regard for Jayshankar's courage. Within himself, he had identified danger, uncertainty, an uncharted future and a steady heartfelt emotion with which he could analyse human beings. Danger and uncertainty were constant companions of Sujoy Banerjee, Jayshankar Jha and Anjan Kar. They had always welcomed the uncharted future with open arms. And they had shared with one another a steady heartfelt emotion, selflessly.

Su: I want to know about you, Jayshankar. You, your family... how you happened to join this profession and how you made a place for yourself...

Jayshankar: Let me tell you something about profession, Sujoy. Like air, water and light, a profession is also necessary for a man to live his life. To carry on in life and look after a family, one has to take up some profession or the other. It gives you wealth and purchasing power. It gives you the strength to face adversities. That is what life is about. What can be a greater success than being alive on your own means...being alive without being at the mercy of someone else? You are a man...you take care of your family. That is the purpose of your life. You will have to adopt some profession and you will also have to like it.

Su: Does everyone find a profession he can like? Do all people get a chance to choose a profession they will love? Aren't there professions which make people hate themselves?

Jayshankar: A profession will not always meet the heart's desire. The heart will have to school itself to like it. You will give love because you have it in you to love.

Su: Still...we do have some values, some regulations. There are some professions in which virtues and sins are intertwined.

Jayshankar: Who has made these regulations? Man himself, right? It's not as though God came down from the heavens and laid down some rules and regulations for humans, is it? Man created his own social norms and they are all temporary. With time, these norms change and so do the yardsticks and concepts of virtues, sins, rights and wrongs. For me...if any deed makes me repent and suffer in retrospect then that is a sin. And if something brings peace and content... or none of those...simply brings your bread and butter, then that is right.

Su: Sometimes I don't understand which makes me suffer in pain and which makes me happy. Pain and happiness mingle into one and I am unable to differentiate. There are some things which make my life uncertain, they tarnish my world and pose hurdles in my path...I want to crush those. But then, I am filled with qualms. Discontent chases me around.

Jayshankar laughed loudly. His guffaws pierced the core of the Kaikhali darkness. He took a sip of his drink and said, "I need rum, brother. This whisky is no fun."

Sujoy grunted an apology. He knew Jayshankar did not prefer whisky and he had brought a bottle of rum for him; but the bottle was still in the car. He felt bad for his slip. Perhaps these were happening because of Sree. Sujoy called Manjil and asked him to bring in the bottle. In his leisure time, Jayshankar liked rum but while working he preferred the local brew. The strong, pungent and almost poisonous liquid gave him an adrenaline rush and woke up the maverick in him. He proceeded with the task at hand with dedication and an indomitable drive. After the job was done, he liked to draw on some *charas*. His complexion appeared flushed and his eyes reddened; his limp body gave a false impression of weakness. Slowly, a kind of dull pain spread through his body. An obscure feeling descended on him. The fumes from the charas-filled cigarette slashed his body into pieces. One of those parts succumbed to slumber. It slipped into deep sleep in an attempt to escape all emotions and rest. It severed all ties with good and evil. But another part of him stayed awake; alert and normal. It went about performing life's other responsibilities. It took care of business, it talked and laughed; and, it planned the next job.

Manjil brought the bottle of rum. Jayshankar, happy with his favourite drink, prepared himself a glass of the dark liquid and gulped down a good portion at one go. Then he said, "Do you know why you can't separate joy and pain? This is because you are extremely knowledgeable. Your bookish knowledge has thrown many questions at you for which you have no answers. You have read volumes and forgotten how to look at things in a straightforward manner. Do you know the real meaning of virtue and sin? Your sin can never be mine. Similarly, I cannot give you a drop from my cache of virtues. Because these things are different for each human being, their feelings too are different. If all sins were equal then, since our society dictates certain actions like killing to be sinful, wouldn't we all be sinners? Wouldn't the butchers who kill cows, goats, hens everyday be sinners too? And what about all those who have other roles to play in these killings?"

Su: It is an accepted norm that man will not kill man. This has been agreed upon keeping man's welfare in mind. Going against this rule is a sin.

Jayshankar: That is just a way of thought, brother. We have coined this question about sin. People like us. So, why can't we change what we ourselves have made? If killing humans is a sin then all judges are sinners. All national leaders, army leaders and soldiers are sinners. But we don't call them so...do we? A judge is the emblem of law for us. Soldiers are national heroes. So where does that leave us? If we must judge a sin then it should be done by the motive behind it. Not by the actual act of killing. If you kill someone in self-defence then you will not receive death sentence.

Self-defence! Right! Sujoy thought, so far all that he had done had been in self-defence. Why should he be a sinner? He had time and again proven to himself that he had not sinned. Had Jayshankar sinned? No. Because he was nothing but a medium. A professional. Only those who were cold-blooded killers could be sinners.

Gradually, Sujoy found himself quietly agreeing with Jayshankar's point of view. Or, perhaps, his heart and mind had been waiting in eager anticipation to agree with this kind of a justification. He thought, Jayshankar was right. Good and evil were relative and depended on man's own comprehension and perception. All the norms that are to be practised in a nation, make up the civil and cultural yardstick of that nation. But these norms were not permanent, they were not necessarily flawless. In fact, national norms and personal norms could well differ. What the population collectively practises is the national norm. It is necessary to maintain peace and order; it is necessary to keep people's greed and self-interest in check. It aims towards general welfare through equality. But, in reality, this purpose is hardly served. Since man is a slave to these norms, and not the other way round, human misery increases in the attempt to enhance social development. The true aim of these norms may well be social prosperity through individual realisation, but this does not happen. Man is simply forced to live by thousands of rules and regulations. And he is thrown into a deep end of dilemma. The established norms do not give man peace. Again, when he tries to gain peace from his personal norms, the social ones prove to be obstacles in his path. Hence, in such conflicting circumstances, good and evil become matters of personal choice and opinion. Man's own discernment rules. But, the realisation of sin is a profound one, very difficult to escape from. It gradually pushes man into a deep swirl of darkness.

Sujoy watched Jayshankar sip his rum while relaxing in a reclined position. Then, in an attempt to emerge from the depths of his thoughts, he said, "Tell me about yourself. I want to know about you."

Jayshankar closed his eyes and started a return journey along his life's path. Thirty-seven, thirty-six, thirty-five, thirty-four.... Gradually he reached the stage when he was eight; and various memories crowded around him. Sujoy listened intently as Jayshankar recounted. Jayshankar's life entered and mingled with his own life. He realised that man actually lived many lives within the realm of his own life...the lives of many people were intertwined with his own.

Jayshankar: My father worked in the Khidirpur fish market. He earned quite well. Our house in Khidirpur was Bapu's. He used to rent it initially, then he bought it. I was eight when Bapu brought me to Kolkata from Katihar. I was his only son after seven daughters...you can well imagine how pampered I was. Bapu couldn't stay away from me for long. He would frequently rush to Katihar and his work in Kolkata suffered.

Finally, he decided to bring me to Kolkata with him. Ma cried a lot...she even proposed that the entire family move to Kolkata. But Bapu did not agree, he did not want his daughters living in the dodgy neighbourhood of Khidirpur.

Su: So you are from Katihar?

Jayshankar: Yes. I was born in Katihar. My grandfather had some land…very little. The family ran on Bapu's earnings which he sent from Kolkata. Our family gave importance to education so all my sisters attended school. In Kolkata, Bapu admitted me to St. Jude's Missionary School. My three eldest sisters were married with much pomp before I reached the tenth standard. When my fourth sister was to be married, my grandfather passed away. Grandmother had died when Bapu was young. After grandfather's death, Bapu was greatly heart broken. He became careless towards his business and sat at home for a long time. I was in class ten. Since that time I started living alone in Khidirpur. I cooked for myself. Bapu wasn't there to discipline me…not that he was very strict. But with him around everything went smoothly. Not because of lack of discipline, I believe it was more out of loneliness that I hooked up with Kailash. At the time, Kailash was honing his skills, he took me to the spots once in a while. Can't say I liked it a lot…but there was a strange fun in it…a kind of madness. He attracted me with his ability to blur the line between life and death. He was amazingly sharp and alert. I have learnt a lot from him.

Sujoy's cellphone rang. He moved to the window, phone in hand. It was Sree.

Sree: Bapi, guess where I am calling from?

Su: Tuition class.

Sree: Oh Bapi! You are wonderful. Bapi, I want to tell you something.

Su: Go on. Hope it's good news.

Sree: Yes, Bapi. And you are the first person I am sharing this news with. Guess why?

Su: I guess that's your wish.

Sree: Oh no, Bapi...because I believe you are my best friend. I love you, Bapi.

Su: More than you love your Ma?

Sree: Bapi! You are jealous! Anyway, listen to me...Baldy has proposed to me, and he has gifted me an extraordinary painting. He painted it...and it's my portrait! He is a very talented artist. He should have an exhibition in your gallery.

Su: Slow down, Sree. One after another.

Sree: Okay, Bapi. Now listen, Baldy has proposed and he wants me to be his lifelong partner. Like you and Ma.

Su: Oh. So, what did you say?

Sree: Initially I brushed him aside. But when I saw the painting I started loving him. You will understand what I am trying to say once you see the painting.

Su: Very well. I am kind of busy now. I'll see the painting when I reach home and then we'll talk. Have you called Ma?

Sree: Hmm...but Ma has switched off her phone. She doesn't like her phone ringing when she is at Aniruddha's place.

Su: So, I am not first. You called me after you tried calling your mother.

Sree: Bye Bapi. I love you.

Su: Hang on...who is Baldy? Do I know him?

Sree: Of course, he comes to our place often. The tall and dark boy. You once said that he had nice eyes.

Su: Oh...so he is called Baldy.

Sree: No, no. His name is Siddhartha. We call him Baldy! Bye Bapi.

Sujoy returned from the window side. Jayshankar too returned from a visit to the toilet and stretched out again. Then he asked, "Was that your daughter?"

Su: Yes.

Jayshankar: Why have you arranged for your wife and daughter to be under surveillance? Are you scared of anyone?

Su: I have my daughter watched because of security reasons. As for Ragini, it is both for security and advantage. I don't know if I have any dedicated enemies but I can feel their existence. I can't say how or why. But, I feel as if there are people who want to hurt me...destroy me. And that can be done best through my wife and daughter.

Jayshankar: What were you saying about advantage?

Su: Ragini has appointed people to watch me both inside and outside the house.

Jayshankar: Like Girin?

Su: Yes...Girin. But the people she has appointed now, tell me everything. They also tell me what they are going to report to Ragini. All these people are part of my business. Yet, I cannot trust them completely. Can I? Ragini doesn't know about this flat yet...but it is only a matter of time, she may get to know about it any day.

Jayshankar: So, Ragini doesn't trust you. But why? You are one of the very few honest men around.

Su: Do you know what is necessary for trust?

Jayshankar: Love.

Su: Yes, love. How can trust grow where there is no love? Ragini is using me to lead a secure life. Why should she trust me?

Jayshankar: But you love her. I know...I can see that. Someday she will understand. Someone who has received love can never understand the pain of unreciprocated love. One day, she will surely realise what you have given her.

Su: Have you ever loved anyone?

Jayshankar's words sounded slurred. Sujoy's voice too trembled. Perhaps, the effect of alcohol mingling with emotions. Sujoy wondered, was he not deserving of even a little bit of love?

Jayshankar: Yes...I'll tell you. Tonight I'll not keep anything from you.

Su: Tell me.

Jayshankar: Remember I said that my father left Kolkata after my grandfather's death? Well, he returned after quite a few months. I know, no one's parents live forever but in my father I saw how a son can mess up his entire existence in grief over the loss of his father. The kind of business Bapu had set up, waited for no one. He returned to find all his clients and even his space taken up by others. It became very difficult for him to re-establish himself. He did not have much money left after marrying off a few of my older sisters. But, he somehow managed to make ends meet, in spite of his preoccupation. In the meantime, I finished class ten and started college. That was when I met you. Bapu died towards the end of that year.

Su: Yes, I remember. You dropped out soon after.

Jayshankar: Yes. And you were the only one from among my college friends with whom I remained connected. Because, you were the only one who visited us regularly after Bapu's death. None of my civilised friends wanted to visit the dingy alley in which I lived. That was when I started looking upon you as a brother. I decided, if the need arose then I would even give my life for you.

Sujoy felt overwhelmed. His emotions got the better of him and his eyes welled up. It could well be expected that people like Sujoy Banerjee, Anjan Kar and Jayshankar Jha did not shed tears. Their varied struggles against life would have destroyed their inclination towards shedding a tear or two. But, nature was strange. It often created some humans in whom harshness and gentleness, emotion and indifference resided together. They could shed tears as well as suppress them.

Jayshankar appeared detached. He took a few sips of rum and then started talking again. The walls were all ears, though they made not a sound, ever. Day after day, they were privy to revelations by Sujoy, Anjan and Jayshankar.

Jayshankar: We ran out of money. Ma sold the plot of land. The money from that saw us through some time. But then paucity was at our door. That was the first time we faced starvation. I felt bad. I was the only male in the house. My mother and unmarried sisters looked towards me hopefully but there was nothing I could do. I did not even visit Katihar in fear. That was when Kailash introduced me to his line of work, and saved me. I started earning. I assisted him for some time and then took on contracts myself. Money came in and I sent some home, though not very regularly. But this business does not fetch money recurrently. When there is work, there is a lot of money…and risk too. In the time between two contracts, the money was spent and life again ran on debt.

Su: I know, you were going through hard times.

Jayshankar: I couldn't borrow from you. You too, were leading a bachelor's meagre life. So, I looked for other ways… which would fetch fast earnings. I had already embraced risk so I had nothing to lose! I started trading ganja…and then charas. Charas was a better bargain.

Su: I had told you not to get involved in the charas business.

Jayshankar: What could I have done? It helped me get my sisters married. What worse could happen to me? But yes, if you had wanted to get involved in it, I too, would have stopped you. To be honest, I did not like your line of trade either. But I know, you had no option.

Su: It is either greed or helplessness which leads a man into these businesses.

Jayshankar: Yes, but we have earned a lot. We have no complaints in that respect. I married off three sisters but the youngest one had an unfortunate life. She was widowed within a year of marriage and returned to us. I wanted to get her married again but she refused.

Su: Who did you marry? The person you fell in love with?

Jayshankar: Had I married wouldn't I have invited you?

Su: True...but what about the children in Katihar you talk about?

Jayshankar: There are children, but no wife. My widowed sister has adopted four orphans. Do you know how many mothers abandon their new-borns in the hospitals? Katihar is a small place, yet my sister found four such babies there. Three boys and one girl. They have filled up my sister's life and I too, consider them my own. We often take care of puppies and kittens, yet hesitate to take in a human child.

Su: Why did you not marry?

Jayshankar: I fell in love with Kailash's sister. But Kailash did not agree to the match. He said, since I was a contract killer my own life had no guarantee.

Su: Kailash's sister? Did she not love you?

Jayshankar: No. In that respect, you and I are in the same boat. Debi never loved me. But do you know what happened? Kailash had asked for a guarantee for my life...but he was the one who died abruptly. Due to a liver problem.

Su: And Debi?

Jayshankar: Debi married someone else...her own choice. The man had a shop in Fancy Market. But he indulged a bit too much in gambling and soon the business was busted. Now Debi entertains men. In fact, she has been doing it for quite some time. In a way, it was good that I did not marry. In my line, there is money but life has no value. Moreover, with a family in tow, one cannot throw caution to the winds. One day, someone might kill me the way I kill others. This profession breeds many enemies. For instance, take the man who is hiring me...he is my biggest enemy because I know his secrets. I am aware that my enemies watch me. Perhaps, someone from my own team is with them. To be honest, the police are not as big enemies of mine. I need to be extremely careful when I come to meet you. And Katihar is almost out of bounds now. I have not given that address to a single person in my group. I take care of everything myself. I may well say that there is no sin and no virtue...but I was born into a Hindu family, and I studied in a religious environment in a missionary school. In some deep corner of my heart, a feeling of guilt flickers. Not for being a contract killer. No. It is for trading charas. But what could I do? I needed money quickly. There are so many police officers and government officials who have no financial need yet they take bribes from us...in cash or kind.

Su: Don't you love Debi anymore?

Jayshankar: I do. I will love her for the rest of my life.

Su: Then why don't you get her out of the life she is leading?

Jayshankar: Why should I? Debi is not mine. And, because she turned me away, she does not want my help. Instead, this arrangement is better. I can visit her whenever I want.

Su: Do you visit her?

Jayshankar: Yes. I am a worthy client. If I am to visit then she doesn't take in other clients. But, to be honest, I like loving her from afar. I have never been able to love her body.

Su: Don't you always say that no profession should be hated?

Jayshankar: I don't hate. I just can't love.

Su: Do you fear for your life?

Jayshankar: Not fear...uncertainty. I am always ready to depart. I don't care about my life. But I have ties...my mother, sister, the children, Debi.... I will leave a document with you today. I have put aside some money for my sister and the children. There is also a flat in Park Circus. I have saved some money for Debi too. I have given you power of attorney, you can take decisions on my behalf. If something happens to me, please look after them.

The businessman in Sujoy became alert. How far would he be able to utilise this power? What if Jayshankar died and he was not informed; and, by the time he got to know, what if there wasn't time to get the death certificate? He said, "It's all very well that you are giving these papers to me but please also leave copies with your sister. And the accounts of your money."

Jayshankar: Yes, I have everything. Do you remember the shop where we got our cigarettes? I bought that shop quite some time back. I am not burdening you with anything undoable. But, since you insist, I will send the papers to my sister. Who knows what might happen!

Sujoy felt like crying. The few drinks he had downed had made his senses limp and now they could hardly hold the tears back. But he did not make any sound; only his features contorted. He stood up, his body swaying. Then he walked to Jayshankar and sat down beside him taking his friend's hand in his. Jayshankar, murderer and drug dealer, said, "Sujoy, don't feel sad. I understand that I will have to be prepared for sudden death. I have seen death so up close that sometimes I can smell it. How long can I carry on this way? I am getting old. New killers are coming into the scene with new weapons. They are more daring. I may live for only a day or I may live till I am hundred...who knows!"

Su: You will live. As long as I am alive. Then we shall depart together. Give up your profession and your business and join me. I will send you to Siliguri. You will be nearer to Katihar.

Jayshankar: No, it's not possible anymore. There is no such option left for me.

Su: Why?

Jayshankar: You are intelligent. So, why don't you understand this? Didn't I tell you that those who give me work are my biggest enemies? If I give up this profession then those very people will have me killed by someone. I have no way out. Tell me something…if there is God, if there is right and wrong, then will my children have to bear the burden of my sins?

Su: No, Jayshankar. Because you have not sinned.

Jayshankar: We had some norms…we took some oaths. First, we would not kill children. Second, we would not rape. Third, we would not betray. Till date I have not broken any of those promises. I have not deviated. Hence, I have not sinned, have I?

Su: No, you have not sinned. Sri Ramkrishna has told us to think of God when guilt troubles us.

Jayshankar: Do you believe in God?

Su: Don't know.

Jayshankar: I too, don't know.

Jayshankar took out some papers from the bag on the bed. Bank documents and the deed for his flat. The phone rang. Sujoy answered.

Anjan: Where are you?

Su: At the den.

Anjan: Who's there? Jayshankar?

Su: Yes.

Anjan: Listen, Aniruddha Kanjilal wants to talk about some paintings. Will you come with me?

Sujoy: Has he asked for me?

Anjan: No.

Su: In that case it is better I don't go.

Anjan: I need to talk to you, Sujoy.

Su: Yes, very soon.

Sujoy took the papers from Jayshankar but did not look through them.

Jayshankar: Please have a look. There might be mistakes.

Su: Later…if I find mistakes, I'll ask you to meet me. We will get that opportunity, don't worry.

Jayshankar: Very well. There is one thing I would like to know. I have never asked you to justify any of your orders… but, I have one question.

Su: Ask.

Jayshankar: Why did you kill your brother?

Sujoy poured some whisky into his glass. He topped it up with water and then downed the entire contents at one go. Then he said, "He was blackmailing me about Pulak Biswas."

Jayshankar: He knew?

Su: Yes, he guessed. But that wasn't all…

Jayshankar: What else?

Su: He tainted my daughter's honour. Day after day. For a few years, he…

Jayshankar: What! What did you say?

Su: He…Sree...

Jayshankar: You did the right thing, brother. You have not done any wrong. I know, you cannot do wrong.

Then they took leave of each other. Their roads diverged from Kaikhali. Before leaving, Jayshankar said, "I too, don't know a lot about you, Sujoy."

Su: Will tell you. Next time.

As soon as they left Kaikhali behind and took VIP Road, Manjil speeded up. Sujoy's phone rang again…an unknown number. He answered. It was a lady's voice.

"Sujoy-da?"

"Yes, speaking."

"This is Dibyangana. You took some paintings from me…do you remember?"

"Of course. Tell me, how are you?"

"Can you come and meet me on the evening of the fifteenth? Please? If you don't mind...if you have the time...I mean, I need to talk to you..."

"Okay, Dibyangana, I will come. But if I get caught up with something urgent, can I call you?"

"Yes, but if someone else answers then just say it is about paintings you wish to talk..."

"I understand. I'll come. Is this your number?"

"Yes. I won't be able to call you again, Sujoy-da."

"Okay Dibyangana. I'll try my best."

12

ON Sunday, Sree went out saying that she was going to Aquatica – a water park – with her friends. On the same day, Sujoy was to visit Dibyangana. He had already spoken to Anjan about it. Anjan had encouraged him to go and find out what Dibyangana had to say. Was it about paintings or something else? Perhaps something personal! But why would Dibyangana share anything personal with Sujoy in the course of their very short acquaintance? Amidst his various engagements, Sujoy did not have the time to ponder on this. He had to visit Siliguri once a month and was also planning on opening a business centre in Guwahati. Though he was yet undecided about Guwahati, because spreading the business outside meant spending more and more time away from Kolkata. Also, each state had its own rules and regulations for trading. Perhaps it wouldn't be as easy to do business in Guwahati as it was in Kolkata and Siliguri.

But, most importantly, his leaving Kolkata meant exposing Ragini and Sree to dangers. Leaving them unprotected. He did not know who he feared or why. It could well be his personal perception as a man, that without him his wife and daughter were insecure. But how could he decide how necessary and justified this feeling of his was? Sree was a free bird. And Ragini independent. Beyond anyone's control. How could their security then be dependent on Sujoy's presence? Yet, Sujoy thought himself to be indispensable for the well-being of his wife and daughter.

Till the time it was proved that this was an illusion, Sujoy would deem his presence important.

Moreover, a business centre would require him to be there as much as possible. Even with the art gallery, although Anjan looked after its administration, Sujoy's presence was required almost every day. Of late, Anjan had succumbed to certain preoccupations due to which he was making mistakes. Sujoy guessed it was because of Anjan's domestic situations.

Dibyangana had just mentioned the time as 'evening', she had not specified a particular hour. Sujoy decided to visit at seven. But that became uncertain when Sree and her friends, Siddhartha included, returned from Aquatica with fallen faces. There were eleven of them—three girls and eight boys. They couldn't explain what had happened to Sree. The friends had planned to meet in front of Nicco Park at eight in the morning and then go on to Aquatica from there. If anyone ran late then the others would wait till nine but after that they would carry on. It would be up to that person to make his or her way to Aquatica. So, when Sree did not turn up by nine, her friends left without her. She finally made it to Aquatica around one. But she was unable to provide a valid reason for being late. After enjoying the artificial wave pool with her friends for a while she suddenly moved away and sat down on the sand. She rested her head on her knees and answered her friends' queries with, "I feel depressed...very depressed..."

And then, Sree could not be brought back to a normal state. She closed her eyes and moaned, "Ahh...don't like anything...nothing! Go away...all of you go away. Leave me alone...I am very depressed!"

Ragini pulled Sree close. Sree whimpered, "Ma...oh, Ma..."

Ragini asked, "What is wrong, Sree? I am here with you...nothing can hurt you..."

"Ma...I feel strange..."

Ragini said to Sree's friends, "Please make yourselves comfortable. I will put Sree to bed."

Then she closed the door to Sree's room. The boys and girls sat around the dining table. They had long since crossed the threshold of the living room into the inner quarters of this house. They discussed amongst themselves:

"She was the one who was most eager for the day out."

"Actually she is very sensitive."

"Have any of you said anything to her? Siddhartha? Where is Baldy?"

"Hey, no...Siddhartha hasn't said anything. He is as surprised!"

"Sree is an artist. Artists often suffer from depression."

"Oh dear, Baldy is also an artist! What will become of them?"

"This has never happened to her before!"

"Maybe it has...we are not with her all the time, are we?"

"Triloka will be able to say. They are in the same school."

"Triloka, has Sree been in depression like this before?"

"No Samya, I have never seen her like this. Wonder what's wrong!"

Sujoy was listening to their conversation from his room. Now he got up. Ragini had already taken Sree under her wings. Was there anything for him to do? Would Sree need to see a psychiatrist? Suddenly, Sujoy remembered Siddhartha. Where was he? Sujoy had seen his paintings. The boy held promise. But now, after all the experience he had gathered through life, he was no longer moved by promise of talent. The existence of talent could only be acknowledged if it continued into maturity.

Was Ragini then truly gifted? Wasn't the torch of her talent still burning bright even in middle age? Sujoy believed,

Ragini was in a different category. She was not a talent; she was a desire for talent. She was not an artist; she was the aspiration to be an artist. Some people keep on writing and finally become writers; some people carry on singing and eventually become singers. Ragini had become an artist by continuing to paint over a long time. She was not an artist in the truest sense. Dibyangana was a true artist. Her dedication was towards fulfilment. But Ragini's dedication was for limelight. Did Ragini understand the difference? Sujoy did not know whether all those who had skill but no talent were actually aware of their respective limitations. Except for Anjan Kar he had not seen anyone being candid in this respect. Ragini could not tolerate any adverse criticism of her work. She believed herself to be immensely gifted.

To be honest, most creative people thought themselves to be the powerhouse of talent among their contemporaries. If someone else appeared larger, then much doubt was expressed about that person's aptitude. It was a bizarre and complex mentality. Creative people were envious of one another's fame. Yet, the scriptures highlight some basic virtues of a true artist. Over the ages, through cultivation in thousands of artists, these virtues have been recorded. People desired not only beauty in the art form but also in the artist's personality. For humans, the Almighty Creator is merciful as well as beautiful. Powerful yet compassionate. Similarly, His child, who is an artist, will have to possess all five virtues—patience, obedience, dedication, thoughtfulness and modesty. Most artists did not have these five virtues in them. Often, it seemed as though no creative person had all these qualities. But, of course, there were exceptions. Like Aniruddha Kanjilal. He commanded allegiance but he was not ruled by envy. Like Prajit Mukherjee. He had dedicated his life to creation and to imparting knowledge. But Ragini was not one of those exceptions. Ragini was beyond elucidation.

Incomprehensible. Of late, Sujoy had been seeing more and more glimpses of Ragini in Sree.

He now turned his attention to Siddhartha. The boy was found in one corner of their living room. Sujoy sat down facing him and noticed that he appeared morose and grim. When Sujoy first saw the boy, he had liked him. He had appeared different; not like every other boy or girl. He had seemed to regard Sree in a different light. Today, too, Sujoy felt the same about Siddhartha. He said in a soft voice, "I am Sree's father."

"I know, Uncle."

The boy bent down to touch Sujoy's feet respectfully. He had a head full of hair. Why did they call him Baldy? Sujoy felt a surge of affection. Adolescence made everything possible. It was the age for meaningless happiness and carefree activities. It was also the age for infinite dreams, deep hurtfulness and boundless rage. It was the age for extreme paradoxes. Didn't a vaulting desire for knowledge drown many a youth in adolescence? Again, those who gained complete maturity in this age, faced a lot of pain. Because they were torn between naiveté and maturity. They were childish as well as practical. A childlike longing for pampering mingled with independent intellect in them. In their social circles these youths were the most mysterious. Both Sujoy and Ragini belonged to this category. And, possibly, Siddhartha too, was one of them.

Siddhartha sat still and silent, gazing at the floor.

Sujoy asked, "What exactly happened?"

Siddhartha recounted the events while Sujoy pondered on them. Sree had left home at half past eight to meet her friends. In that case, where was she for all the hours in between? Perhaps some place which she wanted to keep secret from Sujoy, Ragini as well as Siddhartha. Would Jayshankar know? Probably not. Because they did not keep vigil twenty-four hours a day. They merely kept themselves informed about her whereabouts. Sujoy tried to analyse. Sree was very frank and free with Ragini. In fact, she was quite without inhibitions where he was concerned as well. She had even described to him the first kiss she shared with Siddhartha. Then, what could Sree have to hide? A deeper secret? Suddenly, a thought flashed through Sujoy's mind—was Sree visiting Aniruddha Kanjilal without her mother's knowledge? Panic welled up in him; and to hide that panic, he asked Siddhartha, "What are you thinking? Has something happened between the two of you?"

Siddhartha lowered his head, taking a while to open up to Sujoy. Then he said, "Nothing has happened between us, Uncle. I like to avoid disagreements."

Sujoy studied Siddhartha carefully. The boy had conveyed a lot through that one sentence. He had hinted that instances of probable disagreement did come up often. Sujoy realised how mature the boy was and felt as if he was looking at a reflection of himself. But...perhaps, Siddhartha was more mature than he had been at that age.

Siddhartha spoke up, "Can I say something? Hope you won't take offence."

"No, tell me."

"Uncle, is this how depression sets in? Does one actually realise that she is going into depression? Is it like malaria or chicken pox?"

"Have you seen her this way before?"

"Yes. Perhaps I should have told you earlier."

"What did you see?"

Sree's other friends peeked into the room but hurried away when they saw Sujoy in conversation with Siddhartha.

Siddhartha said, "There have been about three such instances. Once, we were at Nicco Park when she suddenly sat down on the ground and started to moan...I quickly came away with her. After a couple more times, I started looking up about depression."

"And what did you find?"

Siddhartha smiled a little. Then he said shyly, "I am not very knowledgeable but I can tell you what I gathered from my studies. To be precise, depression falls under, what we may call, psychosis. It may manifest itself in two ways—either hyper-excitement or extreme desolation. In some people, both these conditions can be seen. It is called cyclic insanity. Psychosis has different types. In case of manic depressive psychosis, there are three types...manic psychosis, melancholia and manic depressive psychosis. These can set in due to various reasons. They could be present from birth or occur due to some deep-rooted cause. This disorder can also happen due to the death of a near one."

"You appear very well informed. Have you read up an analysis by Freud?"

"Yes, all these are there in that book."

"Id, ego and super-ego..."

"Yes, according to Freud, under normal circumstances, these three exist in a balanced manner. But in case of manic psychosis, ego completely denies super-ego and falls in the trap of id. A person is then driven by the pleasure principle and denies law and society. He dwells in an imaginary world without any limitations. But melancholia is quite the opposite. In melancholia, ego surrenders to super-ego and tries to deny id. In that condition, the feeling of guilt is enhanced and frustration sets in."

"Do any of these symptoms match Sree's?"

"No. She is not frustrated...neither have I observed any feeling of guilt in her. But the fact remains that she is unhappy with everything around her."

"Look, if she is suffering from some mental disorder then we need to take her to a psychiatrist. Psychology and psychiatry are vast fields. Don't take any decisions based on your meagre knowledge."

"No, Uncle. I am not taking any decisions. It makes me sad when I see her like this. Do you know what I sometimes feel?"

"What?"

"Sree doesn't like me all the time. Often, she might be with me but she would be thinking about someone else."

Sujoy smiled a little. How the times had changed! Would he have ever found it possible to converse with Ragini's father in this way? Could he even do it now? But he liked the spontaneity in the boy. He could make out that the boy was mature yet remarkably simple. He said, "Love teaches you to wait…and be patient."

Siddhartha's features brightened. He said, "I'll remember that, Uncle."

Sujoy got up, as he had to get ready. Sree's friends too, wished to leave. Ragini came out of Sree's room and assured them, "She is sleeping. Don't worry. Why don't you all come again in a few days?"

Ragini and Sujoy faced each other. They spoke only out of necessity and discussed whether Sree needed to see a doctor. Ragini was against taking Sree to a doctor. According to her, Aniruddha Kanjilal was an expert on child psychology and she would rather take Sree to him as the man reserved much affection for Sree. Sujoy could not bring himself to agree and soon, like many other such instances, a disagreement sprouted between them. Finally, Ragini pulled out her most precious weapon and said, "She is my daughter. I will decide what is best for her."

"She is my daughter too, Ragini."

"One doesn't become a father just by biological connection."

"What else do I need to do to become Sree's father?"

"Why don't you try and find the answer to that?"

It was quite easy for her to say these things. Apparently, he had not been a good father. He did not know how to be one. He should try and realise what kind of a man his uncountable follies and weaknesses had made him into. All that he had done for the family were eclipsed by what he had not done; and those pointed at his lowly, failed existence. Grievances. An unending stream of grievances. All of the grievances targeted Sujoy Banerjee who had tried his best to deplete himself for the welfare of his family. Yet, the cruel and sordid grievances did not stop. They gradually closed in on the man and subjected him to inhuman torture.

Sree came out of her room and said, "If you can't talk to each other properly then why do you talk at all?"

Then she returned to her room and banged the door shut. Ragini went off to her art room. Sujoy looked at the clock. It was close to half past seven; he would not be able to reach Dibyangana's house before half past eight. He was late. But he readied himself. Depressive psychosis...depressive psychosis...Siddhartha's words circled aimlessly in his mind. He compared himself to Siddhartha.

During the infancy days of his and Ragini's relationship, his conduct had been riddled with inconsistency because he couldn't understand Ragini. Her belief in afterlife, her desperate efforts to marry Sujoy...everything was beyond his comprehension and Ragini remained a mystery. Even today, Ragini was equally complex and unfathomable. But, perhaps not entirely incomprehensible.... After twenty years with her, Sujoy had understood this much that behind all of Ragini's insanity, fickleness and incoherent behaviour was a well-planned endeavour towards wish fulfilment. Was Sree too like her mother? Siddhartha was trying to understand

Sree; but, Sujoy had not done the same years back. He had not questioned any of Ragini's unjustifiable behaviours. Why? Was it because of his immaturity? Or, was it because of his immense self-confidence? Things which had given him nothing but a humiliating marriage and a life punctured with complexities.

13

WHAT do I do with this life?

Sujoy pondered on this. Who was the first person in the world to be faced with this question? And who did he expect to answer for him? In all probability, the person who raised the question was also the one who had the answer. Perhaps, every individual had to find the answers to his own questions. Disease, grief, old age and death had thrown some fundamental questions at the Buddha. He spent years in deep meditation seeking self-enlightenment. The answers he came up with did not conquer death, did not halt old age, did not wash away grief from all hearts; in fact, he himself died of disease. But he left behind experiences and thoughts which made human life more meaningful. The dreadful question – what do I do with this life – did not remain as dreadful.

In this manner, while trying to decide what to do with the life he had received, man created another existence for himself. He started to believe in it and instil meaning into it. He made rules and regulations so that he could connect to that more meaningful life. The result was heaven and hell, virtue and sin. Where was heaven? And, where was the horrific hell? Where resided the power which kept a tab on the virtues and sins of all the people in the world? The proof about its presence or absence was yet to be established. And from the deep gorge of this uncertainty, emerged doubt. This doubt watched the momentary existence of life through time. It searched for success in that momentary existence.

And what did that search bring? More questions and a void created by lack of answers; because it was only imagination which could fill that void. It could well be that the fruit of that imagination was afterlife; that afterlife was actually a sacred belief; that it was akin to experiencing proximity with the Almighty.

Often, when a concept is accepted, the belief associated with it takes over human consciousness completely. Man succumbs to these beliefs because the void is unbearable. Perplexity with his own life is unbearable. Alongside the natural inclination to live, the fight against the indifference born of his consciousness is unbearable. Sujoy had long been carrying the burden of that fight. What do I do with this life? He did not know. Was amassing wealth the only purpose of his life? He did not know.

...why do I amass wealth? It is because that is the work designated for me. I used to love painting. What do I love now? I love Sree. I love Ragini. I love business. I love Anjan and Jayshankar. I love the art gallery and exhibitions. Oh! There are so many things I love! There are so many things around me to love. Do I not love earning? I do. But why?

...there is no option but to love earning. I am not an ascetic. Do I crave pleasures? No, no I don't. I am in search of wealth. I am in search of the meaning of life. And the meaning of life is easier to find if one could love. Oh! I love so many things! I love earning because...! Why did I love earning? Did it bring me respect? Security? Increase my value? My purchasing power? No, earning gave me the power to spend.

...earning is my spending power. I love to spend. Spend for the family, for the betterment of business, for art exhibitions, for the art gallery, for the old age home...spending...spending brings me joy. There was a time when I did not have any spending power; I was then insignificant. But, am I now important? For whom? Who awarded me importance? Only those for whom I spend. What about others?

Sujoy took out a five-hundred-rupee note and gave it to Manjil. Why? Well, Manjil often received such rewards for his honesty and allegiance. Could this be called bribe? No. Instead, it could be called assistance. This extra bit, outside his monthly salary, helped Manjil bear the burden of domesticity. Sujoy took care of these petty things while they drove towards Dibyangana's house. At one point he rolled down the window and immediately a young boy appeared beside it. He wore garlands made of packets of nuts around his neck; his hands were laden with various other wares of nuts, peas and lozenges to sell. Sujoy looked at him. Who was the boy like? Pulak? Girin? He couldn't be sure. He rolled up the window again.

...what do I do with this life? I will extend assistance. And, when I extend assistance, a feeling of authority is born in me. I enjoy that. Oh! I love it! So, what do I do with this life? I will extend assistance. And I will revel in the feeling which follows. That's it. That's it? Was that what one was supposed to do with this life?

...was that what one did with this life? Help and revel. And love. I do love. But, is my love selfless? I love Jayshankar. But how much do I love him? If Jayshankar did not need my help, if he did not keep my trust, if he made my heart anxious...would I still love him? I love Anjan. But if Anjan posed a hurdle in my path, would I still love him? Hence, it is evident that I love with some selfish interests and conditions in mind. So, what do I do with this life? I will love my family. My wife and my daughter. With them there is no self-interest associated. Here my love is unconditional and so, it is a success.

But, do I love Ragini? Ragini and I are man-and-wife by social norms. We had established a sexual relationship but do not maintain it anymore. Ragini involves herself in various relationships with her male friends. I do not object. Why? Because it makes no difference to me. If Ragini is happy with another man, I feel relieved. This brings to light two contrasting conclusions. First...I love Ragini so deeply that her happiness brings me peace and I don't feel bad by her rejection of me. Second...because I have banished Ragini from the realm of my love and desires, nothing about her moves me anymore. Yet, I care for her security. I am eager for her to gain fame. Perhaps because I am sold to Ragini. My conscience commands me to remain loyal and alert towards Ragini. Who is this conscience? Is it not me? I command myself. Hence, I am so bound by my values and my beliefs that I cannot violate myself. Man cannot violate himself.

So, Sujoy decided that it was a sin to violate one's self. Then his thoughts sought out Sree. Without resorting to any kind of analysis, he felt that he loved Sree. He denied the age-old saying – man loved himself the most – and concluded that he loved Sree more than himself. Immediately, various untoward thoughts gathered around him. Had some form of abnormality taken root in Sree? Had Sree entered into any sexual relationship? Was Sree deviating from the normal path of student life? She had promised that she would sit for the SAT...but she didn't. Now, she was saying that she will sit for the GRE after graduation. Time and again she was changing her mind. Was it right? Was it a good omen? Was it normal, the way Sree wrapped herself around him without any inhibition about her fast maturing body? Father and daughter...how far could they test the limits of the natural relation between man and woman? Were all daughters so oblivious towards their fathers? And, were all fathers equally anxious? Or, was this an extraordinary situation which existed only within their four walls? Was Sree disturbed by the lack of amicability between him and Ragini? Had his sin touched Sree? Sujoy sat up with lightning speed. What sin? He had no sin. He was not a sinner.

The car stopped at Shyambazar crossing. A young boy tapped on his window. Sujoy turned to look and found the boy holding a piece of yellow cloth. His lips moved. What was the boy saying? He wanted to clean the windows of the car and earn some money while they waited. Sujoy leant forward for a good look. The boy looked exactly like Sumit Banerjee did in his childhood. Again the thoughts gathered.

...so, Chhotda too had returned to the world. Great! Though, I did not want Chhotda to be reborn. People like him were not fit for this world. They were of no use to the world, except for giving birth to destruction.

The death of one Pulak Biswas gave birth to a hundred young boys. The death of one Girin gave birth to a thousand young boys. How many boys had been born by the death of one Chhotda? The world population was increasing in leaps and bounds.

The car cleared the crossing and Sujoy instructed Manjil to take B.T. Road. Then they would turn right at Paikpara. On these roads, one couldn't drive fast. Sujoy's thoughts drifted to Siddhartha. The boy had rattled off the reasons behind depressive psychosis by heart. One of the reasons was the death of a near one. Sujoy's jaw hardened. He forcefully denied all relations between Sumit Banerjee and Sree.

Sree was sensitive and emotional; but, at the same time, she was practical. Sujoy felt, it was quite possible for adolescence to shove one into abnormal territories. Or, perhaps, Sree was so used to being pampered by her parents that she expected the same treatment from everyone. And when she didn't get that, she behaved abnormally. But, above all these thoughts, what troubled him most was how Sree had been inclined to keep secrets. Wouldn't Sree ever tell them where she had been and what had happened?

Manjil stopped the car outside Dibyangana's house. Dibyangana had probably been on the lookout, for the door opened before Sujoy could reach for the calling bell. It was a moment when the stars and the planets were possibly charting out a future about which everyone was oblivious.

Sujoy entered the house and sat down. Three years had passed. Yet, the furniture and décor had not undergone any change. Or, maybe Sujoy was imagining the present décor to be the earlier one. A kind of awkwardness pricked him when he couldn't see any other family member. The feeling waited for Dibyangana to disclose her thoughts. Dibyangana served tea and sat facing Sujoy. She was without make-up and wore a simple white house-robe. Her eyes had dark circles, probably due to some internal ailment. Sujoy felt as if he was looking at an ascetic woman who had renounced everything in life. A morose and deprived woman. Dibyangana resembled a painting herself. A portrait of a despairing ascetic. Pain was beautifully etched in the lines of her face...her pale cheeks, her lips, her nose...and in the light in her eyes. They seemed to say, I am an ascetic woman. Look at me. Know me. Know me through the language of my gaze. I am the bearer of art. I am art itself. Look at me, know me, understand me. Art is not a companion for leisure hours. It is not a fulfilment of luxurious desires. It is not a part of interior décor. Art is the heartbeat for the dead, the sacred touch for the tainted and the divine nectar for the sinful soul.

Sujoy looked at Dibyangana; his eyes must have expressed some curiosity for Dibyangana said, "The rest of the family is away honouring an invitation."

Sujoy grunted an almost inaudible acknowledgement in want of anything to say. Dibyangana continued, "They will be back around eleven. If they return while you are still here then we shall talk about my art exhibition. Is your gallery doing well?"

Sujoy: Yes.

Dibyangana: Sujoy-da, today I have called you purely for personal reasons. I am going through difficult times. If I can't escape then the only option for me will be death.

Su: I don't get you, Dibyangana.

Di: Let me explain.

A tumultuous storm raged within Sujoy's heart. Many years ago, another person had approached him with her personal problems.

Su: Why are you sharing your personal issues with me? You don't know me well.

Di: I don't know why I felt like trusting you...why I felt that you would not expose me. It's just a feeling. Sujoy-da, I have made some mistakes while taking practical decisions in life. But my gut feeling has never been wrong.

Su: I am honoured, Dibyangana. I will try to be worthy of your trust.

Sujoy sought support from the sofa handle as he rested his weight on it. A furtive tremor ran through him, troubling him with angst. Alas, this life of his! He wondered what else life had in store for him.

Di: Brata and I have never shared a healthy relationship. For the first two years of our marriage I was caught up in trying to understand myself, to try and find out if I loved Brata at all. Initially, I tried to love. Later, my efforts turned truly genuine and I wanted to love him. And, it was then that I realised he had never wanted me.

Su: Why? Of course, only if you want to tell me...

Di: I want to tell you...that's why I have asked you to come. You won't understand the problem if I don't tell you everything. As long as I had feelings for him, I did not tell anyone. Besides, I feel like telling you.

Su: Go on.

Di: He has been involved in a relationship with his cousin from a very young age. His cousin has not married.

Su: Oh!

Di: She tried to commit suicide after Brata got married to me. Of course, at the time, I did not know the reason.

Su: How long have you been married?

Di: Six years.

Su: You mean, you have been living this way for so long?

Di: What could I do? My brother and his wife will not take me back. I don't have any money of my own. Also, caught up in the fever of painting, I did not continue my studies. I am not eligible for any job.

Su: You are born to paint. You did the right thing.

Di: But that too didn't work out, did it?

Su: It will. You have been living this way for so long... what are your parents-in-law doing about it?

Di: They know everything...they have always known. They had thought that once Brata was married he would break out of the obsession. When that didn't happen, my mother-in-law reminded me that a woman must know how to lure her husband! They always watch over me so that I do not spill the beans to anyone. I can't go anywhere, can't make friends...can't even make a phone call. In fact, I am not even allowed to mingle with their own relatives. The relatives of this family think I am a snob. Hence, they prefer to avoid me. My predicament is worse than a prisoner's. My mother-in-law worries that I might get involved with another man and tarnish the name of the family. She is blinded by her love for her son. I'm sure she understands that I am not happy here! I wanted to call you about six months ago. But got an opportunity only the other day.

Su: What is your situation now?

Di: Perhaps better. Because, last year Brata got involved with a girl at work. The girl...well...Brata had to spend a lot of money to get out of the mess. At that time, I wanted to file for divorce but Brata did not agree. They want to put up the picture of a perfect family for outsiders.

Su: You file a case. The law is in favour of women now. And, you have genuine grounds.

Di: Where will I live? I cannot stay with my brother. Sometime back, I had contacted a lawyer from my brother's place. He demanded three and a half thousand only to send a notice! I don't have any money.

Su: The lawyer intended to take you for a ride, Dibyangana. It doesn't cost that much. Moreover, nowadays, there are organisations to help women like you.

Di: Please understand my problem. Where will I put up if I have to do these things? Also, I cannot bear minimum travel expenses. Sometimes I read in the papers about daughters-in-law being killed. I feel very scared. Will these people kill me? That would be their easiest way out of this. I feel scared...

Su: This is hell, Dibyangana. Get out of here. You are so talented. With my meagre understanding, I can still predict that you have good prospects. Your paint brush holds great promise. Your biggest strength is your individuality. If you can take your art the right way then one day you will be a name in the world. Don't think you will be able to do that from this house. For an artist to flourish, independence is very essential.

Di: I want to get out, Sujoy-da. By any means. I can't take it anymore. Sometimes I feel like committing suicide.

Though not a god-fearing man, Sujoy sent up a silent but silent prayer.

Su: Dibyangana, you have done the right thing by approaching me. I can't tell you anything for sure right away but I will do something. First of all, you will have to gather courage. Leave this house immediately. Then I will take care of everything.

Di: Really, Sujoy-da? I don't know what will happen. But I will leave this house for sure. How will I contact you? I will not be able to use the phone.

Su: Dibyangana, it's almost ten o'clock. Should I be staying longer?

Di: Please stay, Sujoy-da. I will not be able to contact you again.

Sujoy raked his fingers through his hair, seeking time to think. Then he said, "Look, the way you have trusted me with your problems, I too need your word for something. If you can't agree to that then I won't be able to help you. By the way, how did you get my mobile number?"

Di: I called your home. A girl answered. When I said I needed to talk about paintings, she gave me the number.

Su: Did she ask for your name?

Di: No.

Su: Good. Don't call my place again. And, don't tell anyone that I am helping you. Especially people close to you.

If we happen to cross each other's paths somewhere then behave like a casual acquaintance.

Di: Very well.

Su: Listen, you will leave this place after three days. It's Sunday today. You will leave home at ten o'clock on Thursday morning. First of all, you will go to the local police station to file a complaint. Tell them that you are forced to leave home because of mental torture. You will have to make your brother accompany you. Tell him that he does not have to take any financial responsibility for you. He will just have to be with you when you leave home and also at the police station. If he seems reluctant then threaten him that you will demand your share of your father's property. If your brother asks about your security then take our gallery's name. Tell him that you have a job there and you will be staying at the gallery's hostel. Don't give the hostel's address to anyone. Will you be able to do this?

Di: Yes. I will simply *have* to do it. Are you sure things will work out?

Su: Instil confidence in yourself. Now listen, are you going to take a lot of stuff with you?

Di: No. The bare minimum.

Su: Okay. Take a taxi and ask it to wait at the police station. After you are done there, ask the taxi to take VIP Road towards the airport. I will wait for you at Lake Town bus stop. Ask the taxi driver to pull over when you see me. Any problems, call me on my mobile.

Di: And then?

Su: Then everything is my responsibility. Don't worry about that. You do your bit. It will be difficult. Your brother, his wife and your in-laws will pose many hurdles. You will have to find the strength to cross them. I will wait for you till four in the afternoon.

Sujoy took out some money from his wallet and said, "Keep this…there is about a thousand. You will need it."

Di: No, no. I don't need this.

Dibyangana's head was lowered, her face appeared flushed and her hand shook. She was feeling extremely ashamed to be accepting assurance and assistance from someone she hardly knew.

"Don't be ashamed…" said Sujoy. "This is not the time for such things. You have managed to be strong enough to tell me. Now do the rest. Wasn't it difficult for you to tell me everything and ask for my help? The money doesn't matter. Dibyangana, a life of creative fulfilment awaits you."

Dibyangana's eyes welled up and overflowed. She clutched the money in her hand and tightened her fist. Sujoy's heart brimmed with compassion for her. He realised how helpless the girl was! And Dibyangana, while contemplating suicide, had reached out for this one last straw. Didn't she think for once that Sujoy might well refuse to help? Wouldn't that have been more expected and normal? Sujoy felt a lump in his throat and, at that moment, he welcomed Dibyangana into his life.

14

MAN has an inner religion by which he lives his life. Love and logic are permanent parts of this religion. The rest is prone to change. Man accumulates these from the circumstances of his birth and these accrued conceptions, faith and thought processes may or may not be changed by man's personal experience, logic and adoration. Those who do not welcome change are considered orthodox. But everyday life does not trigger a person to be welcoming or averse to change. That quality surfaces only when he is faced with dire circumstances. When, while travelling the regular path, he suddenly has to choose from among many conditions. And what he chooses says a lot about him. Through it, he knows himself and also projects himself. This entire process may or may not work by the rules of logic.

The traditional reasoning, which is accepted by everyday life unquestionably, is bound by certain limits. Personal reasoning seeks to break those limits and establish itself. Personal logic or love-induced emotions carry a person to certain heights where he rediscovers his own life. And this rediscovery sows the seeds of independence in him. He experiences the conflict between his own existence and the existence of many other contradictory forces; he tries to ascertain the lines of his own existence. When an existence tries to be at par with contradictory existences, it actually increases its own immobility. And, in the process, it intensifies the conflict between social stagnancy and advancement. This conflict is forever dynamic. Forever alive. And, extraordinary men shine forth through the tumult of this conflict. Men like Sujoy Banerjee.

Sujoy recounted everything about Dibyangana to Anjan. After a pause, Anjan said, "This was bound to be Dibyangana's fate. She is an artist through and through. Artists love life. They are against bondage. You know, if artists and writers were to forget about revolting then despair would set in. Sujoy, there can be nothing better than what you have done. You have again proved what kind of a man you are. I feel emotionally overwhelmed and drained. Sujoy…I don't feel good."

Sujoy took a deep breath. 'Feeling good' was an almost impossible endeavour. Instead, one could decide the level of 'not feeling good'. If an adult, matured man desired love then for him despair was the ultimate feeling, despair was the answer to his prayers. Happiness remained out of his reach. Despair always stood ready to be welcomed. Hence, let despair be his desire. Sorrow be his friend. These things were not scarce.

Anjan said, "I am lucky in one respect…I have friends. But Debola has destroyed me."

Sujoy added, "We are friends. We have our friendship to fall back on and share our grief. Have you noticed how, whenever we meet here, we share sorrow and revel in it?"

Anjan: To be honest, since I can share my pain with you I forget to discuss other things. I am not well, Sujoy.

Su: Today, I too have to say that I am not well. I don't know last when I felt good. Early on, I felt good whenever my daughter was with me. But she is gradually moving away from me…don't know where. I can't reach her. Aniruddha Kanjilal is swallowing me up. Prior to this, I have tolerated the greedy clutches of many others. But why? To tolerate wrong is to sell one's soul. Today, I am a free slave.

An: You have said this before. I want to know why. I have to know fast. Nowadays, I feel I am not going to be here for long. I am truly losing the desire to live.

Su: Anjan, I know you are not well. I will certainly listen to you. But we have a responsibility to fulfil before I do that. What should we do about Dibyangana? She will not like to live on my assistance for long.

An: True. It will hurt her self-respect. We can give her a small honorarium for painting.

Su: That too would be a kind of assistance, in a different wrapping. We need to get her a job.

An: We can employ her at the art gallery. She will like working there.

Su: We'll have to give it some thought. Dibyangana is pretty, young and separated from her husband. How will Ragini and Debola take this?

An: The old age home! I can put in a word for her there. Perhaps we will need to donate some more.

As the discussion progressed, the old age home seemed most suitable. There, Dibyangana could get a job reading out newspapers and magazines to the elderly. But the home had a pay structure. To start with, Dibyangana would not get more than seventeen hundred. Hence, she would have to earn some more elsewhere. Sujoy shouldered that responsibility. It was decided that he would give Dibyangana an initial five thousand for one painting. Anjan would look into the sale of her work. He still believed that Dibyangana had it in her to be a successful artist in future. This arrangement would be made a recurring one. And, Dibyangana would use Sujoy's Kaikhali flat. Although it may seem that a lone woman would be unsafe in a flat in this deserted area, in reality, the men discarded that fear after some thought. After all, how safe had Dibyangana been in a populous neighbourhood amidst well-organised security?

Hence, away from the knowledge of the world outside, two businessmen charted the course of artist Dibyangana's fate. Could they be attracted to Dibyangana? Could they lust after this helpless woman? These possibilities did not find mention in their discussions. Instead, Anjan returned to personal issues. He said, "Why are you not being careful about Aniruddha Kanjilal? Why do you allow Ragini to visit him?"

Su: I don't have any say in this, Anjan. Ragini is independent. She chose me of her own free will and now she has rejected me the same way. We have not had normal conjugal relations after the first year of marriage. How can I control Ragini? Instead, Ragini and her father control me. It was for Ragini that I resigned from politics. And, it was also for her that I sought a way out of poverty. Yet...anyway, Ragini believes in afterlife. I have been a wedge between the person she was to marry and her...

An: I know. I have heard but I thought it was a rumour. Do you mean it's true?

Su: Yes, it's true. I have fulfilled all of Ragini's wishes. I am still doing so. I have never gone to another woman. Yet, Ragini does not trust me. Whereas she has sought out many men, time and again.

An: Why did you not object?

Su: Why should I? Every person must decide what price he should pay for which relationship. What do I stand to gain by objecting? Will I get Ragini back? Instead, my beggar's plea will be flashed for all to see. I will not be able to beg for a relationship. Ragini does not want to lose me as a husband. I don't know the real reason behind that. But I try to analyse by my own understanding. Once, to abolish all possibilities of losing me, she invited a tantric sannyasi home to perform a ritual sacrifice—a full-fledged yajna.

An: How ridiculous!

Su: She religiously chants mantras and visits the Tarapith temple to keep me in her life. Truly, her behaviour is ridiculous and unexplainable. I don't know what purpose I am serving in Ragini's life.

An: Don't you feel the pain, Sujoy?

Su: No. There was only one instance when I felt the pain. Since then, Ragini has not been able to hurt me anymore. I guess, my feelings of pain and pleasure are quite dull. I am probably living this life in a very indifferent and uninvolved manner. My father-in-law helped me a lot in setting up my business...money, advice, company...as needed. I will always remain grateful to him for that. But, in spite of his help, some documents were still stuck in the government office. The business was up and running, and if I did not get those documents I would incur losses. Ragini did not care about what I did and how...all she wanted from me was money. Perhaps, she heard of my situation from her father. One day she wanted to know all details of the problem I was in. I told her everything. And, within a couple of weeks the documents were in my hand. Later, I learnt that Ragini took help from Bikash Purokayastha. Her first husband. The man I had kidnapped and threatened with death if he did not divorce Ragini.

An: Oh my god!

Su: He and Ragini maintain a relationship. They have always done it.

An: But how? Why?

Su: I don't know, Anjan. All I know is that beyond a certain limit, independence becomes waywardness. By nature man desires to be wayward. Even you and I. But we can't cross that limit and hence, lead this secret life.

An: Do you know that Ragini is going to Delhi next month with Aniruddha Kanjilal?

Su: No. Why is she going?

An: Kanjilal has an exhibition in Delhi. Most probably, Ragini's work will also be displayed there along with two other artists.

Su: Good. In that case, I will not have to host an exhibition every year. I was doing it only for Ragini.

An: Only for Ragini? Is it not because you love art?

Su: Do I really love art? I don't think so. Then why did I give up painting?

An: Why did you give it up?

Su: The day I learnt that Ragini has always been in a relationship with Bikash, I loathed myself. I thought, how could I paint when I was not a complete human being? The colours vanished and I did not feel like picking up the brush again.

An inevitable silence descended between the two of them. It was one of those times when there weren't many words left, and thoughts too, played truant. Everything around seemed purposeless and meaningless. Millions of people were going through the same life motions. They had done it in the past and would continue to do so in future. A compulsive life cycle. The only things beyond this monotony were human thought processes and the exchange of feelings.

Anjan heaved a sigh and said, "Debola had once tried to jump off the terrace."

Su: Then?

An: She changed her mind thinking of the children. Do you know, nowadays she seems to find various women's stuff in my pockets and my wallet?

Su: What do you mean?

An: An earring in my shirt pocket. A ladies' handkerchief in my trousers pocket. And, very surprisingly, a chit with a certain Sutapa Sanyal's name and phone number on it...and also a handwritten request, "Please come, I wish to see you."

Su: Where did these come from?

An: I too was at a loss. I thought I would go mad. Every time she found one of these things, she brought the house down with her raving and ranting, she threatened to commit suicide and howled her heart out. Finally, I realised where these things were coming from.

Su: Where?

An: From within my house. Debola herself was arranging and placing them.

Su: What! But why?

An: To prove that I deserved to be doubted. Sometime back, I had advised her to see a psychiatrist. She flared up and accused me of wanting to prove her insane so that I could file for divorce. Now, she wants to stamp me guilty.

Su: It is an unbearable situation! Where are we headed, Anjan? There is such profound darkness around us!

An: There is no darkness around you, Sujoy. You are strong. You love your work.

Su: No, you don't know, Anjan. As a man I have no existence. And, I have many skeletons in the cupboard. In my college days, I murdered a fellow student.

An: You must have had no other option. Else, you would not have killed. It is not possible. We all kill in some way or the other. Did I not kill Kajal? Isn't Debola killing me? Isn't Ragini killing you?

Su: Won't society call these murders! Or sins!

An: Who is this society, Sujoy? Aren't we too part of society? You and me? We have accepted the norm that it is a sin to kill a human being. But can any of our lives be completely sinless and strictly on the path of law? No, it can't. And that is precisely why we have laws and penal codes.

Su: Anjan, I would also like to believe that the concept of right and wrong is temporary and often cleverly implied. It is to a great extent personal. Not social. Every man identifies sins according to the rulings of his own conscience. The rest he agrees to as part of social norms necessary to maintain social harmony. To be honest, society is a momentary existence of some conflicting processes. Man is yet to find a supreme ideal which will bring together all these conflicting processes from all ages and nations. In fact, most of the conventional norms are not to the liking of the human heart. If society is dedicated to the welfare of man then why are its rules against the desires of the heart? Our teacher, Deb-babu used to say that if the rule and the heart cannot agree and unite then the rule will never be attractive. I have always kept those words in mind. I have tried to understand 'well-being' in my own way. I don't know if I am right or wrong. But, I can say this much, I have no feeling of guilt.

An: You are right, Sujoy. Whatever you feel is right. You are responsible towards your family. You are benevolent and fair towards your employees. You extend a helping hand even to those who are unrelated to you and you are compassionate towards your friends. I know, your personal life is painful but you are very strong. You have risen above your mortal existence with that strength. You shoulder the responsibility of many people. Please be responsible for me too!

Su: What do you mean, Anjan?

An: Sujoy, you are an honest and pure man. Please do not turn me away. When my days were spent in playing, studying and painting...when I had no way of knowing the real meaning of life...at that time, I had learnt by heart an extraordinary *shloka*. I still remember it. Among the various ways of being purified in body and soul, the most important was being honest in acquiring wealth. To not acquire the wealth of others by adverse means. The man who can amass wealth in an honest way is pure in the truest sense. If one's earnings are not by honest means then in no way can he purify his body and soul. You are such a man. Now, it is time for me to understand the real meaning of life. And that cannot be done if I don't distance myself from this life. Sujoy, I don't know how long I will live. But, I would like to leave with you all details of my assets and a power of attorney to take decisions on my behalf. If something untoward happens to me, please look after Debola and my sons.

Su: Anjan! Nothing will happen to you. Please don't make me anxious by saying such things. And don't burden me with so much responsibility. Greed is a dangerous and powerful vice. No one can say when it will raise its ugly hydra head. What if I were to take advantage of the power you are vesting in me? What about your lawyer and accountant...?

An: If the need arises they will get in touch with you. I know you are not selfish. Sujoy, you are my last hope and faith. You cannot deceive me...the world cannot turn so cruel! Sujoy, Debola is self-centred and dwells in a world of her own. Our sons are not more important to her than herself. Please look after my sons.

Anjan wept. He covered his face with his hands and wept while despair shrouded Sujoy. Why did his two closest friends want to be bearers of such agonising news? Why did they want to dump all responsibilities on him and relieve themselves? How would he survive without his friends?

Sujoy tried to soothe himself. No, this could not happen. It would not happen. Anjan handed a file to Sujoy. Sujoy took it but did not open it. And then, Anjan enveloped him in a strong embrace and said, "You have been a brother to me, Sujoy."

Sujoy prayed, "Please let me get the opportunity to return this file to Anjan."

15

SREE was still caught in recurring bouts of depression. In the meanwhile, Aniruddha Kanjilal visited her twice. And on both those occasions, Sree appeared slightly cheerful. But more than Sree, Ragini appeared excited. Aniruddha Kanjilal paid a visit to Ragini's studio and offered advice and suggestions. At these times, if Sujoy was at home, there was nothing much for him to do except make polite conversation. Mainly about politics and national issues under the scanner. Alongside, he could also specially request him to keep their art gallery in mind. Kanjilal had already assured Anjan about that but Sujoy knew, such illustrious personalities always enjoyed basking in extra attention. On one such occasion, Kanjilal conveyed the good news that Ragini would be visiting Delhi.

Sree's depression troubled Sujoy greatly. He panicked and thought about it at all times. Sree's depression was perhaps not only an ailment but the result of some other ailment. Her close friend Siddhartha and other friends dropped in regularly. Sree went out with them; she painted too. Apparently, everything seemed normal. But Sujoy could sense the change in Sree. Of late, Sree did not come to him often.

At present, Sujoy was travelling towards Lake Town. Dibyangana was supposed to come today. He decided he needed to keep Manjil acquainted with the situation. He looked at Manjil. But...it was not Manjil. Girin was driving the car. Sujoy frowned. Today, he was on a special mission. Why did Girin have to present himself today?

...Girin, why are you making things difficult for me? Girin, you will not be able to harm me anymore. I have taken away that power of yours. I had no option. You were posing hurdles in my freedom. You had started to control my life. You were slowly becoming the master of my destiny. How could I give you that right, Girin? I had to remind you that you were nothing but a chauffeur. The driver of a machine. You were in the world only for that purpose. But you forgot that and tried to become the driving force of my life. So, please do not take offence, I had to see you off.

Sujoy rolled down his window. Outside he saw a procession. Young boys were marching in a parade, beating drums, wearing feathers in their caps. All the boys on the right looked like Girin. And, all the boys on the left looked like Pulak. Sujoy searched for another face but could not find it. Then he looked ahead. Manjil was in the driving seat.

Sujoy called, "Manjil, please stop for a while. I need to sit in the front. I have something to say to you."

Manjil stopped and Sujoy changed seats. Whenever he had anything important to say to Manjil he always came over to the front. Manjil waited for him. "A lady will be coming today," said Sujoy. "She is in big trouble and has asked for my help. I am doing whatever I can. You know her... Dibyangana. From now she will stay in the Kaikhali flat. I am sure you know why I am telling you this."

"I do."

Manjil parked at the roadside in Lake Town. Sujoy told him to wait outside and watch out for Dibyangana's taxi.

Then Sujoy's thoughts wandered. How could Dibyangana trust him so much? Sujoy felt a kind of wonder; he also felt good. He realised that having been able to do this bit today, there was a flicker of joy in the core of his heart. It was the kind of joy which he had almost forgotten. But why did he feel this happiness? Immediately, he felt afraid. Perhaps, even discomfort.

He tried to divert his thoughts. Anjan and Jayshankar had trusted him completely. What more could a man want in life? Jayshankar knew Sujoy better than Anjan did. With Anjan, Sujoy had been able to share only Pulak Biswas' story. Nothing else. It was not easy to share all secrets, even with a very close friend. Perhaps it was impossible. So, was Jayshankar's trust stronger? No, it was not possible to decide in this manner. A person always observed another person within certain boundaries and decided whether to trust him or not accordingly. That trust or distrust was ultimate in the context of that observation.

Manjil waved. Dibyangana had arrived. The taxi driver was asked to follow Sujoy's car. After reaching Kaikhali, Sujoy dismissed the taxi. Dibyangana looked tired. She had few belongings which Manjil and Jishu carried to the flat. Dibyangana looked around her. Perhaps the isolated area, away from the city lights, appealed to her. "It's a wonderful place! I still can't believe it! Finally and truly, I am free," she exclaimed!

The sun seemed to break through the dark clouds on Dibyangana's fatigue-streaked face. Sujoy felt an urge to keep gazing at the joy on her face. But he lowered his gaze and said, "Let us move straight to the important things."

He told Dibyangana what he and Anjan had decided about her. Then he added, "Don't give this address to anyone. I will visit you often and you have my phone number too. I will also call you at the old age home. Is there any chance of trouble from your husband's side?"

Dibyangana: Don't think so. By the way, I didn't go to the police station.

Sujoy: What! Why?

Dibyangana: My father-in-law pleaded with my brother not to involve the police. He requested us to come to a mutual settlement. My mother-in-law returned my jewellery to me. She was crying...I actually felt quite bad. After all, I have lived all these years with them.

Sujoy noticed the sadness on Dibyangana's face. Then he asked, "Will it be a mutual divorce?"

Di: Yes.

Su: Will you demand alimony?

Di: No.

Su: Why?

Di: I am repulsed by his money, Sujoy-da.

Su: But you have a right to it. He has wasted so many years of your life.

Di: No, he has not wasted anything of mine. But for this, I would not have known the world in which people like you exist. Tell me, would I have known you if I was not married to him? Moreover, will his money be able to wash away all my pain, all that I have lost? I can live on meagre means. This flat...how much do I have to pay?

Su: Nothing. This is my flat. And the adjacent flat belongs to Anjan Kar, who bought your paintings. He will buy more from you in future. Initially, you will get five thousand for the work. I will give you the money today as advance payment. To start with, you will do one painting and Anjan will buy it.

Di: The old age home will give me seventeen hundred... that will be enough for me. You don't have to give me any advance. Let me finish the painting...

Su: Seventeen hundred is not enough. And, you are not at anyone's mercy. Consider this a small investment on our part. When you are a famous artist, our gallery will be proud to showcase your work. Right now, you will have to buy many things to set yourself up. Get the flat in order before you join work. Jishu will help you. Take care. I will come again soon. And paint...and enjoy your freedom.

Dibyangana's eye welled up as she watched Sujoy descend the stairs. How could a man be so nice? Was it possible?

Sujoy sat in his car and put a hand over his chest. The surge of happiness he felt proved to be almost painful. Why did he feel this way, at this age? Dibyangana's face floated into his vision repeatedly. He looked out of the window and tried to think of Sree and Ragini. The usual control he had over himself threatened to slip away.

16

SUJOY was in the front seat of the car. In the rear sat Ragini with her arms around Sree. After a long time, they were together as a family, in a single car. Family! As though living together entitled people to call themselves a family! Sree's Higher Secondary[14] results were declared three days back. She had scored seventy-seven per cent marks... excellent results considering the arts subjects she had chosen. Almost at par with her Madhyamik results. But, there was no joy anywhere. What would Sree study now? They had not decided. Which college would she go to? They had not decided. Nothing had been decided because the situation was not conducive.

Sree was still in a daze. Was she in pain? Did it hurt? Surely not. She had been under anaesthesia. Sujoy's chest felt constricted, painful. He needed peace. What could he do? Where could he go? Dibyangana's face flashed in his mind.

Once home, Ragini settled Sree in bed. Siddhartha was waiting. He too, had wanted to go to the nursing home with them but Sujoy did not agree. In spite of repeated asking, Sree did not reveal the name. All she said was, "No one forced me. Whatever I did was of my free will."

Ragini rebuked, "Didn't I teach you the use of pills?"

"It happened all of a sudden, Ma."

---

14 The final board examination at the end of the 12th standard in senior high school, awarding a pass certificate to all successful candidates. This is followed by university.

Sree was straightforward and sharp in her comments. She said, "I want to be a mother."

Sujoy and Ragini both scolded her with the same words, "Don't be crazy!"

"What is crazy about it? Nature has given me the right to be a mother."

"The society runs on some norms, Sree. Not on your wishes."

"Which society, Ma? There are so many pregnant women lying abandoned on the streets. Which society looks after them?"

"Sree…anyway, we have to live by these social norms."

"Abroad, any girl can be a single mother. Why can't I?"

"Don't be silly! What is possible abroad is not done here."

"Then what is possible here, Ma? When are you leaving for Delhi with Aniruddha? Sometime this week?"

The exchange between mother and daughter carried on for long. This was the first time Ragini had gone against Sree. But Sujoy knew that she would be able to convince Sree. And she did. Tomorrow, Ragini would leave for Delhi. A venomous thought tortured Sujoy. Why was Sree keeping the name a secret? Sujoy suspected but could not bring himself to utter the name. Siddhartha was in the living room, sitting with his head bent low. Was it Siddhartha? No. Impossible! Sujoy went and sat in front of him.

Siddhartha: Is she alright?

Sujoy: Yes. How did you know?

Sid: She herself told me.

Su: Do you know who it is?

Sid: No, Uncle. I asked her…I even tried to force it out of her. But she wouldn't tell me. I threatened to call off our relationship if she didn't tell me. But, in reply, she claimed that was what I actually wanted. She thinks because I have scored more than her in the exams, I want to be rid of her. Can you imagine this, Uncle! Would our relationship have changed because I happened to have scored one per cent more marks than she has?

Su: Do you suspect anyone, Siddhartha?

Sid: No. I can't even think about it. But, she said she did it of her own free will. Didn't she think of me even once?

Su: Did you ask her that?

Sid: I did. And her answer was strange. She said, after thinking about me, she realised that I am not her first choice in life…I am second. But that did not mean that there couldn't be a third person. She said, she has never made any such promise to me!

Siddhartha sobbed and his features contorted. Sujoy felt sorry for the boy. How old was he? Just over eighteen? He had scored seventy-eight per cent marks; this was his time to be happy. But now, within these circumstantial boundaries, what concept would he develop about life as such?

Sid: Our friends are all decent. Such a lowly act by any of them…

Su: Why do you call it lowly? Sree was not forced.

Sid: Even then…it is cheap. Sree is still young. Moreover, she is kind of crazy and emotional! How much does she know about these things? Should anyone support her crazy whims?

Sujoy looked at Siddhartha affectionately. What a pure and soft heart the boy had! Would Sree find anyone to love her more than this boy did? Sujoy took Sidhhartha's hand in his and said, "Go home, Sidhhartha. Concentrate on your life. And be with Sree so that she does not make any more mistakes. Have you decided where you want to study?"

"I'd like to go to Presidency. Of course, if I get the chance."

"You will. My blessings are with you. Always stay beside Sree."

"I will, Uncle."

Dibyangana would surely be back at the Kaikhali flat by six. She worked at the old age home from nine in the morning till four in the afternoon. Sujoy left home at around six. While thinking of Sree, Sujoy's thoughts had wandered to Dibyangana. As they reached Lake Town, Sujoy suddenly realised that of late he had not been thinking of Girin, Pulak or Sumit as often. He felt relieved. As if an ailment was ebbing away. But, what about this longing to visit Dibyangana? Was it a new ailment? Was he treating one sickness with another? He wondered if Dibyangana thought him lustful because he visited often. The thought pained him. Yet, he couldn't bring himself to ask Manjil to turn around. Dibyangana's company gave him peace and contentment. He had been unaware of how long he had craved for this state of mind.

Dibyangana noticed the car and opened the door to the flat. She wore a simple white cotton salwar kameez. Her damp hair hung loose around her shoulders. She was without make-up or jewellery...she looked beautiful. Sujoy smiled a little and asked, "How are you?"

"Do you believe in telepathy?" asked Dibyangana.

Sujoy: I've never given it a thought. Why?

Di: I was thinking about you and here you are! You haven't come for three days.

Sujoy wanted to ask if she felt bad when he didn't visit. But hesitation held his words back. He looked into her eyes and asked, "Is there a problem?"

Di: No, Sujoy-da. I like it when you visit. I haven't been very social.

Su: Then be social. Visit the art galleries. Go to your art teacher sometimes.

Di: Very well...if you say so.

Su: Why should I have to tell you? You are now a free bird. You will have to decide these things for yourself. I may not be able to come regularly. Go visit your teacher...you will feel better. Spread your wings and explore the world. Don't feel reluctant, don't wait for anyone. Make your mind a blank canvas. Dibyangana, will you permit me to have a drink at your place?

Di: This is your flat, Sujoy-da. Why are you asking for my permission? You speak so beautifully, Sujoy-da!

Su: Sounded nice, did it? Actually, it's not that. I didn't really say it nicely. There is something beautiful in you...else, no one has ever told me that I speak beautifully. Politics and business have burnt away whatever beauty was there in me. And, don't talk about the flat in that manner. It may belong to me but you live here. If you don't like my drinking here then I can go to Anjan's flat.

Di: I have no problem.

Manjil fetched whisky from the car and Sujoy prepared himself a drink. The alcohol relaxed his senses and loosened his control; words poured forth. Sujoy felt as though he knew Dibyangana from long back. He felt, this woman was a complete companion with whom one could share everything. He tried to study Dibyangana and find out what was so special about her. What was it about her which drew him to her today and made Sujoy not feel the need for Jayshankar or Anjan's company for his mental peace? Instead, he was drawn to this woman. While searching for an explanation, Sujoy longed to surrender to the flow of circumstances and relieve himself of all burdens. He thought, the endeavour to find the reasons behind all desires was nothing but added complication. He asked, "What have you been thinking, Dibyangana? Do you think I am bad?"

Di: Why, Sujoy-da?

Su: Why not? Here I am, drinking in your flat. You can't refuse even if you don't like it. Perhaps you would like to paint now but you are forced to give me company. Maybe you are thinking that I am taking undue advantage of your situation.

Di: I have placed my faith in you blindly. I have no doubts about you. Besides, I do not feel bad in the least. To be honest, you should feel bad because I am taking advantage. How much do you know me? I could well have dishonest intentions. I could easily break your trust.

Su: No, you won't do that. I can assess people. Dibyangana, I feel as if you are very close to my heart. Believe me, I come here only because I feel at peace here...not because I lust after women.

Di: I know. I understand.

Su: There is no woman in my life except Ragini. Many of my acquaintances used my Kasba flat to have fun but I have never done that. I never wanted to.

It started to rain. Dibyangana rose to close the window and asked, "What would you like to have with your drink?"

Su: What do you have?

Di: Fried fish.

Su: That would do fine.

Dibyangana served him two pieces of fried fish. Sujoy noticed that it was one of the cheaper varieties available in the market. Perhaps she had given him her own share. Sujoy asked, "Can I ask you something? I want to know...Didn't you ever want to become a mother?"

Dibyangana lowered her head and replied in a feeble voice, "I did. I shared the news with Brata when I was three months gone. I had thought that since I was three months pregnant, Brata would not refuse. But Brata did not agree so it didn't work out."

Su: Did you abort it?

Di: What else could I have done since the father did not want a baby? There was no love between us and the baby too would not have been born of love.

A kind of daze descended on Sujoy and made him feel relaxed. It was the kind of daze which set in when a man was drawn closer to a woman in oblivion. It was a plea to find relief from the complex twists and turns of life. Sujoy talked. Dibyangana listened.

Su: My daughter wanted to be a single mother.

Di: What do you mean! She is so young!

Su: No, she is now grown up. Quite grown up! You know, my daughter is a wonder. If you ever talk to her you will realise that she is quite an extraordinary child. She stood tenth in Madhyamik. And in Higher Secondary she has scored seventy-seven per cent even though she did not put in much effort. She is also a talented artist. Yet, today, I feel very sorry for her. Who do I share this pain with? Today I am…

Di: Talk about it. If it makes you feel better then tell me… without any qualms.

Dibyangana took Sujoy's limp hand in her own. A tsunami crashed ashore in Sujoy's heart. He broke down, "Today I took my daughter for an abortion. My eighteen-year-old daughter!"

Di: How? Why?

Su: She is a strange girl! She won't tell us who is responsible for it. She just wanted to be a mother. What guts! Yet, she is still so naïve. And her boyfriend, Siddhartha, is such a beautiful person at heart. I have never seen a boy like him.

Di: You mean, it's not her boyfriend?

Su: No.

Di: Oh!

Su: Can you tell me why she did this? She maintains that whatever she did was of her own free will. No one forced her into it.

Sujoy started to weep. Dibyangana slowly walked around to stand behind his chair and ran her fingers through his hair. Her fingers tangled in Sujoy's head full of curly hair. Sujoy leant backwards and tried to suppress his tears. He sighed, "Oh! Feels so nice. My head is splitting!"

Di: Don't drink anymore.

Sujoy: Will you please switch off the lights, Dibyangana?

Dibyangana switched off the lights and returned to bury her fingers in Sujoy's hair. Sujoy's head rested on Dibyangana's smooth belly covered only by a layer of cloth. Sujoy said, "Can I have one more?"

Di: No.

Sujoy: Okay. Since you say so. It feels so nice. Do you know what I want?

Di: What?

Sujoy: It is raining outside, the lights are off and I am drinking whisky...and, I am in the company of a woman who has come to be close to my heart. What could I possibly want?

Dibyangana remained silent though her fingers trembled slightly. Instead of waiting for her answer, Sujoy said, "But I will not get into a physical relationship with you. Do you know why? Because our minds are not in complete sync yet. So, our physical relationship will not last."

Sujoy left Dibyangana at around ten-thirty. Today he had shared much of his innermost feelings with Dibyangana, possibly because of his relaxed senses. Was it a blunder? Would Dibyangana be able to take everything in her stride? Would she misunderstand Sujoy? Sujoy rested a hand on his forehead and lay back in the seat of his car. This was not the time for such thoughts. His heart was overflowing with sweet content. Perhaps this feeling of peace was fleeting but he longed to be in constant proximity to it. Was he destined to be blessed with this content? Did any father find peace after getting his daughter's abortion done? Hence, Sujoy felt guilty for having found some peace. And, soon, the feeling of content left him. He fretted and wanted to reach his daughter quickly. Upon reaching home, he found Sree asleep. Ragini was busy packing for her trip the following day. All of a sudden, Sujoy felt extremely repulsed by Ragini.

17

FOR quite some time Sujoy had neglected his work. Phone calls poured in from his Siliguri office; a visit was long overdue. He decided to go once Ragini returned. Often he thought about wrapping up the Siliguri chapter of his business. What was the purpose, after all? He realised that despair was slowly settling in. He sometimes felt a sharp stab of pain in his chest. Warning signs of heart ailment? Perhaps. But he did not go to a doctor.

His father-in-law had sent word that he wanted to meet. Since business in Siliguri flourished, Sujoy had risen in stature in his father-in-law's eyes. The man had been thinking of dividing his assets for quite a while now. His sons had not shown any interest in his business. They had immigrated to America on the strength of their respective merits and settled down there.

Till quite recently, Sujoy had found his father-in-law almost unbearable. The man's dominating attitude, his manner of speech and the disregard with which he came forth made Sujoy want to curl up. Yet, Sujoy couldn't even ignore him because he was the man who almost pulled Sujoy up to establish him in the world. Of course, in the best interest of his daughter. Perhaps, that was why Sujoy had to surrender to some degree of servility. Still, at the end of it all, this man had a definite role to play behind the satisfaction which Sujoy derived out of his own spending power.

It was time for Sujoy's annual art exhibition. He could well host it in his own art gallery but he thought of a different one and had called Anjan to discuss the same. Anjan had said, "Once your exhibition is over, I am going to rest for a few days."

Since then, the same longing has been a bee in his bonnet. Rest. Has he ever taken rest? He has always gone out to work through minor ailments. He has worked at least half a day on all holidays. Was it now possible for him to take rest? Responsibilities were mounting. Workload increasing. So, instead of taking rest, Sujoy wanted to immerse himself in work. A strong longing to visit Dibyangana pulled at his heart. This was a first for him. Was it good or bad? The desire made him anxious. Till the time there was no other woman in his life, he lived fearlessly. Was Dibyangana the new woman in Sujoy's life? The other woman? Was she his weakness?

There was a sound at the door. It was Sree. She was in his room after many days. Sujoy felt pleased and said, "Come."

Sree came in, wrapped her arms around his neck and kissed his cheek. Then she rolled onto the bed. She was in her nightdress. If one looked properly then all the folds and planes of her body were evident. Sujoy looked away. He thought of asking about who the man had been...but then discarded the idea. Sree had joined Jadavpur University to study comparative literature. Sujoy asked, "You didn't take the SAT. Hope you are going to appear for GRE?"

Sree: No! What is the use?

Su: What! Have you changed your mind again?

Sree: You are loaded. If I am not around then who will spend your money?

Su: That is what you used to say when you were very young.

Sree: I still think that way.

Su: If you go to the States then I will get a chance to spend some money.

Sree: No, I am going to study here. I can't live away from you, Bapi. I have given it a lot of thought.

Su: But someday you will have to live without me. Won't you get married and leave for your husband's home? Be with his family?

Sree: I will marry a boy who is willing to stay with my family. And why should I have to get married at all? It will just be another relationship like yours.

Su: You shouldn't be picking on your parents' relationship, Sree.

Sree: Why not? Am I not the fruit of that relationship?

She lay on her back and started to explain why she did not want to appear for GRE. One of her friends had cleared GRE and was going abroad. The day he was called for his visa interview, they had all accompanied him to the US Consulate. The entire street was under heavy police surveillance and her friend was subjected to strict security checking. The robotic coldness, the complete lack of coutesy and a glaring emotional disconnect displayed by the security personnel – many of them Indian – had been disheartening and had put Sree off. The sun shone down mercilessly. The accompanying parents of the interviewees had to sit on the pavement across the road and wait. Once an interviewee went inside, he or she did not emerge before a couple of hours had passed. It was hard to believe that the little stretch of road was actually in India.

The parents' faces had drawn looks as they waited in anticipation of their drop of heavenly manna—the good news of a US visa being granted. The moment one of their wards came out, all the parents flocked around the candidate shooting queries about the interview process.

Most of the parents did not know how to converse in English but they had to try since they were standing in front of the US Consulate! Pride dripped from the glowing faces of the parents whose children were granted visas. As for the children, some were overjoyed, some agitated and haughty—none behaving normally. Yet, their eyes sparkled with an impossible dream.

"What is the dream?" Sree asked. "What dream, Bapi? More success, a better job, lots of money! In the end, it is all about money. I don't need money. My father has already done that job for me! Oh my sweet, sweet Bapi..."

Sree rolled up to Sujoy and hugged him. Then she kissed him again and gushed, "We haven't visited Haur for a long time, Bapi. Hope the house hasn't fallen apart."

Sujoy: No, the house is looked after regularly. Your uncle has taken the responsibility and I am helping out financially.

Sree: Why did Chhotjethu commit suicide?

Su: It's difficult to say why people commit suicide.

Sree: Was his death really a case of suicide?

Su: Yes. You know that he left a note, don't you?

Abruptly, Sree changed the topic and said, "I have completed eighteen. Now I am independent, right?"

Su: Weren't you independent even before eighteen?

Sree: Are you still angry with me, Bapi?

Su: No.

Sree: Yes you are. Fine...tell me, which is a worse crime, to give birth or to kill the embryo.

Su: It's not that simple, Sree. It is important to understand the motive behind each. Did you enter into a sexual relationship only to become a mother?

Sree: If I say yes?

Su: The way you said that proves otherwise. Then why are you so concerned about right and wrong?

Sree: If sex serves no other purpose then do you disagree with its necessity?

Su: No, but there is a right time for everything in life. It helps to plan out your life properly.

Sree: The way Ma did?

Su: Sree!

Sujoy shouted. Sree stood up and started to laugh. Then she said, “I know, Bapi. I know everything.”

She left the room. Sujoy sat still as a statue. Who had told Sree? Ragini herself? Sujoy paced the length of the room restlessly. He pondered why Sree and Ragini were not normal in their manner of thinking. Was it because they were creative? Sujoy lay down on the bed abruptly. Various thoughts swarmed inside his head. He did not know whether they were meaningful or not. He just continued to think. He realised that people were bound by personal limits before which they were helpless. Was an independent life then not possible at all? Independence was bound by an ever expanding limit; it was in no way limitless. Only imagination could touch true independence. But for that one needed immense mental strength and the power of imagination. Also, one could not realise freedom on his own. He could only establish his imagination with the help of someone else. Then, who was Sree depending on to expand the horizon of her imagination?

...if Ragini is the one Sree is depending on then will Sree ever find the true meaning of life? Don’t believe so. To be honest, I am quite perturbed by Sree. Man’s conscience functioned by some inborn practices. These gave birth to some tendencies, without succumbing to any influence of society or nature, without being dependent on anyone. And these tendencies were what marked a man as different from others. These set him apart because they were different from the ordinary practices which ruled society and family. But for Sree, this was not the case. I am certain of that because Sree is ruled by illusion. She does not experience doubt. Doubt is constructive while illusion is destructive. Two people are bound in a relationship by social situations and emotional attractions. Sree is indifferent to social situations. She is driven by emotions only. Should I not identify this as a mental disability? Wouldn't I be doing Sree harm by not identifying this as such?

I am hurt by Sree's behaviour. But, I am not intimating her about her mistakes. As though, her predicament makes no difference to me. Yet, who is dearer to me than Sree? Not even myself. Still, I am clinging on to my ego. If one cannot overcome ego then what value would humanity be able to command? What would be the importance of love, affection and respect? What would be the meaning of the two friendships I am so proud of? Would I give my ego more importance than Anjan or Jayshankar? No. I never do that. For Dibyangana would my ego...no! I will not think of Dibyangana. Could Dibyangana enter the realm reserved for my near and dear ones so soon, upon so short an acquaintance? I don't know. I don't want to know. But Dibyangana ruled my thoughts. All the time. I can neither accept her nor think about rejecting her. Hence, I will keep Dibyangana aside and think of Sree.

Sree is driven by emotions. At the core of every emotion lay conflicting forces of light and darkness. At the moment, Sree was shrouded by dark emotions. I, Sree's father, would lead her into light from darkness. I can. I have to. I believe in it. I believe in it without a doubt.

Various such thoughts and analyses crowded Sujoy's mind. The half-asleep state he was in, gave him a magical calmness. But Sujoy knew, this was no relief; it was nothing but temporary escapism. Man made numerous plans based on hope. But hidden behind all those plans was escapism. Hope actually led man to seek shelter in escapism.

At that moment, a sound floated to him from far away… the tinkle of a cycle bell from his childhood. Where was it coming from? What was that sound? Sujoy started awake. The phone was ringing. He rushed to answer. It was two in the morning. Who would call at this hour?

At the other end was someone from the police. Sujoy was asked to go to Nilratan Sarkar Hospital as soon as possible. He was informed of an accident involving a man whose description hit Sujoy with a familiar pain in his chest. His head reeled and his hands and legs trembled. Was it Jayshankar? Was he alive? Extreme anxiety and agony twisted his insides. While getting ready to go out, he sent up a prayer. But to whom? He was not a pious man. Yet, at that moment praying to the Almighty was perhaps his only option. Oh God! Let it not be Jayshankar!

He took along enough cash and even in the midst of anxiety his common sense prevailed. He called up Supratim. "Don't worry unnecessarily," said Supratim, after listening to him carefully. "It may not be anything complicated. I'll pick you up from your place and then we'll go together."

Sujoy had to wait fifteen minutes for Supratim to arrive. In the meanwhile, insurmountable waves rose in his horizon. He wondered how to overcome the waves. He felt as if a great calamity was about to swallow him up. His hands and feet felt clammy. He woke up Sree and Nayan-mashi, and informed, "I am going out. Don't know when I'll be back."

Sree asked, "Where are you going at this time, Bapi?"

"Supratim is on his way here. One of our friends has met with an accident. You be careful and don't open the door to anyone."

"Who is it?"

Sujoy felt irritated and snapped, "Do you know everyone?"

Sree walked up to him. She looked into his eyes and put a hand on his chest. Then she said, "Is it bad?"

"Of course it is. But I don't know to what extent."

A car horn sounded outside and Sujoy left in a hurry. Supratim was at the wheels. At this hour he was not surrounded by any security personnel. Sujoy climbed in beside him and Supratim started shooting questions.

–When did you get the call?

–Who called?

–What did he say?

–Was your card in his pocket?

–A paper with your name and number? Good.

–Is he not alive?

–Did it happen in front of Nilratan?

–Okay. If you don't know him then the matter is solved. But if you know him then only reveal that fact if he is a very close relation. I'll manage the rest.

The body was not covered. Jayshankar's eyes were half open. Lifeless though. His face was streaked with dirt. He had been lying on the road on his face. The checked shirt was drenched in blood, its original colour and pattern lost. The lower part of his body from stomach downwards was covered because that part had been crushed and almost severed from the rest of the body. The stomach and intestines had burst and half-digested food particles had mingled with the blood and flesh. What did Jayshankar eat? For dinner? He used to like paneer.

It was a taxi. First, it drove onto the pavement and rammed into him. Then, without any effort or intention of saving the man, it ran over his back, crushing his body.

It happened in front of the hospital and there were some eye witnesses. Also, a few of the hospital employees recognised Jayshankar. He used to visit the children's ward often around eleven at night with fruits for the poor children. He gave his name as Jay. No one knew how or why he had started this practice of bringing in fruits but it had been going on for a good few years now. Like the old branching neem and tall deodar trees and the pond inside the hospital premises, Jayshankar too had become a part of it. The employees thought of him as a crazy man who fitted in nicely with the variety and mystery of the hospital. The sprawling hospital building was full of sorrow, mishaps, eccentricity and relief. No one had the time or inclination to worry about Jayshankar's whim. On the contrary, they wove stories around him...he had a son who died in this ward... he had a brother he loved a lot. Jayshankar was gradually growing into a myth.

Sujoy's eye welled up. He bit down on his lip. Supratim stood close to him. The police officer present there saluted Supratim and asked Sujoy in a humble voice, "Do you know him, sir?"

Sujoy shook his head. No. He did not know him. But, in his mind, he said, "Jayshankar, forgive me, brother. I know you will understand. I know...!"

Supratim went out with the officer to talk further. The officer stood in attention as he listened to Supratim. Sujoy looked at Jayshankar. His face was devoid of colour and disfigured. Jayshankar had looked like a calendar pin-up model. Full of life. Simple and straightforward. He had believed that conquering all adversities was the meaning of life.

Sujoy dragged himself out. He had to be strong. Supratim was still in conversation. Sujoy thought to himself, Jayshankar had been prepared for this death. Who had killed him? Who had taken his life under cover of an accident? Was this how all dues of life were repaid? A shiver ran down Sujoy's spine. This was the first time he was unnerved by death. He tried to steel himself. Not a drop of anxiety should slip through.

He remembered his responsibility. He was yet to go through the papers Jayshankar had given him. Jayshankar's aged mother, widowed sister and adopted children lived somewhere in Katihar. What would they do now? Who picked up the reins when someone died? No life was eternal. Sujoy felt his control slipping away. Tears gathered in his eyes. In his hurry he had forgotten to carry a handkerchief.

Supratim was coming towards him. Sujoy commanded the tears to retreat. He would have to be in control. He got into the car. Supratim started to drive. Then he looked at Sujoy and said, "Feeling bad, Banerjee?"

Sujoy was startled. Supratim stepped on the accelerator and said, "Cry...go on. You will feel better. Human life... huh! I know you recognised him."

Sujoy stared ahead in silence. He did not know what to say. His wits seemed to be on strike. But his senses were active in their own way. He heard the word, "Cry"; his soul heard it too. He longed to cry. And soon, tears flowed from his eyes. His lips twisted. Supratim held his hand in a strong grip and gave him a few moments to himself. Then he said slowly, "Jayshankar. I guessed...that is why I did not let you come alone. We have been friends for too long!"

Sujoy looked at him. Words were still a far cry. Supratim said, "He was a big police target. It's all over now. You will not be summoned again. I have the paperwork with me. The body will be sent to the morgue. It will remain there."

Sujoy cleared his throat and said, "Please Supratim, can you do me one more favour? Jayshankar owns the Shankar Paan Bhandar near Osmaan's meat shop at the Khidirpur crossing. Please send word across."

"Okay."

After a pause, Supratim said, "Let me tell you the statement I have given. I said, you are associated with various kinds of social work through the old age home, the art gallery. So, it is quite possible for someone to have your name and number on him."

A chill ran down Sujoy's spine. He looked at Supratim gratefully. Supratim continued to talk, "I once befriended a hard core criminal. I was deeply saddened when he died. He used to recite Kabir's *doha*s...I still remember one very well."

> *My eyes are my hut, my irises the bed.*
> *On it I have dropped the veil of my eyelids.*
> *This pleased my beloved.*
> *Had my beloved lived abroad,*
> *I would have written to him.*
> *But he lives in my body, my heart and my eyes.*
> *Where is the need to send news to him?*

The car stopped near Sujoy's house. Sujoy tried to say something before getting out but he had lost his voice. Supratim stopped him midway, and said "There is no need to tell me anything. Try to get some sleep."

Supratim waved and drove off. Sujoy stood there and watched the disappearing tail lights. Suddenly, the car stopped. Supratim turned around and drove back. Then he beckoned to Sujoy. As Sujoy bent down to look through the window, Supratim whispered in his ear, "If you are planning to visit Jayshankar's home then don't do so in the next six months. And, whenever you go, keep me informed."

Then Supratim sped off leaving Sujoy dumbfounded. As the car disappeared from view, Sujoy rang the doorbell. His eyes overflowed!

18

SHAME on the destructive and torturous city! It did not hear the voices, it did not accept discipline, nor surrender to its god. It was ruled by wild, animalistic passions, which devoured all and left nothing for the morning to shine upon. Its emotions were of vaulting arrogance and betrayal, its inhabitants had tainted the pure and abused the system. Its eternal, central master was pure and sacred; he did not sin; he came forth and laid down his justice with the morning shine; he was above all errors. But the sinners did not know shame. I have uprooted the errant population; their high fortresses have been demolished, their paths made barren; no one travelled those paths anymore; their cities are devoid of life. I have dictated that you will be fearful of me, accept my rule; that will save your home and hearth from destruction. But they continue to rise by morning light and spoil every effort; destroy all good work.

That is why the Omnipotent says, wait for me till the day I rise to rob you of it all. Because I have ruled that one day I will gather all mankind, join all nations and pour forth my fury on them. The world shall burn and be devoured by the heat of the fire and wrath raging within me.

Sleep eluded him till the wee hours. Night gradually receded, the stars faded into the slowly spreading daylight and the morning sky was hued in red. An unearthly vision was resplendent in the eastern horizon; but it was not visible from Sujoy's home. In a sorrowful and anxious state, Sujoy wanted to feel how painful the death must have been. Did he lose consciousness early on? Or did he experience the extreme agony of his insides being ripped apart?

Sujoy's insides swirled and he felt like throwing up. He rushed to the bathroom and squatted on the floor. The undigested contents of his stomach gushed out and tears ran down his cheeks. Continuously. As he cleaned his own vomit, he thought how apt it would be if it was possible to discard life's painful incidents and memories in this manner. How much peace and rest that would bring!

His wilting body forced him to return to bed. His legs and head felt very heavy. Suddenly, he felt as if a soft body held him. A body with a lot of compassion and affection. His eyelids were so heavy that he could not open his eyes to look. A magical hand wove through his hair. Dibyangana! Stay...stay beside me! For a while longer. The hand stroked his forehead, cheeks, lips and stopped upon his chest. What a wonderful feeling! Such peace! Dibyangana, was it possible to fall in love again at this age?

His eyelids were glued. Gradually, Sujoy drifted away from all present tensions and worries. Girin walked along the train track...his strides gradually becoming longer...till they became eternally long....

...Girin, did you feel as much pain as Jayshankar did? When you fell off the train, when the lower part of your body was ripped to pieces, when your head split and your evil brain oozed out...the brain with which you had made my life unbearable...did you feel a lot of pain, Girin?

Girin's flesh and blood, bones and marrow were splattered upon Sujoy's vision. The flesh and blood smelt putrid and the bones and marrow swarmed with maggots. Sujoy wanted to flee, away from Girin. He wanted to escape from the awful dead body. He was running. But where could he run to? How could he free himself from Girin? He had to escape to the field in Haur. But a hand was wrapped around his waist; it would not let him flee. He yanked the hand away and ran...there it was, the field! Oh dark field, please take me into yourself. Let me be one with the grass, the soil and the dust. The soft arms of the field welcomed him in an embrace. He returned the embrace and lost himself in it. He felt sleepy, the fear had vanished. It was time for peace and calm because he could again see the pair of divine humans.

Abhi: An exogenous body. It bears the weight of the world. Its responsibilities are many! The more I have seen, the more amazed I have been. I have saved and piled up the bark of the trees to show you. I was not around for quite some time, the trees have taken offence. They have aged and have lost some of their colour. I showered them with affection and pleaded with them to regain their lively green hue. O trees, creepers, grass...how long can I stay away from you? You have bound me with your love. Soon the trees regained their colour and brightened up.

Upo: Was your beloved better than the trees?

Abhi: My beloved is the tree. My children are trees. Trees, grass, fruits, flowers are my progeny. Trees gave birth to me. I am the father of trees and the child of flowers. They can feel my presence. They know when I touch them. They weep when I am unwell. The other day I saw an untimely bunch of flowers on the Kiran tree.

Upo: Kiran? Did you name it so?

Abhi: No, it was named by someone else. It is a flowering plant from Mexico and belongs to the *Euphorbiaceae* or the 'splurge' family of tropical flowering plants. The leaves directly branch out from the stem. The radially symmetrical unisexual flowers bloom at the confluence of the leaves.

Upo: How beautiful! Plants too are like migratory birds. How they travel from one place to another! The other day I saw a flock of lovely Siberian whistling ducks – the Shonapakhi – rising from a paddy field near Memari, flying in the sky in a pattern resembling the rise and fall of waves. These birds are rarely seen here. Having tasted their sweet flesh, man has killed many of them.

Abhi: Man has always been adept at killing.

Upo: Yes, always actively involved in killing.

Abhi: Killing is his victory, his *joy*.

Upo: Man achives a good, auspicious victory...what is termed *sujoy*...through killing!

Abhi: Ah, *joy, joy*, *sujoy*...Sujoy.

Upo: Sujoy, *sujoy, joy*!

Sujoy's body trembled as the dream broke and he woke up. Sree was lying very close to him, her arms around him. She watched him open his eyes and move his lips. She watched and then said, "Go to sleep, Bapi. You are tired."

She moved closer to him, creating more intimacy. Sujoy felt Sree's nearness, and with it, a pressure. What was it? He couldn't understand. He tried to sit up but Sree held him back forcefully. She pulled his head down to her chest. Sujoy realised, she was dressed in a flimsy nightdress held up by thin straps. With his nose buried in her bosom, Sujoy felt suffocated. He shoved her aside and sat up. He couldn't remember much. Couldn't grasp anything meaningful. All he knew was that he had to get out of there. He had a lot to do.

Sree put her arms around his neck once again. Then she pressed her lips on his and pushed him down. "Today you are not going anywhere, Bapi. You are tired. I have given Nayan-mashi a few days off. Till Ma returns...it will just be the two of us and we will spend time together."

Sujoy asked, "What is the time?"

Sree: Half past eleven.

Sujoy: Oh! It's so late! Why didn't you wake me up earlier?

Sree: You haven't slept through the night. Today you are not going anywhere. From now, it will be only you and me. Till Ma returns, please be only mine, Bapi.

Sujoy: Don't be crazy, Sree! I have lots of work. Didn't you go to college?

Sree: Classes haven't started yet. The admission process is just over. I have called your office and told them that you will not be going in.

In a way it was good. To not go anywhere. He wanted to be alone with himself. Perhaps, his subconscious too wanted the same. So he did not contest Sree's wish. Did Sree understand that this could be his wish too? But how? Was Sree then waiting at the threshold of adulthood, poised to become a responsible woman? He turned on his side and raked his fingers through Sree's hair creating narrow white partings. Sree rubbed her nose and her face against Sujoy's arm. Sujoy felt uncomfortable. He dropped his hand to her smooth bare back. Sree snuggled closer and said, "Stroke me, Bapi. Oh...don't stop, Bapi! Stroke me!"

Sujoy stroked her back absentmindedly. His eyelids felt heavy and drooped. He saw Jayshankar, lying there with a pale face. A lifeless heart beneath his bloody shirt. The heart was no more, it used be there. The man was no more, he used to be there. No more. Voices rose around Sujoy...no more, no more.

What is no more, Sujoy?

My hands are no more.

What is no more, Sujoy?

My legs are no more.

What is no more, Sujoy?

My eyes are no more.

Jayshankar, I am blind and deaf without you. I am incapable. I did not know, I am an incomplete man without you. I knew that I was solely dependent on you but I never felt it this way. Perhaps, this too is a beginning. The beginning of a life without you, without your help, without your presence in all spheres. I don't know, Jayshankar…!

Sree: Bapi, keep on stroking. Why are you stopping? How can you stop? Is my silky-smooth back not attractive to you, Bapi?

Sujoy: Why did you give Nayan-mashi the days off? I feel like having a cup of strong tea. I have a splitting headache. Who will make me tea now?

Sree: I will, Bapi. These few days I will do everything for you.

Su: How many days? You don't know any cooking or housework, Sree.

Sree: I do. I'll be able to do everything. Nayan-mashi has cooked a lot and kept it in the fridge. We will finish that first and then eat out. You and I. These few days…only you and I.

Su: Fine. Then make me a cup of tea. Can you light the gas?

Sree: Sure. Don't take me to be a complete novice.

Sree's dress rode up her legs as she got off the bed. She wore nothing under. Sree was somewhat too carefree and flippant. Sujoy felt the flicker of a premonition amidst his various thoughts. It seemed so improbable that it added to the darkness in his heart. It bobbed up and down and finally settled in his mind's vision. But it was so impossible a notion that Sujoy crushed it immediately. His fatigue and his despair faded. He regained much of the control over himself and sat up. His thoughts were agitated; his yearnings disjointed; his aversions active. Sujoy was a hurt man who was hiding his pain. He was trying to gather the strength and the penchant to conquer the adversities of life without Jayshankar by his side. Jayshankar had known that he would leave soon. Sujoy realised that now he would have to wade through life without a Jayshankar beside him. He would have to traverse this long life which stretched ahead. Man was obligated to life by the duty to complete the journey.

The afternoon passed in agonised thoughts of Jayshankar. Sujoy had just decided to take a shower when Sree said, "When I was a child, I used to scrub your back for you. Come Bapi, let me scrub your back today."

Sujoy struggled to discard the uneasy feeling, "Yes my child..."

"Don't call me child. I am Sree."

"Yes, Sree, my child...scrub my back..."

They spent some time in the bathroom. Sree lathered Sujoy's back with soap. She too got covered in soap bubbles. Water sprayed over her hair and dress, moistening her skin under her dress and making it glow. The soaked dress clung to her wet, glowing skin. The sight made Sujoy's ears go warm. He pushed Sree out of the bathroom and shut the door. He then turned the shower full on and stood under the spraying needles of water. A sorrow greater than that of losing Jayshankar threatened his world. An agonising moment of an ugly suspicion...a crude possibility knocking at his door. He did not want to fall prey to this ungainly moment of sorrow. What kind of accursed moment was this in his life? He came out of the bathroom to find Sree lying face down on the bed, sobbing her heart out. Her tears moistened the pillow and the bed was damp from her foamy, soaked dress. Sujoy stroked her hair and then turned her face towards him. Sree sobbed, "Why did you...you... throw me out? Why? I have been waiting...waiting for so long to spend time with you. Alone with you. Bapi, I want you. Don't you want me?"

Sujoy took Sree in his arms. He overcame the sense of premonition and steeled himself for odds. Though, he was not clear what he was steeling himself against. He remembered an ailing Sree holding on to him and pleading, "Stay with me, Bapi." Today too, was a similar day. Today too, Sree was unwell. Hers was a deep-rooted ailment. Sujoy's heart became restless with compassion; it got drenched with affection and pity for his child. It was time to get over his grief and dedicate himself to taking care of his daughter. Fulfil the duties of a father. Or perhaps, fulfil the duties of humanity. He thought of his dear friend Jayshankar.

...Jayshankar, my brother, the duties of a father have overtaken my grief. They are pushing you out of my mind. I know, you will understand, like you have always done. Jayshankar, you carry on, I will follow soon. Just a few years from now...

Sree said, "Bapi will you listen to me? There is a lot I have to tell you. Bapi, don't you want me?"

Sujoy gathered her close and said, "You are a crazy girl, Sree. My crazy child. What is there to want or not to want? You are my world. Without you does my life hold much value? Any purpose?"

Sree: I have a lot to tell you. I want to tell you everything today. I have been waiting for long.

Su: Okay, Sree. It's almost evening, you'll catch a chill in these wet clothes. Go and take a shower while I get dressed. Then I'll listen to you.

Sree: Before that, tell me where you went last night.

Su: A friend of mine met with an accident.

Sree: Who is it? Tell me the name.

Su: You don't know everyone, do you?

Sree: Tell me the name, Bapi. I need to know everything about you.

Su: Shivarajan. His name is Shivarajan.

Sree: How is he? Is he alive?

Su: Yes, he is alive. He is jubilantly alive. Some people can live life king size, Sree.

Sree: I'll go take a shower, Bapi. Then we'll talk...lots.

Su: Yes dear.

Sree: Bapi...

Su: Yes?

Sree: Help me take a shower.

Su: Do it yourself today. I'll help you some other day. I'm very tired today, darling.

Sree: Promise?

Su: Yes, Sree. Promise.

Sree left to take a shower. Sujoy stood by the window. The city looked mellow in the light of the setting sun. As far as his sight stretched, there were countless houses, with countless lives in them. There was no clamour anywhere. As though, all the pain and panic of the world had been laid to rest. Eternal peace seemed to reign. From a bird's eye view as this, it was difficult to say that there were still many shortcomings in thc process of creation.

A gust of wind blew in. It had a distinct smell...of Kaikhali. Sorrow followed and crashed against his heart. A pain spread though his chest. Had termites found their way to the secret treasure hidden and protected by his ribs? And, at that moment, to drown the pain of losing Jayshankar, Sujoy longed to go to Dibyangana. He tried to tell himself that this longing was meaningless. When his daughter was in the grip of a serious illness, this yearning to be with the other woman was not at all important or appropriate.

Sree returned after her shower. She looked like a bunch of fresh Gulmohar flowers in the bright yellow dress she had changed into. Her damp hair hung around her shoulders and her eyes were bloodshot—tinged lightly with red from the water spray. She took out food from the fridge and started to heat it up. As though she was adept at it! She laid the table. As though she did it every day! Sujoy felt as if a young Ragini was going about her chores. When was Ragini due back? Perhaps she would call at night to talk to Sree. Sujoy sent up a prayer for Ragini to return soon. But, the next instant, he felt it was not necessary; Ragini's quick return would only give him the opportunity to succumb to an escapist mentality. He felt, it was more important to understand Sree properly. He wanted to understand her. Because Sree was gravely ill. He did not know where its remedy lay, with whom.

Sree called him to dinner. A very homely picture temporarily unfolded in Sujoy's house. A normal domestic dinner scene. Sujoy thought of making some phone calls to his various offices. It was quite strange that no one had called so far. He walked to the phone and noticed that the plug had been pulled out. Sree came to him and said, "I took it out. Today I have cut you off, Bapi."

Sujoy looked at his daughter affectionately. His age had awarded him with much experience. Sree said, "Come, Bapi. Let's eat."

"I have to make some important phone calls, Sree. I'll do it after dinner."

"No, you won't. Today, you will not call anyone."

"I have to. You know my friend met with an accident, don't you?"

"Okay, then just one call."

"No, three calls. At least."

After dinner, Sujoy called up his office. Then he called Supratim. Supratim asked, "How are you now?"

"Good. What happened there?"

"All arrangements have been made. I heard many people turned up to take the body away. The body will be released at six. Don't worry, everything will fall in place. Go back to work from tomorrow."

"His family will not know..."

"Let me see what I can do. But you listen to me and stay away from this affair."

Again despair descended on him. A heavy melancholy. The peaceful Kaikhali flat came to mind. Sujoy walked to the window with the phone in hand. His mobile had been switched off since yesterday. Today seemed to have a sign on it saying, 'intermission'. He dialled Anjan's number. Busy.

A group of boys were returning from the playing field. Sujoy watched them; none appeared familiar. A shiver circled his heart. Unfamiliarity. Would he never again find any young boy familiar? Without reason, he thought of Dibyangana. Was Dibyangana a young boy? The evening darkened, Anjan's phone number remained unavailable. Sree called, "Bapi...Bapi..."

She pulled the phone away from him. She had allowed too much of his time for others. No more. Now it was her turn to talk. She pulled out the phone plug and did not let him switch on the light. Then she pushed him onto the bed and said, "Listen to me, Bapi."

Sujoy lay on his back. He wore a fine kurta and the scent of sandalwood emanated from his body. His body reeked masculinity. A two-day stubble covered his cheeks. Streaks of grey flashed in his head full of curly black hair. He spread his arms; like a divine man. He was a pure, confident and aggrieved man. Sree lay with her head on his arm. Her eyes had a dreamy look. She said, "Bapi, I won't be able to live without you. Bapi, no one...no one else...I have seen many and I have realised that I love you. Only you."

The premonition was now clearly visible in front of Sujoy. He said, "I know, Sree."

"No, you don't. You don't know anything. I dream of you. You have been in my dreams for a long time. You come to me in my sleep. I am then a forest lass, revelling in freshly blossomed youth. I am walking along the forest path. The forest where my father left me. I am waiting for him to return. Waiting with my love. He is the man in my life. With him in mind, I have taken off my bark skin clothing and decorated my body with wild flowers. I have seen my reflection in the pond. Beautiful! This is me! I will offer him this beauty of mine. Here he comes. Here comes the man. The man...you, Bapi. Look at me, Bapi. Take me. You are my dream.'

Sujoy: Why doesn't Siddhartha come anymore?

Sree: I am not in touch with him. I don't need him, Bapi. If you are with me, I don't need anyone else.

Su: Why are you not in touch with him? Why don't you need him? He is an extraordinary boy. I doubt you will ever get a friend like him.

Sree: I don't need anyone if you are with me.

Sujoy: You do, Sree. Every relationship has its own definition.

Sree: Who has decided that? Man himself, right? I don't believe in these man-made norms. I am a woman. I am free. Complete. I have the right to get for myself the man I like.

Su: You do. But there exists not just this one relation between man and woman, Sree. The various relationships are expressed in unique ways. Like the one between father and daughter, mother and son, brother and sister. Even that between a boy and a girl who are friends. The body does not necessarily intrude. The angle of sexual attraction is kept dormant in these cases. This is a product of civilisation. And this makes humankind beautiful. You have to understand this.

Sree: I don't agree. This is a natural occurrence. Nature does not know father, brother or friend. Nature only knows man and woman. Read *Volga Theke Ganga*[15] and you will find....

Su: *Volga Theke Ganga* is an extraordinary piece of literature about human evolution. What you are trying to say relates to ancient times. At that time, humans were conscious only of self-defence, hunting, leadership and forming groups. Civilisation is an advancing phenomenon. It cannot go back in time. We cannot discard what we have achieved.

Sree: Civilisation is a make-believe concept. In reality, man has not changed at all. The man-woman relationship existed even among the extremely powerful and civilised divine personalities. I can show you the Puranas and the Vedas to prove that.

Sree rose and returned with a book. Then she started to read, "In the *Rigveda*, from a conversation between Yama and Yami, we find a valuable narration of ancient times. In the *Rigveda*, Shishumar is imagined as a tree. Yama sits atop that tree and drinks *soma-rasa* along with other gods. Yami tells Yama, 'In the deserted island amidst the vast ocean, you are my companion.' The first man and woman came into this world

15 Bengali translation of *Volga Se Ganga*—a landmark collection of twenty short stories in Hindi by the great Marxist scholar of cultural studies, Indo-European societies, languages and Buddhism – Rahul Sankrityayan (Kedarnath Pandey) – published in 1944. It is considered to be a classic collection in Indian literature, particularly in modern Hindi literature, the stories portraying the evolution of human civilisation from 6000 BC to 1942. The Bengali translation was published in 1954.

as lovers. Yami tried to lure her brother, Yama, into a sexual relation with her so that mankind did not become extinct. But Yama had immense restraint. In a very modest and soft manner he reminded his sister of the correct path of life. He reminded her that it was illegitimate and prohibited for blood-related men and women to engage in sexual relationships. Having explained this, he could prevent his sister from taking part in a sinful act. But it is not known how this legend ended."

Sujoy exclamied, "The explanation for your thoughts is in there, Sree!"

Sujoy's voice sounded weak and grave. As if he had taken a vow to cling on to limitless patience. The words from a daughter which could enrage a father beyond all boundaries, failed to break through the wall of patience Sujoy had erected. Because, as a man he was unique; he had promised himself that he would free his daughter of her ailment. But Sree did not notice these things. Today was her day to shed all inhibitions. Today she wanted to gain something. Something which could also create a great rift between the benefactor and the beneficiary. It could very well destroy them. So, she said, "No it is not, Bapi."

Su: It is. Read carefully, give it some thought. You will understand.

Sree: No, it is not in here. The story remains incomplete. Both Yama and Yami were brought up with the same ethics. But Yama followed rules while Yami liked to break them. That does not tell us what is right and what is wrong. Through the times, many rules have been made in the world. Some people have followed them while others have broken them. For me, there is only one rule and one ethic…that I love you. I want you. There is no right or wrong in love.

Su: Sree, these rules make up our civilisation. Understanding these is what civilisation is about. These rules, this understanding, this civilisation are not without mistakes. They are not unquestionable. Because evolution is dynamic. It is a constructive process. Human society is still evolving. Through civilisation we have discovered a divine truth...it is called relationship. Relationship between one human and another. Sexual relation between mother and son, brother and sister, father and daughter is not possible. It is unreal, a false and perverted concept. This thought of yours hints at your demented mentality. Sree, please leave! I cannot stand you in your present demeanour.

Sree: Bapi, love me!

Su: I love you more than myself. But I am tired today. At this moment, I can't stand you. You are matured enough, Sree...you should understand. Sometimes a person needs to be alone, it becomes necessary.

Sree: Okay, Bapi. Done. You are tired. I will leave. I have told you what I wanted to say.

In a flash, Sree claimed his lips with her own. Planting a full womanly kiss, she rendered Sujoy quite breathless. Sujoy stiffened; he felt as though all his senses had died abruptly. He remained alone in the dark room. His thoughts awakened and he spent another sleepless night with his thoughts for company.

19

TODAY is a special day in my life. Today, I realised that life offers us new beginnings every moment. As an honest and righteous human being, one had to recognise those points of new beginning and fulfill numerous responsibilities. That is what we call humanity.

Man has only one duty—to transform everything discourteous, wrong and ugly into things that are courteous, right and beautiful. And, without shouldering this responsibility man cannot be faithful to humanity.

I have seen the end of my dear friend Jayshankar. A pitiful and horrific end. Why did I have to see this? Because, for the last forty years, I have accepted all that was happening around me without any objection...all that was destructive and deathly, all that was ugly and painful. I destroyed the ugly presence of those who were not dear to me. But I have never expressed a desire to identify and wipe out the ugliness present in the people dear to me. Jayshankar's death has taught me a lesson. It is wrong to wait eternally for good things to happen in the lives of our near and dear ones. Because life does not give man endless time. The line between life and death can be washed away any moment. Life swiftly transforms into death and ushers in the end. So, I will have to steer every moment of life towards goodness. I have learnt to journey towards goodness because of the death of my dear friend Jayshankar.

My friend Anjan is today dejected with life because he has accepted the inevitability of everything. Once, in an attempt to change the direction of the flow of events, he had become the cause of a death. But that was not a failure. To be honest, failure may knock on his door now if he is unable to shed his desolation and look upon life again with a smile. If he fails to lead Debola out of her abnormality. He does not know if he can do it but he has to keep trying till life reaches the shores of death. Anjan will have to try. I, Sujoy, will have to try. Try to bring in the good and the beautiful.

Ragini, I will bring you back from Aniruddha Kanjilal. You will be an artist in your own right. You will be my wife.

Sree, I will make you better. I will instil order in your disturbed mind. I will make you beautiful and I will bring Siddhartha back for you. Sree, you will realise the purity and uniqueness of various human relationships.

Dibyangana, I will...! What can I give you, Dibyangana? What will make your life better? What do you want? Will you marry again? I love you, Dibyangana, but I don't know what you want. I will find out.

Jayshankar's sister, I will sort out all your problems. You will not face any difficulty. But, first, let me make my daughter better!

The sky was tinged with blue. Sujoy rose from the bed and went into Sree's room to call her. Sree, woken from her sleep, saw Sujoy and mistook his presence to be his consent. She held out her arms to him. Sujoy's senses were alert, his will to do good was strong and his duty towards humanity was steady. He asked, "Would you like to go to Haur, Sree?"

Sree smiled and said, "Yes, Bapi. Haven't been for long. When?"

Sujoy: Today.

Sree: Great, that will be just great! Will you love me, Bapi?

Su: I will. I am going out for a while, lock the door properly. If Manjil comes, tell him to take the day off.

Sree: How will we go to Haur?

Su: By train.

Sree: Wonderful! When will you return?

Su: Once I have taken care of a few things. Manjil will inform the office. How do we let your mother know?

Sree: I have the number for the guest house. I'll tell her.

Su: Good. You go to sleep.

Sree: One small kiss, Bapi.

Sujoy kissed his daughter. He was bursting with inspiration and determination. He took Anjan's file and got into the car. He would be driving after a long time. He rolled down the windows, the wind blew in. Sujoy increased the speed and took VIP Road. The sky was gradually turning red. Dibyangana, Dibyangana...Sujoy was rushing to Dibyangana. He was following his desire. How would Dibyangana's sleep-smeared face look?

But, as he reached the Kaikhali crossing, he turned around. He felt, this time was not for Dibyangana. It was for Sree. Let Sree get better first...then Dibyangana....

...I will find out, Dibyangana. What you want. Do you love anyone? Abhishek, Akash, Iraban, Ipshit, Uddalok, Ushamitra, Ritabrata, Enayat, Aishwarya, Omar...who do you love? If you do...I am angry. I long to see you, yet I am not going to you...it makes me infuriatingly angry. I want you desperately, but I should not, will not want you...this makes me angry. Dibyangana, if you are in love with someone else then I will sure kill your lover. Dibyangana, my daughter is unwell. I have to make her better. Then I promise to unite you with your lover in all goodwill. I love you, Dibyangana. May your lover have a long life....

Sujoy again turned around from someplace near Anjan's house. Beside him, was the file. He touched the file once, and felt that today was not Anjan's day either.

This day was only for Sree. Let Sree get better then Anjan will have his day.

...Anjan, you will have to return to your life. You will have to live. I will bring you back. You are bound to yourself to do this. You are bound to humanity. You are bound to your dear ones. Don't invite death, Anjan. Don't go away. Anjan, hold on till I come back....

Siddhartha sat with a book lying open in front of him. It was a habit of his to wake up at the crack of dawn and study. The book on the history of English literature lay open but his mind was elsewhere. This had been going on for quite a few days now. Since he made the decision about Sree. Yet, he sat down with his books every day. He would have to get back his concentration.

The phone rang. The rest of the household were still sleeping so Siddhartha answered the phone. A deep and excited voice asked from the other end, "Is Siddhartha there?"

Siddhartha: Speaking...

Sujoy: This is Sree's father.

Sid: Yes, Uncle...is Sree alright? And you?

Su: Siddhartha, you gave me your address when Sree was sick. I am near your place. I would like to talk to you.

Sid: I'll be there right away.

Su: Are you sure?

Sid: Absolutely.

Su: Ok, I'll wait for you in front of your house.

Siddhartha hurried out, his hair was dishevelled and he wore a half shirt over loose trousers. Sujoy put Anjan's file on the rear seat and asked Siddhartha to climb in. He started to drive slowly and asked, "Why don't I see you these days?"

Sid: I am not in touch with Sree.

Su: Why Siddhartha? I know you love Sree deeply. You told me that you would be with Sree forever.

Sid: I wanted to, Uncle. But it did not work out.

Su: Why?

Sid: Can any personal relationship be based on a condition?

Su: No. Relationships need to be unconditional. Did Sree ask you to accept a condition?

Sid: Uncle, I can't talk to you about this.

Su: We have already had matured discussions. We have been friends from the beginning, haven't we?

Sid: Of course.

Su: Then tell me.

Sid: Uncle, I was greatly pained by Sree's abortion. I felt extremely humiliated.

Su: Quite natural.

Sid: I spoke to Sree about it. I told her that it was not right to get involved with someone else while in a steady relationship. But she said it was part of her freedom. So I told her, in that case, I could also do the same.

Su: What did Sree say?

Sid: She was very angry. She threw me out of her room. The next day Aunt Ragini called me over.

Su: Ragini!

Sid: She asked me if I realised how talented Sree was. I said, yes. Then she said that because I too was an artist I might feel that I was no less than her. But in reality, Sree was way more talented. She was a genius and geniuses were free spirits. The strong desire for freedom makes a great artist. Aunt Ragini said, if I really loved Sree then I shouldn't try to control her. I would have to let her go, let her be free. She would go away from me, but she would also return. Uncle…I couldn't agree to that.

Su: Siddhartha?

Sid: Yes, Uncle?

Su: Don't you want Sree to be free of these misconceptions?

Sid: I do.

Su: Will you take her back if she wants to come back to you?

Sid: Yes. Unconditionally.

Su: Sree is not well. I will make her better and then return her to you.

Siddhartha looked at Sujoy with wonder in his eyes. There was confidence on Sujoy's face. But Sujoy couldn't say anymore. He said, "Let me drop you home."

Sujoy drove fast. As Siddhartha got off near his house, Sujoy said, "Will meet soon."

Siddhartha smiled. Finally, after this rushed episode, his mind came up with a logical thought, a question. Why did Sujoy have to come to him so early in the morning to discuss these things? He couldn't find an answer. By then Sujoy had disappeared.

20

SREE wore a midnight blue handloom saree with gold borders. A bindi on her forehead and some light jewellery; she had taken much care dressing up. Sujoy couldn't take his eyes off her. When did his little girl become so beautiful? When did she grow up? When did she learn how to wrap a saree around herself?

Sujoy's unwavering gaze made Sree swell up with pride. She cocked her head like a female pigeon, experienced and ready. "I can't risk taking you by train, my child. Let's take a taxi," Sujoy said.

They were on their way. Sree had wrapped herself around Sujoy, her arms linked with his. The taxi driver threw them a glance every now and then. But Sree was overflowing with joy. She thought herself victorious; her patience and expectations were finally about to bear fruit. She thought Sujoy had agreed with her logic and accepted her. Once in a while, she remembered Chhotjethu. She had almost forgotten his touch. After him, there had been newer touches to experience. Now she was looking forward to Sujoy Banerjee's company to wash away the past. She was almost out of her mind in the hope of success.

And Sujoy wondered…Sree, I don't know what to tell you!

There were countless faces of young boys in front of Sujoy. They were not like Pulak. They did not resemble Girin either. They resembled Chhotda. Innumerable Chhotdas were before him.

...but I will explain to you , Sree. I will free your mind of evil. I will instil goodness. I will instil beauty.

As they neared Haur, evening descended. The twilight played over the paddy fields and, in that semi-darkness, Sujoy spotted Mishi-thakuma walking along the ridge of twilight, across the field in the distance, melting into the darkness.

...Sree, I will not take up any other responsibility till you are well. Sree, my dear, when you are well you will feel ashamed of your behaviour today. But I will say that I don't remember anything.

At the entrance to the market, Sujoy clearly saw his mother sitting near the poultry shop with a chopping blade. She was plucking feathers off chickens with great satisfaction.

...Sree, you will paint many pictures! Would you like to join the Government Art College? Would you like to take lessons from Prajit Mukherjee? You will find that a guru does not only guide the talent of his students; a guru is also a learner himself!

His old friend Pulak Biswas was enjoying fritters from a paper bag. Girin sat on a bench at the adjacent tea shop. It was dark. Sujoy dismissed the taxi and walked towards Amal Jana's house with his daughter. Amal looked after their house and Sujoy would have to take the keys from him. Sree talked nineteen to the dozen. About her dreams, her friends and all the things which her world of imagination had conjured up for her. Sujoy listened and pondered.

...what do I tell you, Sree? How do I make you understand? If you don't understand then I will take you to a doctor. If you resist, I will simply force you come with me. If Ragini objects, I will not pay heed.

Sujoy noticed that Sree turned serious as they entered the house. She entered Sumit's room and, holding on to the door, said, "Bapi, I want to be alone for some time."

Sujoy readied himself for a new tumultuous chapter to unfold but outwardly he remained calm and said, "Very well. I am going out."

Sree: You lock the main door from outside.

Su: Okay. I'll be back soon. Amal will send us roti and egg curry for dinner. Will that do for tonight?

Sree: I want to be alone now, Bapi.

Su: Alright, dear.

Sujoy locked the door from outside and went on his way to meet up with old acquaintances. Then he picked up their dinner from Amal's house and returned home around half past nine. The house was in complete darkness. Sujoy felt a pang of anxiety. What was the girl doing in the dark for so long?

He switched on the living room light and put the food away. Then he pushed open the door to Sumit's room. He couldn't see much in the darkness. He switched on the light and immediately his eyes were blinded by the scene in front of him. He covered his eyes with his hands and tried to force words out…"Sree!" His voice sounded feeble.

Sree lay without a stitch on her. She called, "Come, Bapi. Take me."

Sujoy walked towards her in a daze, his body trembling. He wanted to cry. He sat beside Sree and rested a hand on her forehead. Then he said softly, "Get up, Sree. This is not right. Put your clothes on."

Sree hugged Sujoy. She was restless, disoriented. She pleaded, "Take me. I can't bear it anymore."

Su: Put your clothes on. This is making me go mad.

Sree: I am going mad, Bapi. You promised you would make love to me. Okay, if you can't do it then use your fingers. It's nothing but an excretion—a physical need. I go mad without it! Ma has told me that suppression is more dangerous and she taught me by fingering mine! Bapi, Ba...

Sujoy circled Sree's neck with his hands and strangled her. He said, "You and your mother are the filth of this world."

Sree tried to prise his hands apart.

...you have no right to live in this world.

He increased the pressure of his hands. Sree gradually turned blue. Her legs bent.

...you are a stigma on human civilisation.

Sree's tongue hung out. Her teeth bit down on her tongue and blood flowed. Her eyes popped out.

...don't take birth anymore. Please. Please. Please.

Sree lay lifeless. In a horrific state. Sujoy covered his daughter with the saree. A crushing pain gripped his heart. He wanted to throw up. He staggered to the courtyard and flopped down by the tap. Then he threw up. The vomit smeared his face and stained his clothes. He got up. He felt out of breath and broke into a thick sweat. He swayed and stumbled on his way out of the house and to the field. Then he collapsed on the grass. Pain and sweat. Sweat and fatigue. Fatigue and weakness. His lips moved...

...I have sinned. I have killed my daughter. Today I have done something unpardonable by the Almighty. So long I have abided by His rulings but today I have transgressed. Today I have sinned. I am my own master. I am my god. Because He is responsible only for birth. Only for goodness. Only for sacredness. Today I have sinned. Sin. Sin. Sin.

Sujoy lay still. Two divine men came and stood by his head.

Abhi: This world needs you. Upo, you are gradually turning into a bird, you are developing wings. Oh! How colourful are your wings! Your beak!

Upo: This world needs you. Abhi, you are gradually turning into a tree, your arms are becoming branches, your legs turning into a broad, firm trunk. Oh! How green are your leaves!

Abhi: Come, settle on me.

Upo: Yes, give me shelter.

Everything remained unattended. All resolutions. Promises. The world carried on at its own pace, eternally. There were so many others who took resolutions and made promises.

The still body of a man lay under a huge sprawling tree. A bird sat on a branch of the tree. It shed a colourful feather which floated down like a flower petal and settled on the chest of the dead man.

"Tree...tree, can you hear me?" called out the bird.

"What?"

"Are you sleeping?"

"No. Tell me."

The bird wiped its beak on a leaf. It pecked at a couple of fruits. The tree shivered. The bird flapped its wings three times. Then it flew away. It would return to the tree, soon.